The New Patriots

Barry C. Lefferts

To Pat

Best Wishes

Barry Lefferts

The New Patriots

by
Barry C. Lefferts

Taylor-Dth Publishing
P.O. Box 445
Fairfax, CA 94930

www.taylor-dth.com

ISBN: 0-9727583-4-8

Library of Congress Control Number: 2003106329

Manufactured in the United States of America

This is dedicated to my family.

CHAPTER ONE
Bari, Italy   August 1927

Nunzio Cappolla stood on the dock next to the ocean liner, looking out at the endless sea. Three thousand miles across that sea was Boston, America, his new home. He would be taking the ship to get there.

Enzio and Anna Cappolla, his parents, came to see their son off.

"Please take care of yourself," Mama cried.

Papa pressed some money into Nunzio's fist. "Take this. You will need it for refreshments aboard the ship. Uncle Alberto sent it along with the money for your passage. You know how your uncle Alberto and Aunt Nora love you. It's too bad they never had children of their own. They love you as if you were their son. I know they will give you a good home, and teach you everything you need to know about baking, so you can be the best baker in America. Bakers never go hungry, Nunzio. And please, write to us every chance you have. Capisce?"

"Yes, Papa. Capisco," Nunzio answered, tears rolling down his cheeks.

His sister, Maria, was so beautiful, standing next to him, with her jet-black hair blowing in the ocean breeze. What a goddess, he thought, as he grabbed her in his arms and simply stood there, holding her. "Arrivederci, my beautiful beloved sister," he said. "Oh, how I will miss you, but we will be together soon in America. We will all be together in America."

"I love you so much, Nunzio," Maria cried. "Our brother, Bruno, had to take charge of things at the flour mill. That's why he isn't here. But he sends you his love and best wishes, and this bible to study on the long voyage."

The ship's engines were roaring full blast. Their noise, and the sound of the water brushing against the dock, gave Nunzio a feeling of excitement he had never experienced before. He had never been away from Bari, let alone across the ocean. He could not control his anxiety. He looked around at the hundreds of people who were to be his family for the next ten days. Two men across from him were discussing politics.

"Il Duce is doing wonders for Italy," the first man said. "Unemployment has not been lower since the war, and look how the railway service has improved."

"Yes," said the second man. "But at what price? Open your eyes. Look at what's going on around you. That blacksmith's son is the anti-Christ. He will bring nothing but trouble to Italy."

An old couple was seeing their children and grandchildren off. Behind them, two lovers were kissing goodbye.

How many families the great sea separates, Nunzio thought. He looked at the giant ship, its mighty stern, the big chimneys smoking. On the ramp, the captain and his officers were greeting the boarding passengers.

"Nunzio, Nunzio," a voice called. It was Father Bettino, yelling as he peddled his bicycle toward them. "Nunzio, I came to see you off," he yelled again as he stepped off his bicycle. "How could I let my favorite choir boy leave for America without an arrivederci."

"Buon giorno, Father," Nunzio replied.

Father Bettino handed Nunzio a gold crucifix on a chain. "I know you won't be eighteen for four more months, but I won't see you then," he laughed. "So here is your birthday present. Wear it and think of me."

"Grazie, Father, grazie. I will never forget you, and I will never forget Bari. Someday, I will return to visit and will be very rich. I will give you lots of money for the poor people in the Parish."

"I will be looking forward to that day, Nunzio. Until then, God go with you, and inspire and guide you. Love the Lord and the Lord will love you. Buon viaggio, Nunzio," he said, as he climbed back on his bicycle and peddled away.

"Arrivederci Father. Grazie," Nunzio called after him.

His mother was crying. "My bambino," she sobbed. "Dress warm in Boston. It is very cold and damp in the winter, and your Aunt Nora says it snows all the time. People die from influenza, and pneumonia and God knows what else."

"Don't worry, Mama," Nunzio responded. "I'll dress warm, and I'll take care of myself. I love you, Mama," he added. Again the tears rolled down his cheeks as he hugged her. "They're boarding now, I have to go," he said, kissing and hugging his family. "I love you. Arrivederci."

Nunzio boarded the ship. He looked back at his family one last time before he stepped on deck. Everyone looked like angels nestled on a silver cloud, he thought. They kept waving at him, and crying, as the ship pulled away from the pier. Nunzio, tearful, yet smiling, waved back at them until all he could see was the bright sun in the distance. He fantasized that the ship was the palm of God's hand, carrying him to the unknown. He was leaving everything and everybody he loved, to start life in a new and strange land.

At length, he set out to explore the mighty vessel. This thing is like an island, he thought.

When he located his quarters, he placed his suitcase in front of his bunk. He was in the second-class sleeping quarters that he shared with three other passengers. The bathroom was in the hall between the rows of other sleeping quarters. At the end of the deck were a galley for the second class passengers only. On the upper deck was a row of private cabins for first class passengers, and the officer's quarters were across from the captain's cabin. At the end of the deck was the grand ballroom and the first class dining room. At the passenger's briefing, Nunzio learned that all passengers were able to use the grand ballroom, and there would be entertainment nightly.

After two days at sea, Nunzio was very restless and bored. He hadn't yet been able to get into any meaningful conversations with any of the other passengers, especially his two sleeping-quarter mates. They talked politics day and night.

The sea was calm, yet he felt slightly nauseous. He didn't care much for the food. After his mama's cooking it was difficult to eat the food served on the ship.

He couldn't sleep well, either. The constant rocking kept him awake, keeping him tossing and turning all night. He would get out of bed and stand on deck, looking out over the dark and mysterious sea. "How many sharks are out there that would love to sink their teeth in me?" he asked himself. Bruno used to come home from fishing trips, and tell stories about sharks and other creatures of the deep.

Nunzio would listen in amazement. Bruno loved to go fishing, as did most men in Bari. Nunzio could never get excited over fishing. He, Bruno, and the rest of the family worked in the mill, sifting flour for the bread and pasta makers. Uncle Alberto worked in the mill before he left for America and opened his own bakery in Boston. Nunzio kept staring at the water, dreaming about America. I will become very rich and have everything in the world, he thought.

He noticed a young man about his age standing on the deck. The man looked at Nunzio and smiled, "I can't sleep either," he said.

"Buona sera," Nunzio replied. "I have been feeling a bit ill since we left Bari. This is my first voyage, and my first time away from home. I guess I'm not used to it."

"I understand. This is my first voyage, also," the man said. "I come from Corato, my name is Torquato. Torquato Baccio. And yours?"

"Nunzio Cappolla, from Bari. Are you going to Boston?" Nunzio asked.

"Yes," he replied. "I will be going to school in Boston, and then I'll be working for a friend of my father's in New Hampshire. That is not too far from Boston."

"I'm going to work in my uncle's bakery in Boston," Nunzio replied. "I hope to do good there, but I'm scared. Besides that, I don't feel very well."

"You're probably a little seasick. Here, take one of these," he said, handing Nunzio an orange.

"I can't take your food," Nunzio said. "You might want it later."

"There's plenty in the dining room," Torquato answered. "Go on. Eat it. You will feel better. If you still feel sick, just heave over the side, drink some water, and go to sleep."

"You sound like a doctor," Nunzio replied. "What kind of school are you going to in Boston?"

"Electrical engineering. The big thing in America is electronics. Someday you will be wiping your ass with electric toilet paper," Torquato laughed. "My father's friend in New Hampshire has a factory where he makes electric appliances, and I am going to learn how to design them."

"Sounds exciting," Nunzio replied. "What's the name of the school?"

"Massachusetts Institute of Technology. It's on the Charles River in Cambridge, next door to Boston. Here is my letter of acceptance with an explanation of the school's facilities and programs."

Nunzio looked at the paper. "This is in English," he said. "I don't understand any English except hello, goodbye, and my name is Nunzio."

"Maybe I will teach you what I can in the short time we have until we reach Boston," Torquato said with a laugh.

"That would be nice," Nunzio replied. "You're traveling first class, so it would have to be between meals and bedtime."

"I'll tell you what, Nunzio. Come to the first class dining room in the morning. I will clear it with the officials for you to join me for breakfast, okay?"

"Well, are you sure?" Nunzio asked.

"Yes. Now if it's settled, let's both get some sleep. See you domani."

They left the deck and headed for their respective sleeping quarters.

The next morning, Nunzio awoke feeling well rested, and he was hungry for the first time on the voyage. He could hardly wait to have breakfast and see his new friend, Torquato. He took a couple of swigs of water to wash his mouth, and spit it in the basin next to the bunk. He slipped on his brown knickers and a black shirt. His shoes were tight on his swollen feet and he smelled bad. How nice a hot bath would be, he thought.

When he got to the dining room, he was in awe. What a difference from the second class galley, he thought, as he noticed the beautiful pictures on the walls, the milk white tablecloths and the shiny silverware alongside the crystal clear glassware. He walked around the room, looking for his friend.

"Nunzio," Torquato called. "Over here." Torquato was sitting with two men and a lady at the far end of the dining room. "Buon giorno, Nunzio. It's all right for you to join us. I made sure you have a setting. Sit down."

"Grazie, Torquato," Nunzio responded. "I feel a lot better this morning, thanks to you."

"Let me introduce you, Nunzio. This gentleman on my right is Julio Esposito, and the lovely lady is Mrs. Esposito. The other gentleman is Franco Alfano. Signor Alfano is presenting an opera in the grand ballroom tonight, one that he wrote and produced. Isn't that right, Signor?"

"Well, not exactly," Signor Alfano answered, greeting Nunzio. "Have you heard of Giacomo Puccini?"

"Yes," Nunzio replied. "Didn't he write Madam Butterfly, and La Boheme?"

"Yes. And before he died he was writing an oriental fantasy titled Turandot. And, well, I took the liberty of finishing the opera. It was recently performed in Milan and in Puccini's home village of Lucca. Now I am going to America to seek backing for it. Perhaps it will play the Boston Opera house. In the meantime, you can see it on the ship tonight, and let me know what you think."

"Would you do an aria for us now?" Signor Esposito asked.

"Here? Now?" Franco laughed. But he agreed and promptly began to sing. As he was singing, the other passengers in the dining room approached the table. One of the onlookers was a young and very beautiful girl. Torquato and Nunzio noticed her at the same time. Her eyes caught Nunzio's, and he couldn't help blushing.

Having noticed his friend's shyness, Torquato leaned over and whispered to Nunzio, "Have you ever made love to a girl?" he asked. Nunzio blushed again, and didn't answer.

Torquato laughed. The girl leaned over, resting on the back of one of the chairs. Her large, firm breasts were visible through the white cotton dress.

"Am I dreaming?" Torquato asked the girl. "Have I died and gone to heaven to be looking at such a beautiful angel?"

The girl giggled and put her hand over her mouth.

"What is your name?" Torquato asked.

"Loretta," she answered. "Loretta Camarco."

"I am Torquato, and this is my friend Nunzio. That gentleman singing is Franco Alfano. He's singing an aria from an opera by Puccini, and will be presenting the entire opera in the grand ballroom this evening. Would you like to join us tonight in the ballroom?"

Loretta looked at Torquato, and then looked at Nunzio. She smiled and paused for a minute. "You are strangers," she said. "Nice girls don't go out with strangers."

"You can't be serious," Torquato replied. "We're in the middle of the ocean. And besides, everyone on this ship will be at the ballroom. I just want you to sit with us."

Loretta looked them over again. "Okay," she said, relenting.

"Would you like some tea?" Torquato asked.

"Yes, I wouldn't mind having some, thank you," she replied. As she reached for the tea she bent over, exposing her lovely, round firm breasts. Her nipples accidentally brushed against Nunzio's shoulder.

Nunzio blushed with excitement, and crossed his legs to hide his erection.

Loretta sensed his reaction, and giggled to herself.

"Why are you going to America?" Nunzio asked.

"I am meeting my father there," she answered. "My mother died last month, and my father went to stay with my cousin in Boston. Now he has a job in a restaurant and sent for me to come work with him."

Torquato interrupted. "I am going to school in Boston to study electrical engineering, and Nunzio is going to be a baker."

"How nice," Loretta said, putting down her tea.

'Now, if you'll excuse me, I have something to do. I will
see you at lunch, perhaps, and we can talk again." She got
up and left the dining room.

"Come, Nunzio," Torquato said. "Let's go out on the
deck and get some fresh air."

They excused themselves and walked out to the deck.
Nunzio took an orange and put it in his pocket to eat
outside.

Outside, they saw Loretta standing near the entrance
to the deck. "We meet again so soon," Torquato said.
"Would you join us on deck?"

"In a while," she answered, as she headed for her
cabin.

The sea was calm and the sun was shining bright. It
was a beautiful morning. Many passengers had already
crowded the deck. Musicians were playing Italian folk
songs, and everyone joined in the singing.

Torquato looked out at the ocean. "You know," he
said to Nunzio, "about this time in 1492 a Genovese by the
name of Christopher Columbus sailed to find The West
Indies, and he discovered America."

"Yes, I know," Nunzio said. "We studied that in
school. There are many Italians in America. Some in high
office, like Fiorello Laguardia, the Congressman, and that
big shot in Chicago, Al Capone."

"Al Capone is a gangster," Torquato said. "They say
he goes around killing people. There are many gangsters
in America. Many of them Italian, from Sicily mostly, but
a lot of them are Irish, and a lot of them are Jews."

"I've never met a Jew," Nunzio said. "But, Father
Bettino told me all about how they killed Christ, and how
they have horns like the devil. He said that only other
Jews and the devil can see the horns. He said that when
Jesus comes back to earth, he will know who the Jews are,
and deal with them."

"Do you believe that story, Nunzio?" Torquato asked.

"Well Father Bettino wouldn't make it up. He knows everything about everything," Nunzio responded.

"If you studied your bible, you would know that Christ was a Jew, and what your priest taught you is medieval bullshit. I am a Jew, Nunzio, and I can't remember ever seeing a fellow Jew with horns. Nor can I remember meeting the devil."

"You are a Jew? But your name is Torquato. You're from Corato. How can you be a Jew?"

"There are many Jews in Italy, Nunzio," Torquato said. "They're as loyal to Italy as your family has been. The Hebrew people go back to the beginning of the Roman Empire, and your Catholic church began in the Jewish temples. Didn't you study any of that in your school?"

"We studied the scriptures and the teachings of Christ," Nunzio replied. "The nuns told us that anything outside of faith in Jesus and the Holy Roman Catholic Church are lies told by the devil and his demons, the Jews. They said that to believe those lies means you would be doomed to burn in hell."

"That is ridiculous anti-Jewish rhetoric, Nunzio. My ancestors have been in Italy since Charlemagne, around the year 800, only three hundred and fifty years after the fall of the Roman Empire. Always, they were second-class citizens. They survived the persecution, the inquisition, the lies, the hate." Torquato was getting very emotional as he paused. He glanced at Nunzio and continued. "In 1867 my great-grandfather loaned King Victor Emmanuel V a lot of money, and helped him revise the economy of Italy. For that he was made a Baron. My family settled in Corato on the land King Victor granted him in return for the loan. My grandfather chose to have our names be Italian and, although my great-grandfather was extremely pious, my grandfather preferred to keep a low profile as a Jew. I was educated in England, in a boy's preparatory school in

London. Each year on the Jewish high holy day of Yom Kippur, I would meet my family in Rome at the synagogue to pray to God, Nunzio. Yours and mine. The father in heaven. And each year the Pope would leave the Vatican to pay us a visit. Yes, the Pope would visit us demons, Nunzio, and he would have a small army of loyal good Catholics with him. He would go up to the rabbi, our priest, and stand behind him. He would kick him in the ass. Yes, Nunzio, the Holy Father would kick a poor old Jewish rabbi in the ass while he was observing the highest holy day of the year. Was this to entertain God, or perhaps Jesus? Last week was Yom Kipper, and last week the head rabbi got his traditional kick in the ass. I'm sorry if I seem too emotional. I can't help it. I get that way when I think about the injustice and the humiliation Jews must bear just for being Jews."

Nunzio stood in silence for several moments. "I don't know what to say. I'm sorry, Torquato. I guess I have a lot to learn."

"Now that you know I am Jew, the first you have ever met, can you still be my friend?"

Nunzio looked bewildered. He stared at the ocean, turned toward Torquato, and said, "But the Pope preaches love and brotherhood."

"Yes, brotherhood to other Catholics," Torquato responded. "But what about brotherhood to non-Catholics? Surely, there is enough room in heaven for us all. Our beliefs may be different, Nunzio, but our creator is the same. When we are living in Boston I would like for us to be friends."

"I would like that," Nunzio said. "I would like to be your friend, and I would like for you to teach me English."

They clapped their hands together, and stood smiling at each other.

Loretta arrived. "Am I interrupting something?" she asked. "I could come back later, if you two love birds would rather be alone."

Nunzio and Torquato dropped their hands and turned toward Loretta. "Ah, the angel has arrived," Torquato said.

Nunzio smiled.

"I will be glad when we arrive in Boston," Loretta said. "I can't take much more of this ship. I wasn't born to be a sailor."

"And what were you born to be?" Torquato asked.

"The wife of a prince. Do you know one, sir?" she laughed.

"I have a prince of a wine downstairs that I would like to share with both of you," Torquato said. "Alcohol is illegal in America, so we better drink all we can before we arrive. Can you imagine a restaurant without a wine cellar?"

Torquato left, and returned with the bottle of wine with three glasses. "I would like to prepare a toast. To my two new friends, the young Signor Cappolla and the Angel Loretta." Torquato raised his glass, and they all sipped the wine.

"Salute," Nunzio said, as they tapped their glasses together. "To our future home, America."

"To America," Loretta and Torquato chanted in unison.

That night, they went to the grand ballroom together. Torquato cleared it for Nunzio to join him and Loretta in the first class section. Since both he and Nunzio were built about the same, and both of them were the same height, Torquato was able to lend Nunzio a suit befitting an aristocrat.

For the rest of the voyage, the three were inseparable. Torquato tried to get Loretta romantically interested in him, but had no success. "I would like us to be good friends," she kept telling him. She also made it clear to Torquato that her father had no love for Jews. Torquato assured her that he was used to that situation.

Torquato taught Nunzio as much English as he could in the little time they had.

Torquato, "Buono in English is good."

Nunzio, "Good."

Torquato, "Il abito, the suit."

Nunzio, "The suit."

Torquato, "La camicia, the shirt."

Nunzio, "The shirt."

Torquato, "Buono, Nunzio, buono."

"Good, good," Nunzio replied. "Si, is good, yes, good."

"Domani, America, Nunzio. Tomorrow we will be in America."

Nunzio repeated, "Tomorrow in America. Boston, America and Uncle Alberto and Aunt Nora."

CHAPTER TWO
Boston Harbor

Nunzio joined the rest of the passengers and officers in the grand ballroom for a briefing while the U.S. Custom officers cleared the ship.

Medical examiners were mainly concerned if anyone had typhoid, small pox, bubonic plague or any other communicable disease. They were to be kept in a quarantine area until it was certain they were not carrying any of these diseases.

"Alcohol consumption is illegal in the United States of America," the customs official announced. "Attempting to smuggle alcohol into the United States can result in deportation. Do not try it. Please list all items you are bringing into the United States on the forms provided. Thank you."

Nunzio nervously filled out his forms and prepared to disembark. Torquato and Loretta were right behind him. The tall, lanky, blond-haired man introduced himself as Immigration Officer Von Kepper. Beside him was a translator.

"Scandinavian," Torquato whispered.

"Ladies and Gentlemen," he hollered. "Those of you who will be residing in the United States please form a line to the right. If you are visiting the United States as a tourist, or are here on business, form a line to the left. Have your papers ready and in your hand. Those of you without papers will have to report to the room down the hall with the letters WOP on the door. Are there any questions?" Half the place started talking at once. "Hold it, hold it," the officer yelled raising his hand. "One at a time, please." His interpreter started taking questions from the people in line.

Several hours later, Nunzio, Torquato and Loretta were finally finished processing. "I can't believe it," Nunzio said. "I'm in America. I'm actually standing in Boston Harbor in the United States of America. I feel so strange, Torquato. How about you? How do you feel? And you, Loretta?"

"I'm cold," Torquato replied. "That's how I feel. "Downright cold and damp, and I'm tired. But I'm also as excited as hell to be here."

"I don't know for sure how I feel yet," Loretta said. "Ask me tomorrow."

"Listen you two," Nunzio said. "I'll be working at my uncle's bakery. Cappolla's Italian Bakery, 705 Hanover Street. They told me their house was on top of the bakery. Don't ask me how they put it up there," he laughed. "You both come to see me there soon, okay?"

"And here is my address in Cambridge," Torquato said as he handed them each a paper with his address on it. "I'm between Harvard and MIT."

"My address is 402 Salem Street," Loretta told them.

"Torquato?" Nunzio had a puzzled expression. "This paper says David Fairchild, Esquire, Elegant Estates. Is David Fairchild a friend or a relative? You never mentioned him on the ship."

"I told you the story of my family and how we became barons. Well, the Fairchilds of Europe, Philip, Aaron, and Benjamin Fairchild are all my cousins. My family is one of the leading banking families and wine producers in the world. My Hebrew name is Dovid, which in English is David, and so in America, Torquato Baccio will be known as David Fairchild. I hope that won't make a difference to you Nunzio, or you Loretta?"

"For my money, you can go to the Washington Capital and call yourself Calvin Coolidge," Loretta wisecracked.

Nunzio laughed. "Baron David Fairchild, the hornless Jew from Corato. I'm going to find Signor Alfano and see if he can write an opera about you." Nunzio started to sing, "Oh, what happened to Torquato, the smart-ass Jew? He went inside the closet and came out as a person new. With a wave of the hand and a turn of head no more Torquato."

The three of them laughed and embraced. "I've got to go now," Nunzio explained. "My uncle wrote that I should take a taxi to the bakery, because he could not close the bakery to pick me up. So arrivederci Torqu..., excuse me, I mean David." He looked at Loretta. "And if you are still Loretta, arrivederci to you."

"Good luck, Nunzio," Torquato said. "I'll be over to see you sooner than you think."

Loretta, noticing her father, cried out, "Arrivederci, both of you," as she ran into her father's arms. "Buon giorno papa," she said, and hugged him passionately.

"Seven-zero-five Hanover Street, Cappolla's Bakery please. My English not so good, so mi scusi, por favore," Nunzio said to the taxi driver.

"Name's Gino," the taxi driver replied. "I speak Italian, my family's from Roma."

"Ah, yes Roma, that's wonderful," Nunzio said. "My lucky day. The taxi driver is Italian."

Gino pointed to a row of statues. "See that, that's the Boston Commons and that's Copley Square. This is where America began. It's a great city, you're gonna love it, only be careful. The Irish, they run this town. The Sicilians, they run the illegal alcohol, and the Jews sell all kinds of stuff, in the streets and door to door. The Irish hate the Italians and the Jews, and the old-time Anglo Americans hate all the foreigners, but the city works. Somehow it works."

"You paint a nice picture, Gino. Everyone hates

everyone, just like in Europe. I should feel right at home in America."

"This is Hanover Street," Gino replied. "The north side of Boston, the Italian section." Nunzio looked at the row of apartment building, garbage cans overflowing in the streets. The pushcarts lined the curbs. "Verdura!" one man yelled as he displayed his vegetables. "Carne, carne," another man was singing, as he held up a slab of beef on a rope. There was spaghetti and fruit and ices and rags and shoes, anything a person could want was being sold from pushcarts.

"Here we are. Number 705," the taxi driver said, when they stopped in front of the bakery.

Uncle Alberto saw the taxi pull up and came running out of the bakery. "Nunzio! It's you! You're finally here. You look wonderful. So handsome, just like your papa. How much do I owe you, Mr. Taxi Driver?"

"Twenty cents," Gino told him.

"Here's a quarter, keep the change."

"Come inside Nunzio. Your Aunt Nora is on pins and needles, waiting for you."

"Bambino. Bambino mio," Aunt Nora shouted when she saw Nunzio. "Como sta?"

"Buon giorno, Aunt Nora. I am fine. It is good to see you both. I bring love from everyone in Bari. And, I brought you a gift that Mama made." Nunzio opened his bags, and dug to the bottom to retrieve a handmade quilt.

"Bello, Bello," Aunt Nora said as she gave Nunzio a big kiss and hug.

Uncle Alberto put his arm on Nunzio's shoulder, "There is so much to talk about Nunzio. I want to show you around the house, the shop. I want to show you all of Boston, but first I show you your room. You can put your things away, and then you manga. Aunt Nora fixed your favorite pasta e fagioli, with fresh bread, hot out of the oven."

After dinner, Nunzio was too stuffed to do anything. He had not had a dinner like this one since he left Bari. Uncle Alberto took him on a tour of the bakery. The two large ovens in the rear of the baking area were for the long Italian breads. The smaller oven was used to bake the rolls and cakes. The long table was for rolling the dough. There were flour sifters, rows of shelves where the canisters and utensils were stacked, so much involved in running a bakery.

"We use only the best ingredients, Nunzio," Uncle Alberto told him. "We start baking at three o'clock in the morning and we open the shop at seven."

In the front was the retail shop, there was a half dozen counters full of fresh cannoli, cheese cake and various pastries. On the back walls facing the counters were shelves of bread and rolls.

"Two pennies each," Uncle Alberto explained. "And the long bread is four cents. Business is very good, Nunzio. Your Aunt and I have been investing our money in the stock market. That is like owning shares in different companies and as they do well our stock value goes up and we make a profit. That is how we bought this building and that 1926 Pontiac automobile you see parked outside."

"It's beautiful," Nunzio replied. "When do we go for a ride?"

"Sunday, we go to church, then we go out for a New England seafood dinner. Then I will show you Boston. But for now, I think we should all go to sleep. Tomorrow we wake up two-thirty in the morning and you begin learning your new trade. Nunzio-the-Baker. How do you like the sound of that?"

"Two-thirty in the morning? I heard there was such a time, but I thought it was just a fable. And now you tell me there really is a two-thirty in the morning, uncle."

Uncle Alberto laughed. "You'll get used to it just like

your aunt and I have. Come, let's go to bed. It's good to have you here."

"It's good to be here. I miss mama and papa and Maria, but it is still good to be here. I'll see you in the morning."

Nunzio looked out the window of his room. "Buona notte, Bari. Good night, America." As soon as he got into bed he fell asleep.

CHAPTER THREE
Cambridge

Torquato finished brushing his teeth and drank a glass of tomato juice. Nervously, he put his papers together. This was his first day of school, and he was David Fairchild, son of the Baron of Curato. I'm going to do fine, he thought. He looked around the three-bedroom house he was sharing with two other engineering students, Robert Nash and Donovan Atterson, both from New York, and both very Protestant. He was in the same situation in London, and managed to survive, so I'll survive here, too, he rationalized to himself.

"Good morning, David." Donovan chanted.

Jesus, does he ever sound like a girl, David thought. "Good morning, Donovan. Ready for the big day?"

"Oh, yes, ready. But, please call me Don, only mummy calls me Donovan. Guess who's addressing the new class today as head of the welcoming committee?"

"Who?" David asked.

"Why none other the Honorable Alvin T. Fuller, himself," Don answered.

"That's wonderful. Who is Alvin T. Fuller?"

Before Donovan answered, Robert came hopping down the stairs. "You don't know who Alvin T. Fuller is? You Italian guys don't know anything. Why, he's only the Governor of Massachusetts, and he's going to welcome us to MIT."

"That's nice," David replied. "The Prince of Wales welcomed me to school in London, so what's the big deal?"

"Are you sure it wasn't the Prince of Darkness?"

Donovan remarked. "Come on, were going to be late if we don't hurry."

The three of them shared the same homeroom class. Mr. Dudley welcomed them to MIT and informed them of the Governor's welcoming committee to be presented at assembly. They were given a list of the books they would need to purchase. The curriculum for the semester was given, and then they were taken on a tour of the school. Outside, the view of the mighty Charles River gave grandeur to the brick walls of the school. They crossed to the assembly hall where Governor Fuller was seated near the podium next to the president of the school. The few female students gave proof to the fact that it was one of the few co-educational engineering colleges in the United States.

"Ladies and gentlemen," the Governor roared into the crowded assembly. "We have here amongst us today some of the best minds from the four corners of the world. We are here for one purpose, or rather one common purpose, to learn. Yes, to learn how to create a better world, or perhaps, through engineering, to improve on the world that God has created. Yes, God created a fantastic world and has given us the ability and the resources to expand on what He created. You are the future of this country and this planet. On behalf of the people of the great state of Massachusetts, I welcome you to the Massachusetts Institute of Technology."

The assembly rose and applauded. The next speaker was the president of the school and then the rest of the faculty was introduced. After they adjourned, David, Donovan and Robert went to the bookstore to fill the list of supplies.

They needed to buy books containing the collected works of Joseph John Thompson and John Fleming, along with James Clark Maxwell and Henrik Rudolph Hertz.

"Before you can design electrical instruments and

appliances you must know what electricity is," Mr. Dudley had told them. "And that is what I want you to concentrate on this semester."

"That comes to twelve dollars," the cashier told David.

He looked at the honey-blonde haired girl with the small round face and small frame and paused for a moment. As he counted out twelve one-dollar bills, he looked up and said, "My name is David Fairchild, and I would like very much to know who you are. Perhaps over a cup of coffee?"

The girl smiled, "I'm Sally Marcus, and I don't date strangers, but thank you anyway, Mr. Fairchild. Now, if you'll excuse me, there are people behind you."

"Those are my roommates, and we're not strangers anymore since we know each other's names. I will come back tomorrow and ask you again."

Sally just smiled and waited on Donovan.

"You work pretty fast," Robert said as they walked outside.

"That girl really excited me," David replied. "What did you think of her, Don?"

Donovan just looked nervously ahead and replied, "I have no time for girls right now. I'm here to learn engineering. Aren't you?"

"Yes," David said. "But not twenty-four hours a day. I've got to have a little fun."

"She looks a little too skinny for me," Robert said.

"Classic beauty, that's the way I would describe her," said David. "Graceful and classic. I can hardly wait until tomorrow to see her again."

"Tomorrow you'd better know how Joseph John Thomson discovered that atoms contain particles of electricity, and never mind the dumb girls," Donovan said.

"I know that Benjamin Franklin flew a kite, Donovan. Why don't you do the same," said David.

The New Patriots

"This country doesn't care who they let in, do they?" Donovan asked.

"Must not. You're here," Robert said. They laughed as they walked back to the house.

CHAPTER FOUR
December 23, 1927

It was Nunzio's eighteenth birthday -- two days before Christmas. So much has happened in the last two months. He enrolled in night school to learn English, Uncle Alberto was teaching him to drive, and he could even understand the street signs. He'd learned so much about America. Uncle Alberto took him on the Freedom Trail to explain the American Revolution and all about Paul Revere and Benjamin Franklin. He was at the site of the Boston Tea Party, and the homes of great American poets and philosophers, Longfellow and Emerson. He had never heard of any of them, but still, it was exciting.

Every morning, except Sunday, Nunzio was downstairs at the bakery by three o'clock. He helped Uncle Alberto sift the flour and prepare the dough for baking.

Moses, a helper, would clean the ovens, sweep the dust off the floor and carry the heavy trays to the oven. Moses was the first negro Nunzio ever talked to. He was the son of a slave, and he told Nunzio all kinds of stories about his childhood in Alabama.

"Only 63 years ago the Civil War ended, and all slaves were freed by President Abraham Lincoln," Moses told him.

Nunzio couldn't believe that a great country like America actually had a civil war and kept slaves.

Nunzio was happy his birthday came on a Sunday so he could have this day off. He was playing with the crucifix on the chain around his neck. "Father Bettino gave me this for my birthday," he told Uncle Alberto as they stood outside the church.

"Yes," Uncle Alberto answered. "And it's going to be one hell of a day. There's going to be a block party on Hanover Street the likes of which you've never seen. Musica and food and musica. Oh, and your friend Torquato, or David, whatever he calls himself, is coming. I forgot to tell you he called," Uncle Alberto said, just as Loretta and her father were coming up the walk.

"That's wonderful," Nunzio smiled in delight. "Did you hear that Loretta? Torquato is coming to the party."

"That's nice. I'm looking forward to seeing him, I spoke to him last week. He said he was in the bakery to see you right after I left. I must have missed him by two minutes."

"That's right," Nunzio said. "He had his girlfriend with him. Her name is Sally. Seems like a very nice girl. A Jew like Torquato. They look good together."

"Let's go inside," Aunt Nora said. "Mass is beginning."

Father Vincent DiSalvi was not at all like Father Bettino. But, he was a good caring priest and he gave Nunzio a warm welcome. Nunzio felt very good about the people in the parish, most of whom were customers in the bakery. There was Rosa Ladato and her five kids. Her husband never came to church. Always visiting the bootleggers, he would do odd jobs for a couple of bottles of booze. And there was Mr. and Mrs. Madino, who owned the meat market. Mr. Madino was always complaining about the Jewish peddlers undercutting his prices and stealing his customers. Also, sitting close by was Franny Foscolo. Everyone called her the Boston buton. And there was Al Russo, the plumber. And, of course, Dr. DiGiacomo and his wife Marie. They would all be at the party, Nunzio thought to himself. But what about Angelo Donato - the son of a bitch gangster bastard? He wouldn't show up at a Christmas block party. But he would never miss sending those two thugs around every Friday to collect the protection money.

"How come the police don't give us protection?" Nunzio asked Uncle Alberto.

"The police protect the gangsters and the gangsters protect us. We don't pay, we don't have a business. That's the way it is."

"There's more than one America," Nunzio whispered.

"Nunzio, are you daydreaming again?" Aunt Nora asked. "Father Vincent is giving Mass. Please have some respect. Thank you."

"I have a lot on my mind," Nunzio said.

Outside, he told Father Vincent how much he enjoyed Mass and that he was getting used to his Sicilian dialect.

"That's very nice, Nunzio," the priest answered. "How are you coming along with your English lessons in night school?"

Nunzio answered in English, "I am doing fine, thank you. Are you coming to the party, Father?"

"Not bad, Nunzio, not bad. And, yes, I will be there to sing you Happy Birthday. And you Loretta," Father Vincent continued as she came down the steps with her father, "I heard you got a new job."

"Yes Father, it's fabulous. I'm working at Bonet of Paris, downtown. I put the dresses on the racks and assist the models. And my boss said he might let me model after a while. He said I would be a good model."

"I won't comment on that," Father Vincent said. "But, I wish you good luck. I'll see you all at the party. Oh, Franny, I need to see you for a minute. You haven't been to confession for quite some time. Is there a reason?"

"I've been too busy Father," Franny told him. "Maybe next week. Merry Christmas, Father."

"Aren't you coming to Midnight Mass tomorrow, Franny?" he asked.

"Maybe, Father, maybe," she said as she walked

away, her head facing the ground.

"See you this afternoon at the party," Uncle Alberto told the priest, as he got in the Pontiac.

"I'll walk home," said Mr. Camarco. "The cold air feels good, and I need the exercise."

"Papa is afraid of cars, but he doesn't like anyone to know," Loretta whispered to Nunzio.

"Maybe we should walk with him, it's only three blocks and it will do us both some good," Nunzio said.

"Okay," she answered.

"We will see you back at the house. We're going to walk," Nunzio said to Uncle Alberto and Aunt Nora.

"Would you like to stop for some hot chocolate, Loretta?" Nunzio asked.

"I would love some," she answered. "Papa, would you like to join us?"

"No, you two go ahead, I'll see you at home."

Victor's luncheonette had the usual after church crowd hanging around thumbing the comic books and the newspapers, drinking soda pop and coffee. Nunzio and Loretta sat in a booth in the rear of the shop. Nunzio went over to the counter and ordered two hot chocolates.

"Your father seemed to be very much down," Nunzio said to Loretta, as he rejoined her.

"He still hasn't gotten over my mother's death. And my quitting the job at the restaurant bothered him," Loretta answered.

"That was a break for you though, Paul Bonet coming into the restaurant and offering you a job for a lot more money then you were earning. That doesn't happen every day."

"Yes," she nodded and added to herself as Nunzio went to pick up the hot chocolates, "Papa still would like to have me around more often. I'm all he has."

Nunzio put the two cups on the table. "I would like to have you around all the time, Loretta. I was so happy that you live so close and that the restaurant was near the bakery. You know how I feel about you, Loretta."

"Please Nunzio. I like you a lot, but as a friend, a good friend. You and Torquato? We came over on the boat together, and who knows, maybe we will be lifetime friends, but that is all." She put both her hands on his and looked into his eyes and smiled. "Okay?" she asked. Nunzio just smiled back. They finished their hot chocolate, and walked outside.

"Why, I do believe it's snowing," said Loretta.

"Yes, I think you're right," Nunzio replied, attempting to catch the flakes in his palm. "A block party in the snow. That should be a lot of fun."

They walked toward Salem Street and Loretta's house. "I'll see you this afternoon at the party, Nunzio."

As he left her at the door to the three-story brick apartment building, he quivered with excitement. That was how he felt every time he was with Loretta. Walking home with his hands in his coat pocket, the snow coming down hard now, Nunzio thought to himself, my first birthday in America - a block party. Loretta and Torquato will be there, we will all freeze our asses off together, but who cares, it will be so great. Oh how I wish Mama and Papa and Maria and Bruno could be there. "Merry Christmas to you," he said, looking at the sky.

Everyone on Hanover Street was getting set up for the party. There were several hot sausage and pepper stands and Dominic DiAnza was selling pasta, the 25-gallon pot resting on his wagon. Mr. Foscolo, Franny's father, had a table with bananas and apples, and Franny was actually helping him, a rare sight these days.

The street was like a carnival, and with the snow falling it was magnificent, Nunzio thought. Every peddler in Boston was out trying to get the last day's business before Christmas. Although the bakery was closed on Sunday, Moses was busy cleaning, as he did every

Sunday. Since he slept in the little storeroom in back of the bakery, it was quite convenient.

Uncle Alberto and Moses baked 200 loaves of bread and several cakes for the party. Nunzio knew one of them was his birthday cake, because he heard Uncle Alberto and Aunt Nora discussing it last night. He could hear everything through the thin walls of his bedroom, and when they made love, Nunzio got excited. He thought about visiting Franny, like he heard all the other guys did, but his timing was never right. Between working all day, night school and his chores, there was so little time for anything else.

Nunzio stood at the entrance to the bakery. Uncle Alberto was standing by the ovens talking to a man. Nunzio could not see who it was. Then he noticed Angelo Donato's 1922 Rolls Royce Silver Ghost parked outside. What the hell would he want today? He asked himself.

Nunzio tried unsuccessfully to eavesdrop. "Good morning, Nunzio," Angelo said, as he walked to the front of the store. "Happy Birthday and Merry Christmas." He handed Nunzio a five dollar bill. "I'm sure you can find a place to spend this Nunzio," Angelo laughed.

Nunzio did not know what to say or what to do so he mumbled grazie, and put the bill in his shirt. He watched the gangster get into the car, then turned to Uncle Alberto and asked, "What was he doing here today?"

"Oh, he wanted to let me know he was supplying the beer and wine for the party today, free. And besides, you're here two months and already you're the Mayor of Boston?"

"It seems strange that the man who runs the North End would come to you on a Sunday because he wants to be charitable. I guess that's the way they do things in this strange country," Nunzio replied.

"This is the land of golden opportunity, Nunzio. Play your cards right, learn all you can and the sky is the limit,"

Alberto said, as he put the breads in the large paper bags. "Help me pack these, Nunzio, so we can get out to the party. Your friend David should be here soon."

Nunzio grabbed a bag and started packing the breads. "Yes, David should be here any minute. Not to change the subject, but I hope nothing is wrong for Donato to call on you," Nunzio said with a worried expression.

"Don't be stupid. He gave you five dollars didn't he? Would he do that if there was anything wrong?"

"You give those two guys who work for him that much every week, Uncle Alberto."

"You know, Nunzio? I'm doing very well in this country. I'm making a lot of money on the stock market. Every penny I have I reinvest, so maybe in a few years I can let you take over the bakery and your Aunt Nora and I can move back to Bari to live like royalty. Or, if we stay in America, we could live in California where it never snows, and the mountains overlook the ocean. I can buy a little land and grow my own food, just like in Bari. So, don't worry about Angelo Donato. Just have a nice birthday and enjoy the party. Help me take these breads outside. Moses, you can help too."

Nunzio and Moses were behind him carrying the remaining bags of breads. It stopped snowing, and the three inches on the ground left a beautiful white carpet on the street. Nunzio looked down the block and saw Loretta at the Foscolo table talking to Franny.

Just then a 1920 Lincoln convertible pulled up to the bakery, "Happy birthday, Nunzio. Buon giorno, Mr. Cappolla," David yelled as he and Sally got out of the car. In the back seat were Robert and Donovan. "I brought my friends to the party," David said as he embraced Nunzio.

"Hello Nunzio," Sally said, "Happy Birthday."

"Grazie, thank you," Nunzio replied.

Loretta saw them and came running over. David introduced Robert and Donovan and they all joined the rest of the party.

"If mummy saw me now," Donovan whispered to Robert, "the only thing she would leave me in her will would be her pubic hair."

"Well this is 1927, dear boy," Robert replied. "The age of tolerance. Let's just have fun."

"Here's your birthday present from Sally and me," David said, as he handed Nunzio a package.

"Wow! A radio!" Nunzio said, gleaming from the surprise, as he tore off the wrapping.

"Now you can listen to Graham McNamme's report and practice your English," David replied. "This radio is made by Continental Electric. My father's friend in New Hampshire owns the company, remember?"

Uncle Alberto interrupted. "There is much time for talk, Nunzio. Now is the time for a party. Aunt Nora is making a feast for dinner. You can all stay and talk then."

"Great," said David. "And I just happen to have four bottles of Fairchild 1906 vintage to wash down dinner."

"Hey! The band is starting to play," Sally shouted. "Lets dance in the snow, David."

"Is Paul Bonet coming, Loretta?" Nunzio asked.

"He had things to do at the store. I'm glad he let me have the day off. Tomorrow all the fancy people from Beacon Hill will be in to pick up their dresses for Christmas and New Years Eve. I'm not looking forward to working tomorrow."

"You work at Bonet's?" Donovan asked.

"Yes, I do."

"Mummy knew Paul Bonet when he had his store in Manhattan. Even before he started calling himself Paul Bonet. He was Chaim Horowitz then, a Russian Jewish immigrant dressmaker. Now he's Boston's number one fashion designer, Paul Bonet, the Parisian."

"Yes, and Torquato Baccio is David Fairchild. And, Donovan Atterson. Who is Donovan Atterson?" Loretta asked.

"You and Bonet have a thing going?" Donovan asked Loretta.

"We like each other," said Loretta. "I just work for him, and he's going to let me model. After all, he's a very talented and respected designer. It doesn't matter to me who he was, only who he is now."

"What were you and Franny talking about?" Nunzio asked Loretta.

"Just girl talk, that's all. Hey, they're playing Funiculi Funicula. Let's dance."

That evening, after dinner they all sat in the living room telling stories of the events of the past four months. Nunzio had his new radio turned on. "They're playing Italian music," he said.

"That's Enrico Caruso," Uncle Alberto said. "What a voice. Too bad he had to die so young. Six years already he's dead."

"But his music and his voice live on thanks to his recordings," David replied. "What an age we live in. Electricity and Caruso will still be singing arias a thousand years from now."

Aunt Nora brought out the birthday cake. "Happy Birthday, Nunzio," they all chanted.

"This was the best day of my life. Thank you all so much. The only thing missing is my family in Bari. With this glass of 1906 vintage Fairchild, I toast you and them."

CHAPTER FIVE
Four months later

The warehouse on Commercial Street that housed Anglo Donato's office was especially busy for a Friday morning. Four men were emptying the truckload of wine and stacking cases against the wall. Vito Natali was standing lookout on the loading dock. Several of Angelo's soldiers, as he called them, were floating around the warehouse. Gino Arturo was sitting outside the office nervously thumping the newspaper on the brown bench. Angelo wanted to see him first thing this morning, no if, ands, or buts, and he knew he was in for a whole lot of shit. Angelo was on his way in from his mansion in Plymouth, a stone's throw from the spot where the Pilgrims landed. That's about the same spot this wine was smuggled in, Gino thought to himself.

"Here comes the boss now, Gino!" Frankie yelled from the doorway. "He's outside, checking in with Vito."

Angelo walked in without saying a word and opened a case of wine and looked at one of the bottles. "Wonderful," he said to Frankie. "Even Scarface Al don't handle shit this good. All that fucking beer they kill each other for, and here we got premium stuff. Let them have Chicago and New York, eh? We'll take New England anytime."

"You got that right, Boss," Frankie replied, "But I think Mooney and a couple of the boys over on the South End are looking to cut in on us."

"Cut in my ass. Remember what happened to that Patsy Riley creep that cut in? I bet the fish are still nibbling on his dick." They both laughed.

"You know, Boss. That was a great idea using that Cappolla guy's breads to deliver the wine. Nobody suspects a thing," Frankie said.

"You like that, eh, Goomba? Alberto Cappolla ain't no Sicilian, but he keeps his mouth shut and loves money. He's got every stock on the market. But that nephew of his, I keep my eye on him. I can't figure him out. Don't know what he does with his cut. He never spends a dime, and doesn't play the market. Not even a bank account."

"I think he wants to bring his family over from Bari," Frankie said.

"Just what we need Frankie, more Cappollas," Angelo laughed as he looked over toward Gino.

"Excuse me, Frankie. There's a stunod I got to have a talk with in my office."

Angelo, walked toward Gino, "Hey, you dumb fuck. Get in the office." Angelo grabbed Gino's jacket lapels and put Gino against the wall. "You been sticking it in Franny Foscolo?"

"Everyone's been getting a little of that, Boss. What's the big deal?"

"The big deal is you've been getting more then a little. She's five months pregnant and she swears you're the father. You and Danny are supposed to be making your rounds, collecting the protection money. What kind of protection are we selling when you're fucking the client's daughter? I want you to get a new suit today and go down to City Hall and get a marriage license. Danny will be your best man. Congratulations, you're not only going to be a father, you're going to be a husband this Sunday coming."

"But Boss, she's been with a hundred guys. How can she say it was mine?"

"Very easy. She moved her lips and said to my client, Mr. Foscolo, 'Papa, Gino Arturo got me pregnant.' And, being the kind and understanding Lord of the North End and everything that fucking moves in the North End, I told him to get ready for the wedding. Now, of course, you have a choice. We can have a nice funeral instead. Either way, you'll need a new suit. But if you prefer the funeral, I get to pick the suit." Angelo smiled and pinched Gino's cheek, "So, what's it gonna be?"

"I'm on my way downtown, Boss," Gino answered, as he turned around and walked out the door.

"Good choice. Oh, stop at the goldsmith and get a nice ring, and take the day off. Danny will make the rounds with Frankie today."

Angelo was happy with himself for the way he handled the problem. He walked out to the men unloading the wine. "Let's move your asses over there!" he yelled. "This stuff's gotta get distributed today."

The flour truck rolled into the warehouse. The two men opened the back of the truck and started throwing the sacks on the concrete floor. Ralph Cosselano was in charge of this part of the operation. "Let's get the wine into the flour sacks. Six in each like always," he instructed the men.

After the truck was loaded, he told two of the men to follow the truck over to Cappolla's Bakery and get the sacks unloaded.

When they arrived at the bakery, Moses, and the new black man they hired, by the name of Acey, quickly unloaded the sacks. Nunzio and Alberto began stuffing the wine, one bottle into each bread, and six breads into each paper bag. Then Moses and Acey loaded the bags into the Cappolla route truck.

"I'll take Acey with me on the delivery today, Nunzio. You and Moses can get the rest of the breads ready for retail. Nora will watch the front," said Alberto.

"Yes, Uncle," Nunzio replied.

Nunzio watched the truck leave Hanover Street. The speakeasy over on Richmond was the first stop. Nunzio hated doing this, but Uncle Alberto got involved with the gangster and there was no way out except in cement. He thought about the money he was hiding under the floorboard. It was almost four hundred dollars. It was his cut from the operation. Soon he would send for his family and he would at least have a nice nest egg for his future, if he didn't get killed or arrested by the Feds. They would deport him for sure, he thought. He wished there was some way out, but Donato knew every move he made. Every move everyone on the North End of Boston made. He had all the cops on his payroll, and the politicians and commissioners, but not the Feds, or did he? Nunzio wondered. Well, I'm not going to die finding out. It wouldn't do any good. This prohibition is bullshit anyway, it won't last much longer. Christ sake, everyone is drinking illegally, and sons of bitches like Al Capone and Angelo Donato are getting fat. "I'm part of it too," he whispered to himself.

"You say something?" Moses asked.

"Just thinking out loud, Moses. Just thinking out loud."

"Nunzio," Aunt Nora yelled into the back. "Loretta is here. You want to come out front?"

"I'll be right out," Nunzio replied. "Take care of things Moses. I'll be back in a while."

"Don't you worry, Nunzio," Moses said. "I can handle this load. Before you came I had to do everything back here. Of course, we weren't messen' with wine then." Nunzio smiled to himself as he walked out front.

"Hi, beautiful," he greeted Loretta. "Day off today?"

"Franny and Gino are getting married on Sunday and I'm going over to help her get ready," Loretta responded.

"Looks like she's been ready a long time," Aunt Nora interrupted.

"That's funny, Aunt Nora," Nunzio laughed. "Her father made her pick someone, and I guess Gino got the call. I'm sure Donato put the pressure on. Likes to think he's God. So Loretta, how are things going at Bonet's?"

"Great. I'm modeling full time now and taking English lessons from a tutor. And I've been seeing Paul on occasion."

"That's nice. I was going to call you myself," Nunzio said. "You haven't been to church in a couple of weeks now. Your father said you were too busy. And, I haven't seen or heard from Torquato since the block party. Have you heard from him?"

"Yes, he was in town last week and stopped by the shop. He said he was very busy at school and he would call on you first chance he got. We hired a new girl at the shop, Nunzio. Seventeen years old and very pretty. Her name is Rose Kelly. She's an Irish girl. Her father is a cop. I was thinking you might want to meet her."

"Why would you think that?" Nunzio asked.

"Well, for one thing, you never go anywhere to socialize. You go only to church, night school and work. I just thought you might like to meet a nice girl."

"Why would a nice Irish girl, daughter of a nice Irish cop, want to meet an Italian baker?"

"Never mind, Nunzio, it was just a thought. I'll see you in church Sunday for the wedding."

"Right," Nunzio replied. "I just hope I can sit there with a straight face."

Loretta gave him a kiss on the cheek, and said goodbye to Aunt Nora.

"Imagine that, Aunt Nora," Nunzio said, as he took one of the cannolis out of the counter and started nibbling. "Loretta wants to fix me up with the daughter of an Irish cop. I think America is making her a little dubots."

"You got plenty of time to worry about girls, Nunzio. And there are a lot of Italian girls that would give anything to meet you."

"That's true Aunt Nora. I better get back to work.

Oh, by the way, I got a letter from Mama. She sends you and Uncle Alberto her love and Papa and Marie and Bruno send their love too."

"I got a letter also," Aunt Nora said. "I miss Bari very much. Sometimes at night I dream... Oh, what's the difference? This is another time."

Nunzio started to go to the back when he noticed the Rolls Royce pull up. Oh, shit. What does he want? He asked himself.

The chauffeur got out and opened the back door. Angelo stepped out and walked into the bakery.

"Hello Nora, Nunzio," Angelo said. "I need some pastry for the weekend. I'm having guests from out of town. Have you heard about the wedding on Sunday?"

"We heard," Nunzio answered.

"Nice couple," Angelo said smiling. "Let me have a dozen cannoli, two cheesecakes and four breads and some rolls, two dozen should be enough. Here's a ten spot, keep the change Nora. Maybe buy yourself something pretty to wear. You can't wear all those stock certificates Alberto buys, can you?" Angelo laughed. "Shipment go out okay today, Nunzio?"

"Yes, Mr. Donato. Uncle Alberto and Acey are making the deliveries now."

"Good, that's real good."

Just then the front window shattered. The sound was like an earthquake. The top row of breads fell to the floor. The chauffeur ran into the bakery, "Is everyone all right? A car just came speeding down the street, two men opened fire. I didn't have time to get my gun out and they were gone, boss."

"Nora, Nunzio are you okay?" Angelo asked looking over the mess in front of the bakery.

"Yeah, we're just wonderful Mr. Donato," Nunzio replied. "Just wonderful."

"It was probably Rooney's men, but I can't be sure,"

Angelo mumbled.

"Vinnie," he called to the chauffeur. "Let's get back to the warehouse. I'll have some men down here to clean up this mess, Nora, and here's a twenty to fix the window. Call the glazier over on Washington. Tell him I said to get right over. I'm sorry this happened, and I'm glad they missed, real glad."

Nunzio watched the Rolls Royce pull away. "I don't like this whole operation Aunt Nora, we could have all been killed. Whoever did this either knows what we're doing or they just wanted to kill Donato. I hope it's Donato they're after."

"I wish your Uncle never got involved," Nora replied. "But what do we do now? Donato is the king around here. If they kill him, five minutes later there's a new king. I'm going upstairs to rest. Too much excitement for one day."

"What do you think of what happened?" Nunzio asked Moses as he came into the front of the bakery.

"I don't get paid to think," Moses replied. "I just do my work, and when the bullets start flying, I duck."

Several hours later Uncle Alberto and Acey came back to the bakery. "Holy shit," Alberto said, looking at the glacier fitting the window. "Nunzio, what the hell happened here?"

"Your paesano, Angelo Donato, came to buy some cake and bread. Some guys came by and figured maybe he was putting on too much weight, so they tried to stop him with a rifle."

"Was anyone hurt? Was Nora ...?"

"Not this time," Nunzio interrupted. "Nobody was hurt this time."

"Thank God," Alberto sighed. "Thank God."

"Aunt Nora is upstairs."

Uncle Alberto went upstairs and Nunzio finished up in the back with Moses and Acey.

"The window's all done," Joe, the glazier, told

Nunzio.

"Thanks, Joe. Here's your money," Nunzio replied handing Joe the bill. "Keep the change for getting here so quick. We may become a regular account of yours."

"Thanks, Mr. Cappolla."

"Mr. Cappolla," Nunzio whispered. "You're the first person in America to call me that."

Angelo jumped out of the Rolls before the chauffeur stopped the car. He stormed into the warehouse. "Vito, get in the office, we got some problems," he yelled, as he rushed toward his office. "Someone just took a shot at me while I was in Cappolla's Bakery. From Vinnie's description of the car, I think it was Rooney's boys."

"I'll take a few guys with me, Boss. We'll blow that son of a bitch off the face of the earth," Vito replied.

"Yeah, Vito. Then he will send an army to blow my ass into a thousand pieces, and then what's left of me he sends another army for that. Dead men don't sell wine and dead men don't drive around in a Rolls Royce. A lot of people make their living off this operation, and I got a wife and kids over in Plymouth that don't want to go to no funeral, so we got to do something sensible in this situation."

"Like what, Boss? What you got in mind?" Frankie asked.

"Call Rooney. Tell him I want to meet with him somewhere neutral. No men, no guns, just him and me. Tell him I want to discuss our differences."

"Okay, boss," Frankie said. "I'll call right now. When do you want to meet with him?"

"Anytime he says. Right now would be fine."

While Frankie was on the phone, Angelo checked around the warehouse.

"All the stock is in, boss," Vito told him as he glanced at the checklist. "And Gino got his suit and the ring and is all set for his wedding."

"Good," Angelo answered. "This has been one hell of a day."

"Hey, boss," Frankie shouted. "Rooney says how about one hour in front of Faneull Hall?"

"Tell him I'll be there."

Frankie walked out of the office and gave Angelo the collection money he and Danny picked up for the day. Angelo looked over Ralph's delivery sheets.

"Not bad," Angelo said to Frankie. "At least things went smooth with the operation today. Start the car Vinnie, we're going downtown."

Faneull Hall hadn't changed much since Peter Faneull completed it in 1742. It's known as the Cradle of Liberty because of all the historical meetings held there. What a place for an Irish and an Italian bootlegger to hold a meeting, Sean Rooney thought to himself as he watched Angelo get out of the black Rolls Royce. The two men nodded at each other but did not shake hands.

"We can sit on the stairs if you like," Rooney said.

"I can stand," Angelo answered him. "After the way you treated me today, Sean, I'm glad I'm able to stand. What was the idea of trying to kill me?"

"If I wanted to kill you, Angelo, you would be dead. I just wanted you to know how easy it would be if and when I decided to kill you."

"You know I hate gang war, Sean. I had enough of that shit when we were kids. You and me, the Mick and the Dagoes always fighting. There's a lot of money to be made out there, Sean. Why can't we operate without killing each other?"

"You're moving too far south, Angelo. The other day I seen that bread truck over on Newton. What the hell you doing delivering wine over on Newton? That's my turf."

"Bread, Sean. The truck was delivering bread. They eat bread in the South End same as anywhere else."

"Bread, my ass," Rooney replied with his arms up in

the air. "I got your whole operation being watched and we went in after the truck left, opened the breads and there was imported Dago wine. Quit trying to bullshit me. You want to deliver wine to the South End, no problem. I want 50% of the profits and you can deliver all the wine you want. I don't want this to turn into another Chicago, Angelo, but I don't want you fucking me, either. Understand?"

"Fifty percent is heavy Sean. I can handle, say... 25%."

"You want peace, Angelo? Fifty percent and you can have peace. Only just wine. You try to cut in on the booze and the beer and you better call General Pershing, because you're going to need him. Now, is there anything else you want to talk about?"

"Okay," Angelo reluctantly agreed. "I'll send Vinnie down every Friday with your money." he added as he walked toward the Rolls.

Back at the warehouse Angelo sat cursing to himself as Frankie and Vito waited for him to tell them the outcome of the meeting.

"For the time being we pay fifty percent of the profits to Rooney and we can operate freely in the South End, wine only. Let's see how it works out. Besides, Rooney controls a lot of those Mick political bosses and cops." He turned to leave. "I'm going home," he called back. "I'll see you at the wedding on Sunday."

"If I was the boss, I would blow the shit out of Rooney and take over all of Boston," Vito said as he watched the Rolls Royce drive down Commercial Street.

"You ain't the boss, Vito," Frankie replied. "And I don't think you'll ever be the boss."

"Don't be surprised, Frankie, baby," Vito said, patting him on the cheek. "Stranger things have happened. Ciao."

CHAPTER SIX
Monday Morning

Paul Bonet stood in front of his store on St. James Street watching the sunrise as he did every morning. It was his favorite time of the day. Peaceful and quiet. And he could work on his designs without any interruptions. He was admiring the red and gold canopy in front of the store. What a magnificent entrance he thought. Inside the snow white carpet and the royal blue and gold walls with Greek and Roman artwork gave his creations the elegance they deserved.

He had asked Loretta to come in early this morning to model some of his new summer collection, and no sooner had he turned on the lights, he noticed her at the door.

"Good Morning, darling," he said as he helped her remove her coat. "How did you sleep last night?"

"Dreaming of you, Paul, dear," she smiled.

"How did it go in church yesterday with that wedding?" Paul asked.

"Well, her father was too proud to show up, since Franny is five months pregnant. So Alberto Cappolla gave the bride away, and the priest kind of rushed it along. The groom did not look very happy, but they are married. My friend Nunzio and I took the newlyweds out for dinner last night at the Freedom Trail Inn. I almost got Nunzio to do the Charleston. Funniest thing you ever saw."

"I wish I could have been there," Paul said. "Anyway, time to get to work. I appreciate your coming in early this morning, Loretta. I hope I can make it up to you by taking you out for dinner tonight."

"Why that's the best offer I've had so far today," she

laughed, giving him a kiss on the cheek. That was as much physical affection as she had shown him since they met. Paul had been a perfect gentleman, but she knew he would like more than that. She felt the same way, but knew she must control her emotions. Paul is very handsome and doing very well in his business, she mused. Many girls would cut off an arm to be in her shoes. But, I'm not just any girl, she added to her thoughts. When the time is right, I'll know.

"I'm working on the Daffeny Line, Loretta," Paul said. "Would you put on the blue dress and I'll make any adjustments necessary while you have it on."

"Yes, dear," she said, retreating to the dressing room.

"You look radiant, darling," Paul sighed when she returned.

"Are we working, or is this a private showing?" Loretta asked.

"A little of both. You are the most desirable woman I have ever met in my entire life." He went over to her and took her in his arms. He kissed her gently on her lips, stared into her eyes and then pressed his lips on hers harder than before and moved his tongue into her mouth. She returned the gesture, opening her mouth to receive his tongue.

"I'm crazy about you," Paul cried as he pulled the top of the dress down, exposing her magnificent breasts.

"No, Paul. Please don't," Loretta cried. "Not now, not here... like this, please." She pulled away and ran into the dressing room.

Paul sat down on the sofa, staring at the dressing room door. "I... I'm sorry," he shouted.

Loretta came out with her own clothes on and went over to him. "Don't be sorry. I feel the same way as you, Paul, but I want it to be right. Not a quick moment of passion on a sofa in your store. I've never been with a man, Paul." She gave him a gentle kiss and he embraced her with equal gentleness.

"I love you, Loretta. I know that I love you like I have never loved anyone."

"I don't know what to say, Paul. I feel that I love you too, but there are so many things, so many differences," she said.

"What do you mean?" he asked.

"What do I mean? Well for one thing I'm a Catholic and you're a Jew. That would kill my father. He's in so much pain now."

"I'm a Jew by birth only. That has been a problem for me all my life, I can convert if it means being with you."

"And you are forty years old, and I'm only twenty. You are almost my father's age," she said.

"Yes, and I can keep up with any twenty year old on the face of this earth."

"For how long, Paul?"

"Why can't we live one day a time? I want to marry you. I know I can make you happy."

"Marriage? But if we have children, you will be closer to a grandfather then a father."

"I love you, Loretta. If you love me we will make it work."

"I need time to think, Paul. Please give me time to think."

"Take all the time you need. But like you said, I am forty, so don't take too long."

She smiled and gave him a hug. "Let's get back to work now," she whispered in his ear.

As she let go, Rose Kelly walked into the store removing her shawl while she curiously watched Loretta remove her arms from around Paul's neck.

"Good morning, Mr. Bonet, Loretta. I hope my timing wasn't bad."

"Good morning, Rose," Paul chanted. "Glad to see you here bright and early."

"Same here," Loretta said. "Lots of work to do. It should be a busy Monday. Half of Boston will be coming in today to look at our summer dress line."

"I pray to God you are right about that, Loretta," Paul said.

"And which God are you praying to Paul?" Loretta asked with whimsical sarcasm.

"The one that created you, darling. The one that created you," he said, staring into her eyes.

"Nobody can ever accuse you of not knowing the right thing to say, Paul," she said, kissing her fingers and touching them to his lips.

"Shall I set up the new dresses for the models, Mr. Bonet?" Rose asked.

"Yes, Rose. They are all numbered in order, except that blue one. Loretta will show that one first."

"How do you like this one, Rose? I call it Numero Uno Vestito. That's Italian for number one dress," Loretta said.

"It's beautiful, Loretta, and your English has improved a lot," Rose answered.

"Having a private tutor has made a difference. My friend Nunzio goes to night school and still he understands only half as much as I do. Speaking of Nunzio, I want you to meet him. He is very handsome, and I know you will like each other."

"Be a matchmaker on your own time," Paul said jokingly. "We have work to do now."

"I would like to meet your friend, Nunzio," Rose whispered.

Rose proceeded to arrange the dresses and soon after she finished, Florence, Edith and Mona, the three other models, arrived along with the two seamstresses, Gail and Irene. After exchanging hellos and getting ready for the showing, Paul lined the girls up in order behind the red velvet curtain and opened the front door. One by one the glamorous cream of Boston's high society arrived. They were seated in the lounge and were served champagne and caviar. The models paraded around the room as Paul explained each garment. Rose helped Paul write the orders.

"A most rewarding day," Paul said smiling when the last customer exited. "All of you did a wonderful job, and as always, my appreciation will be shown in your pay envelope on Friday," he exclaimed.

Loretta hugged Paul and asked what time he would be picking her up for dinner.

"Eight, okay?" Paul asked.

"I will be waiting," she answered, not wanting to subject Paul to her father's attitude toward him.

Loretta stopped at the bakery on her way home. "Hello, Nora," she smiled. "Thought I would bring my father some cannoli for desert."

Aunt Nora had been shaken up since the shooting and kept looking out the plate-glass window. "How many cannoli would you like?" she asked.

"Two will be fine. Oh, and is Nunzio in the back?"

"Nunzio," Nora called to the back room.

"Buon giorno, Loretta," Nunzio said as he walked into the front. "How have you been?"

"Wonderful, Nunzio," she replied. "Ah, I would like to arrange for you to meet Rose. Perhaps tomorrow night you can come with Paul and me for a cup of coffee, and I can ask Rose along."

"I have school at night," Nunzio explained.

"Surely you can miss one night of school."

"I suppose I can."

"Then if Rose is available, I will call you tomorrow and tell you where to meet us."

"Okay, Loretta," Nunzio smiled.

That night, Loretta and Paul went to the Regency House for dinner. Paul knew what the restricted sign meant. No Jews or colored people allowed. And though it angered him, he went there anyway. They did not know he was Jewish and he did not tell them. Pride was not his greatest attribute. He wanted so badly to be part of Boston's gentile society that he betrayed his heritage. Loretta did not question him on this, because she did not understand.

"Good evening, Mr. Bonet," the maître d' welcomed Paul and Loretta. "Would you and the lady care for a table near the dance floor?"

"That would be fine, Andrew," Paul said.

"We're fortunate to have Earl 'Father' Hines and his orchestra for your dining and dancing pleasure," the maître d' added.

"He is one of my favorite musicians," Paul said.

"Likewise," Loretta proclaimed.

After a dinner of pheasant, too much wine and more dancing than Loretta's feet could stand, Paul looked her in the eye and said without hesitation, "Darling, I could ask you to come to my apartment, but I would prefer to take a room here at the Regency."

Loretta wanted to say no. She thought for a moment that she should tell him she had a wonderful time and to please take her home. All of her principles were on the table and she didn't know how to play the hand. "Anything you want," she heard herself say.

Paul could not control his excitement. Taking her hand, he led her through to the lobby. He fumbled with his wallet and asked the desk clerk for the room key. They walked up to the second floor arm in arm. Paul carried Loretta across the threshold as if she was his bride. They both stood in the middle of the room embracing.

"Are you nervous?" Paul asked as he opened the buttons on the back of Loretta's dress.

"I don't know if I'm nervous or scared, but I can't stop shaking," she said.

Her dress fell to the floor, and she was standing there in her panties. Embarrassed, she folded her arms across her breasts. Paul undressed and took her in his arms. She had never seen a man completely naked before, and tried not to stare at him. She couldn't hide her embarrassment.

"I always thought I would be doing this on my wedding night," she sighed. "It doesn't seem right, Paul."

"When you're in love it's always right," Paul said.

He leaned over and kissed her gently, and placed each of his thumbs in the sides of her panties. He pulled them down to the floor, kissing her all over.

Hot flashes shot up Loretta's body. She had never experienced such pleasures, such feelings. Paul lifted her and carried her to the bed.

"Be gentle," she whispered in his ear, as his hands and his lips explored every inch of her body.

"You're beautiful," he sighed as he continued caressing her. "You have the most perfect body I have ever seen. I want this to last forever."

She moaned in ecstasy as she felt the thrust of entry. She kept rhythm with each of his motions and cried out in her pleasure.

"Oh, Paul. Paul, it's so good, it feels so good. I love you, Paul. I love you."

Suddenly she felt his release into her body and he collapsed in her arms. "I love you, Loretta, with all my heart, I love you."

"I gave myself to you completely, Paul," she said afterwards. "A lifetime of waiting for the right man and the right time, and here it is."

Paul looked at her. He noticed a tear on her cheek and licked it off. "Is something wrong?" he asked.

"No. It was wonderful," she answered. "It could become habit forming. And what a lovely habit," she said as she pulled him toward her.

Paul, again aroused, made love to her.

"We can't stay here all night, Paul. My father wouldn't understand my not coming home. Please, darling, take me home."

Paul kissed her eyes and said, "I understand. Perhaps the day will come soon when we can be together all the time, and I can fall asleep holding you."

"Perhaps," she said as she got up and put on her clothes. "Paul, I would like to have Nunzio join us tomorrow night, and introduce him to Rose. Would it be all right with you?"

"Of course. We can take them to the movies. There is a talkie out called Wings that I am sure we all would enjoy."

"That would be nice," Loretta said. "I love you, Paul."

When she got home she was glad her father was asleep. Loretta lay in bed thinking about Paul. He made her feel unimaginably good. But there was something missing, she didn't know what it was. Maybe it's just me, she thought. I do love him, she said to herself, and she fell asleep.

CHAPTER SEVEN
The next day

Vito Natali loved to drive around Boston and fanaticized about the past. That morning even the rain couldn't stop him. As he drove down Fleet Street, past Paul Revere's house, he could see the old boy riding to Concord yelling, "The British are coming." Or maybe he was really warning the Irish that the Italians were coming.

He passed the site of the Boston Massacre, and stopped the car. He decided he needed to walk for a while. That was no massacre, he thought. If we have to do business with Rooney, there's going to be a real Boston Massacre.

The rain was coming down in buckets, but Vito did not care as he walked with his hands in his pockets daydreaming. "I was a fucking Captain," he said to himself. "Me and Pershing. We kicked some ass back in '17. I can remember Colonel Stanton yelling, 'Lafayette, we are here,' when we hit France. We gave them Germans a couple of new assholes.

"Well, the war ain't over yet. It ain't ever going to be over. It's just a matter of identifying the enemy. The G-men are the enemy, sticking their damn noses in everyone's business. What the hell do they care who drinks what? They're all a bunch of shits. Mayor James Curley is the enemy. Too much power for one man. Rooney for sure is the enemy, and Angelo Donato. The enemy that doesn't know he's the enemy. Well, Captain Natali, time to prepare for war." Vito got back into the car and headed toward Hanover Street. He stopped at Cappolla's Bakery. The rain was beginning to let up as he parked in front. Franny was inside talking to Nora Cappolla.

"How is married life, Franny?" Vito asked.

"Okay, I suppose," she answered looking straight ahead.

Vito had put it to Franny a few times himself, and was hoping the kid didn't have curly hair like his.

"Gino around?" he asked.

"He's in the back with Nunzio," she said.

Vito went into the back and called out, "Hey, Gino, what are you doing?"

"The boss wants me to help with today's shipment. There's a lot of vino to go out today," Gino said.

"Come outside, I wanna talk to you alone," Vito said.

Gino put down the sack of wine and followed Vito to the street.

"You happy about marrying the whore, Gino?" Vito asked.

"You know the answer to that one, Vito," Gino said.

"The boss is going a little crazy on us, Gino. He thinks he's fucking God or something. This deal with Rooney, your having to marry Franny, and his other horse shit. I think it's time for some new management."

"Ya know Vito, this conversation can get us a place in the Charles River with lead boots."

"Hey, fuck Angelo Donato. I helped beat the stunod Kaiser, I'll handle Donato. "Are you in or out? You know if you're out I'll have to kill you. As much as I like you, I'll have no choice."

"Since you put it that way, Vito, I guess I'm in. I hate Angelo anyway. Do you think you can run the operation?"

"A whole lot better than Angelo. Let's go inside. I'll get in touch with you when I have the details worked out. Don't say nothing to nobody. Not that Cappolla kid, or even your lovely wife."

When they got back inside Nunzio was on the

telephone. Loretta had called to tell him about the plans for that evening. He was to meet them in front of Victor's at seven. They were going to have a snack and go to the movies. Nunzio was going to meet Rose Kelly.

"Hey, Moses," Nunzio said turning toward the ovens, "I'm going to see a movie tonight. I've never seen a movie, and I'm going to have a date."

"Sounds like your lucky day," Moses answered.

Gino picked up one of the sacks and turned to Nunzio, "Never mind that crap now, we gotta lot of work to do."

Franny walked with Vito to his car. "Can you drop me at the house, Vito?" she asked. "It's starting to rain again."

"Going the other way," he said. "And besides, the water is good for you. Cleanliness is next to Godliness," he laughed as he got into the car and left.

At seven o'clock that evening, Nunzio was standing nervously in front of Victor's. At about a quarter after seven he noticed Paul Bonet's car. Loretta and a blond-haired girl got out of the car before Paul pulled into the lot. He wanted to walk toward them, but chose to remain standing in front of the luncheonette. They crossed toward him.

"Nunzio, this is Rose Kelly. Rose, I would like you to meet Nunzio Cappolla, my good friend," Loretta said happily introducing the two.

Nunzio was speechless. He just stared at the long, blond hair, the blue eyes and the little freckles on her face and her arms. She's beautiful!

Rose was turning red from embarrassment and, as usual, could not stop blushing.

"Loretta told me a lot of nice things about you, Nunzio," Rose said.

"Likewise," Nunzio answered.

"The movie starts at eight," Paul called out walking

toward them. Maybe we can eat after the show."

"Is that okay with you two?" Loretta asked.

"Fine with me," Rose answered.

"Me, too," Nunzio said.

They walked to the theater. Nunzio kept staring at Rose during the movie. Each time he turned to look at her she turned toward him and smiled. He quickly looked away, nervous and embarrassed. Paul had his arm around Loretta's shoulders and she kept whispering something in his ear.

"That was the best picture I have ever seen," Paul said as they walked out of the theater.

"It's the only picture I have ever seen," said Nunzio. "But my English is still not so good. I cannot say I understand everything they were talking about."

Paul put his hand on Nunzio's shoulder, and asked, "Would you mind taking Rose home by yourself? I need to be alone with Loretta tonight."

"Paul," Loretta complained. "That's not right."

"It's okay," Nunzio said. "That is, if Rose doesn't mind."

"No, I don't mind," Rose said.

Paul handed Nunzio a ten dollar bill. "This should more then cover dinner plus. Take it, and thanks for understanding. See you at the shop in the morning, Rose. Good night."

"Good night, Mr. Bonet. See you tomorrow, Loretta," Rose replied.

Loretta didn't say anything as she walked away with Paul.

"How do you like Boston and America?" Rose asked as she and Nunzio were seated in Victor's.

"I like it fine but I miss my family. And there is a lot of things going on that I don't understand."

"Like what?" Rose asked.

"The way people treat each other over here for one

thing. This prohibition thing. I don't know. I guess I'll get used to America. Were you born here?"

"Yes, my great-grandparents came here in 1845 from Ireland because of the potato famine. We live in the same house on West Newton as my great-grandparents did. My father is a police officer."

"So I have heard. You must worry a great deal, and your mother, also."

"My mother died about five years ago. Pneumonia. We live with my grandmother and my brother. And, yes, I worry all the time. But my father can handle himself quite well. My brother, Jim, is also on the force."

"I would like to meet your family, Rose."

"I'll tell you, my father is not too crazy about me working for Paul Bonet. And I don't know how he would react to you. He doesn't like Jews or Italians. He says that they're all gangsters, and they're ruining this country."

"Do you believe that?"

"I don't know what I believe. There are Irish gangsters and Italian saints and visa versa. I like working for Paul Bonet. I think prejudice is a disease, but it is a fact of life we have to live with."

"In Italy I never knew anyone but Italians, and now my best friend is Jewish. I work with colored men and I'm sitting in a luncheonette having dinner with a beautiful Irish girl. I don't feel any prejudice at all. I think it is stupid. My friend, David, told me stories of the prejudice in Europe, and what he went through even as the son of a Baron and a wealthy family. It doesn't make sense."

"America is the melting pot for all people, Nunzio. Things will get better."

"Yeah," Nunzio sighed. "I would like to see you again, Rose. I'm sure I can handle your father. We are both catholic and..." He paused. He was about to say 'and I'm not a gangster.' Then he remembered Angelo and the wine in the breads, and stopped himself.

"And what?" Rose asked.

"And, I'm sure he will like me once he meets me," Nunzio laughed.

"I'm glad I met you, Nunzio. You're everything Loretta said you were. I can't figure out why she didn't grab you for herself."

"I think it has to do with chemistry. And I'm glad I met you, too. I better get you home now." He paid the bill with the ten dollars Paul gave him, and put the seven dollars change in his pocket. It was pouring when they got outside, so he hailed a cab.

"Your lucky night," he said to the driver. "First West Newton on the South End, and then Hanover on the North End."

"Yes, sir," the driver said smiling.

"I really want to see you again Rose," Nunzio said as they pulled in front of her house.

"Come by the dress shop. Good night," she said kissing his cheek. "I had a wonderful time."

"Drive around town for six dollars worth and then let me out on Hanover Street near Richmond. Here's seven dollars," Nunzio told the driver.

The driver was delighted. He drove slowly in the rain.

Nunzio was daydreaming as he looked out at the Boston streets in the rain. "Rose Kelly, Rose Kelly, Rose Kelly," he kept saying over and over. The more he said it the better it sounded.

He got out of the taxi on the corner and decided to walk in the rain. He saw the police cars and the ambulance in front of the Foscolo's house. He ran over to find out what was going on. Uncle Alberto and Aunt Nora were out front, as well as three-quarters of the neighborhood.

"What happened here?" Nunzio asked Uncle Alberto.

"Awful, just awful," Aunt Nora cried.

Uncle Alberto took Nunzio over to the side and said,

"Gino called Angelo and told him to get right over, that it was an emergency. Angelo called me at the bakery to see if I knew what was going on. I told him I didn't know a thing, so he drove over himself. No chauffeur even. He was inside the apartment with Gino, Franny and the old man, when the fireworks began. Gino managed to roll under the table and didn't get hit. He says he played dead, but got a good look at the gunman. Franny, Angelo and the old man. Dead. They're all dead."

"Who did it?" Nunzio asked.

"I don't know. Gino's over there talking to the cops." Alberto said. "It looks like Vito Natali is the new boss now. Of course, he doesn't know what happened yet, but he will be around as soon as he hears. I'm sure he's going to want revenge on the killers."

Nunzio ran over to Gino talking to the policemen. "Who did this, Gino?" Nunzio shouted.

One of the policemen tried to push Nunzio away. "It was Rooney's men. The same ones who shot up the bakery," Gino said.

Gino got in the back of the police car. He had to go to the station to look at pictures and help identify the killers.

"Don't you worry," one of the policemen, a tall blond Irish-looking man yelled into the crowd, "we'll find the killers, or my name ain't Jim Kelly."

"You're Jim Kelly?" Nunzio asked the policeman.

"That's right. Now move along everybody. The show is over. The Boston Massacre of 1928, that's what the papers will call this one."

The rain was coming down harder. Nunzio shook his head in disbelief. He went to his room and took out his box of stationary. He started to write:

Dear Maria. I don't know where to begin to tell you the events of the day. Let me start at the beginning...

CHAPTER EIGHT
October 2, 1929

Although it was well over a year since the murder of Angelo Donato, Franny Foscolo and her father, nobody on Hanover Street had forgotten. Passing by the scene of the crime, Nunzio could still see the crowd and the ambulance, the police cars, and Jim Kelly.

Nunzio had been dating Rose steadily for a year, and getting along surprising well with Jim Kelly, Junior. And Signor Grandma Kelly was especially fond of him, and had been making him dinners of corned beef and cabbage every Friday. It was a dish for which he had acquired a taste.

Vito Natali was running Boston with an iron hand. He eliminated the Rooney mob, and formed an alliance with the syndicate. There was nobody to stop him.

Loretta and Paul had been married for six months, and Loretta was still modeling at the dress shop. "I will keep going until I am pregnant," she told Nunzio.

David was doing well at MIT, and planned to marry Sally in January. Uncle Alberto decided to liquidate his investments after the first of the year, and retire in style. His stocks were doing well, and he already told Vito that Nunzio will be taking over the bakery when he cashed out.

Nunzio was hoping to bring the family over from Bari. Mussolini had put an end to any chance of free elections in Italy, and although the Fascists seemed to have the confidence of the people, if not the church, Enzio Cappolla was a devout Anti-Fascist, and was ready to emigrate.

Nunzio was getting the wheels turning for them to

leave Bari and settle in Boston. The bakery was expanding, and aside from being used in transporting of the wine, the baked goods were becoming popular around Boston.

Herbert Clark Hoover, an orphan who had become a millionaire by the time he was forty, was President of the United States. He promised an era of the greatest achievements for this country. Everyone would prosper through hard work and wise investments. There was no reason not to believe him. "A chicken in every pot; a car in every garage," he promised.

The country was prospering. The factories were whistling out of their chimneys. America was lending money to European countries, and that money was being used to buy American products. Germany was borrowing heavily from the United States to pay its war debts, which seemed unending.

However, there were many groups, like the farmers and miners, that were not sharing in the prosperity of the 1920's. In the textile industry, working conditions were poor and wages were low.

The economy was being weakened by too much credit. Thousands of people were borrowing money to pay for stocks in the hopes of getting rich.

Alberto Cappolla was one of the biggest investors. Not only did he put his entire fortune on the line, but every penny he could borrow was invested in the market.

Nunzio was taking Rose to the movies, the same theater they had gone to on their first date. They were going to see All's Quiet on the Western Front.

CHAPTER NINE
October 29, 1929

"Nunzio, please hang up the phone," Aunt Nora pleaded. "You can talk to Rose later. The customers are lined out into the street.

Nunzio nodded at Aunt Nora. "I'll call you back later," he said into the phone. "I love you, too. See you tonight."

Nunzio helped Aunt Nora in front, while Moses and Acey took care of the back room.

"The truck should be here with the wine any minute now," Moses said.

"Call me when they get here!" Nunzio shouted.

"Pack four cannoli for Mrs. Bernardo," Aunt Nora said to Nunzio. "I wonder where that uncle of yours is? He hasn't been here all morning."

"Probably at the bank, or with his broker," Nunzio replied, as he grabbed one of the small boxes and packed the cannoli. He dropped one of the cannoli on the floor, and bent down to pick it up.

"You're thinking about Rose, again, " Aunt Nora kidded. "All you think about is Rose. Maybe if you married her, you'd stop dropping things."

"The thought had entered my mind, Aunt Nora," he responded with a smile. "As soon as Mama, Papa and Maria get here, I'm going to ask Rose to marry me."

"What do you think the Irish cop-father is going to say about that?"

"Jim Kelly's bark is worst then his bite. We get along fine. He talks like a bigot, but he doesn't really mean it."

"Does he know about the wine?"

"Jim Kelly drinks a bottle of wine like it was a glass of water. And beer, too. He should have a pipeline from the brewery to his stomach. He makes more from bribes than his paycheck from the police force."

"How do you know that?" Aunt Nora asked.

"I know a lot," Nunzio answered sarcastically, glancing at the front of the store. "Hey! Look who's outside. It's David Fairchild, himself," he said, walking around the counter to greet him.

"Torquato La David," Nunzio shouted, as he grabbed David's hand. "It is so good to see you. How come you're not in school?"

"Examination week," David said. "I thought I would visit you a while, and then maybe you and Rose would join Sally and me for dinner. My treat, of course."

"Your treat? And they say Jews are cheap," Nunzio said, jokingly.

"Is today a holiday or something?" David asked.

"Not that I know about. Why do you ask?"

"Well, the bank over on Commercial is closed, and there was a line of people in front," David said.

"Here comes my Uncle Alberto, I'll ask him if he knows?"

Uncle Alberto brushed right by David and Nunzio, and picked up the phone.

"What's the matter?" Aunt Nora asked.

Uncle Alberto didn't answer her. "Keep trying Mr. Parker's office," he told the girl on the phone. "Keep trying, goddamn it, keep trying," he cried. "He's got to be there. Where the hell could he be? Where the hell...?" he was crying uncontrollably with the receiver in his hand.

"Oh, my God, what's the matter? What's the matter?" Aunt Nora frantically pleaded.

"Don't none of you listen to the damn radio?" Uncle Alberto asked, still crying. "The stocks are dropping like crazy, the market is going berserk. Every stock, every goddamned stock. Everyone who heard the reports are running to the bank to get their money out. The fucking banks are closing to stop the run, and I can't get a hold of that asshole broker, Alan Parker. I want to sell my stock before it's too late, and I can't reach the broker. Fuck, fuck, fuck!"

"Please, such language, Alberto. It will be okay. Please stop crying. It will be all right," said Aunt Nora trying to calm him.

David turned the radio on in the back room. "There's a newscast coming on now," he called to Nunzio and Uncle Alberto. Aunt Nora put the 'closed' sign in the window and joined them in the back.

"Make it loud so I can hear. I'm not getting off this phone 'til I get a hold of Parker," Uncle Albert shouted.

"I repeat," the newscaster said. "The bottom has fallen out of the stock market. The crash has caused losses in the hundreds of million of dollars. Banks are closing their doors and calling emergency board meetings to weigh the situation. President Hoover is asking you not to panic. Please remain calm. You have nothing to fear at this time. This is only a temporary situation, and together we will weather this storm. In a few days things will be back to normal."

Alberto put the phone down. "I'm wiped out," he cried. "Broke, penniless, and I owe more money than... Oh, what have I done? The house, the store, we're gonna lose everything!"

"What do you mean lose everything?" Nora asked. "You heard what the President of the United States said. Everything will be okay in a few days. Please, Alberto. Please stop carrying on."

"Fuck the President of the United States," Alberto said. "The market crashed. My stock is worth shit, and you're telling me to calm down. I'm getting out of here."

"Where are you going?" Nora yelled. "Alberto,

please come back here. Nunzio, go after your Uncle, please. My God! What is happening?"

"I'll go with you," David said.

Uncle Alberto was already down the block, and his car was turning the corner by the time David and Nunzio got into David's car. They lost him at the turn.

"I'm sure he will be all right," Nunzio said, as they returned to the bakery. "How do you think this crash is going to effect things?"

"I'm an engineering student not an economist, but I would imagine if things don't spring back, everyone who has stock in the market is going to lose their money. As for the effect on the rest of the country, and the world for that matter, I don't want to guess. I don't know, but it could be a major problem. I think we better forget about going out tonight, Nunzio. You better stay with your aunt until your uncle comes back. I'm going back to Cambridge. I'll call you in a couple of days. Ciao."

Nunzio got out of the car and went back into the bakery where he tried to comfort his aunt. The truck was in the back, with Moses and Acey unloading the wine.

It was near seven p.m. when Nunzio finally left the bakery and went to see Rose. "I really would rather just walk around and talk," he told her. He wasn't hungry, and he was worried about Uncle Alberto.

"What do you think is going to happen?" Rose asked.

"Well, according to Vito Natali, people will probably drink more for a while, but things should straighten out. The President feels confident that we will have a mild depression and then get back to normal. But Uncle Alberto still hasn't come home. He's never done this before."

Rose took Nunzio's hand. "I love you so much, Nunzio," she said with heartfelt sympathy.

"I love you more then you can imagine, Rose. Let's get married now. I don't want to wait any longer."

"I thought you wanted your family to be here when

we got married."

"They will understand. I want to wake up every morning with you in my arms."

Rose pulled him toward her and kissed him passionately. Nunzio quivered.

"Yes, I will marry you now," she said.

They walked along the Boston Common, neither one saying anything while holding hands and enjoying the night. Everything will be all right, Nunzio thought to himself. Uncle Alberto is probably home right now. When he took Rose home, Jim Kelly, Sr. and Jr. were in the kitchen, drinking beer.

"Pa," Rose greeted her father. "Nunzio and I are getting married as soon as possible. We don't want to wait."

"Are you pregnant, Rose?" her father asked.

"Of course not," she replied.

"Then what's the hurry?" he asked

"We just want to be together, Pa," Rose said.

"You keep messing with that wine business, Nunzio, and the Feds are going to get you on the Volstead Act violation. Then you'll be honeymooning in prison," Jim, Jr. said.

"I'm going to talk to Vito and get out of it. I never wanted to be involved in the first place," Nunzio responded. "Do we have your blessing to get married?

"My blessing? I only want my daughter to be happy. I still think you're a grease ball, Dago, garlic breath."

"Grease ball, Dago, garlic breath, eh? You ever think of becoming a poet? You have a hell of a way with words. But, thanks for your blessings." He chuckled. "Rose, I'll make the arrangements in the morning, and we can get married in a couple of days."

"I love you," Rose replied. "Call me in the morning."

"I will. Good night, Mr. Kelly. Good night, Jim," Nunzio said, walking out the door.

He kept walking home while trying to find a taxi, but there weren't any available. He wound up walking all the way home, all the time thinking about Rose and Uncle Alberto. When he arrived home, Aunt Nora was still up, and Uncle Alberto was not home.

"Did you hear anything at all, Nunzio?" she asked him when he walked in.

"Not a thing. He must have gone somewhere to be alone for a while. Let's go to sleep. I'm sure he will return by the morning."

"I can't sleep without your Uncle," she cried. "I'm going to sit here until I know he's all right."

"Then I'll sit here with you, Aunt Nora."

The two of them fell asleep in the living room. Nora kept waking every fifteen minutes and whispering, "Alberto?" Every time the door made the slightest sound, she would jump up.

Alberto never came home that night. In the morning, they did not open the bakery. Nunzio told Acey and Moses to take the day off and rest up. He and Nora just sat in the living room waiting for Uncle Alberto.

Vito Natali was furious when he heard that nobody was at the bakery to receive the wine. Then, when he heard the reason why, he put every one of his men out looking for Alberto. "Search every inch of Boston," he commanded them.

That evening, Loretta and Paul came over with Rose. Alberto was still missing, and Aunt Nora was sitting with her rosary in hand, praying. She would not talk to anyone. She kept crying and praying.

"A lot of people jumped out of windows when they found out they lost everything," Paul said, which was not comforting to Aunt Nora.

"How did this thing happen?" Nunzio asked.

"Because this country was climbing a stairway that everybody thought had no end. But when we reached the top step, it was one too many and too soon. Right down to the bottom, everything went."

"Will we recover, Paul?" Nunzio asked.

"The President thinks so. But I think there's going to be a depression that will rock the whole world."

"What a pleasant thought," Rose said. "You have a way of cheering people up, Mr. Bonet."

"My opinion," Paul said. "Just my opinion."

Nora jumped when she heard the doorbell. "Alberto," she asked, anxiously.

But it was an Irish cop at the door. "Mrs. Cappolla?" he asked.

"I... I'm Mrs. Cappolla, what is...? My husband, is he all right? What is it? You got my Alberto with you..?"

Rose recognized her brother's voice, "Jim, what is it?" she cried.

"We found a car in the Charles River. The body, we believe, is Mr. Cappolla's," Jim said.

"No! Oh, God, no!" Aunt Nora cried hysterically. "No, not my Alberto! Please, God. What am I going to do?"

Nunzio tried to comfort her, but she was out of control.

"We better leave," Paul said, as he took Loretta's hand.

"I'm staying here." Rose said.

"We'll need you to come to the morgue and identify the body," Jim said.

"I'll go," Nunzio said.

"I'll stay here with your Aunt until you get back," Rose replied.

Nunzio gasped in horror as the Coroner rolled the sheet off the body. It was Uncle Alberto. He stared at the ashen gray, water-washed body a moment before turning away and vomiting on the floor. He wanted to cry, but couldn't. He was in shock.

"I'm sorry," Jim said. "I'm truly sorry."

"How did it happen?" Nunzio asked.

"We don't know for sure, but it looks like he just drove his car into the river. Probably suicide," Jim said.

"Was there a note or something?" Nunzio asked.

"No, there was nothing. Do you have any idea why he would take his life?" the officer asked.

"Stock market, like the others. He had everything invested, and he went wild when the news came on the radio. He just ran out of the house," answered Nunzio, dazed.

"I guess a lot of people are in the same boat. Of course, that doesn't make this situation any easier," Jim said, putting his arm around Nunzio's shoulder.

"Thanks, Jim," Nunzio said.

"Let me drive you home, Nunzio."

"I would appreciate that."

At home, Nunzio stood in the doorway.

Aunt Nora looked at him, her face was red from crying. She walked over to Nunzio. "Was it...?"

"It was my uncle," he answered, sadly.

"Oh, God!" Aunt Nora screamed. "What will I do? I don't want to live without Alberto. I want to die. Please let me die, too."

"Aunt Nora, please. I'm sorry, so sorry," Nunzio said holding her and crying with her.

"I'm staying here tonight, Jim," Rose said. "Please explain to Pa."

"Sure, Sis. He'll understand. If you need anything, just call me."

There was a crowd gathering in the street. Everyone had heard about Alberto and had come to Hanover Street; Vito, Gino and Father Vincent, too, of course. A full moon was in the sky, but there was a dark cloud over 705 Hanover Street. In the days ahead there was going to be a terrible storm over the entire country.

CHAPTER TEN
February, 1930

Dearest Maria:
This is the first chance I have had to write since Uncle Alberto's unfortunate death. Rose and I have been married three months already, and we are very happy being together. Mr. Natali has taken over the bakery and the house, and has been kind enough to allow Aunt Nora to live there rent-free. Rose and I are also staying there, but we are looking for our own place. I am still working at the bakery, but I would prefer to work somewhere else. As soon as I can, I will find another job. That might not be easy, as thousands of people are out of work and companies are closing every day. Many of the banks have failed, and I understand even Europe is starting to feel the Great Depression. Everyday the newspapers tell how the situation is getting worse. People are jumping out of windows, and those who were doing well last year are selling apples on the street corners just to buy bread.
Thank God, Rose still has her job at Bonet's, although business is way down, and my friend, Loretta, said she doesn't know if they can continue paying the help if business doesn't improve. Oh, and Loretta got a big break. She is modeling in a national fashion show. She will have to travel to Hollywood, California, where they make movies. They will be filming it for the news. Maybe you will even see it in Bari. Everyone is so excited. Last night we all went to the movies to see a film named Cimarron, and I told Loretta that someday she might be up there on the big screen, too. She sure is pretty enough. I know you and Mama and Papa were looking forward to

coming here, but this depression has put that on hold. I miss you all so very much, and I want you to meet my Rose. I love her so much, Maria. You will love her, too, even though she is not Italian. You are always in my heart, my sister. Give my love to Mama, Papa, Bruno and everyone in Bari.

    Your loving brother,
    Nunzio.

    Nunzio took the letter to the mailbox, and stopped at the grocers for a few things Aunt Nora and Rose had asked him to pick up. Mr. Morgagni, who owned the grocery, was complaining that everyone wanted credit and that he couldn't stay in business if he had to carry the whole neighborhood.

    "Let them borrow from your pal, Vito Natali," he said to Nunzio. "That's his new business now. Loan sharking, I think they call it. Before you know it, he will own everything in Boston. And that Enzio Carroll is running around town collecting for Mayor Curley. What do you hear, Nunzio?"

    "From you I hear double talk, Mr. Morgagni. I need a box of eggs, a bottle of milk and a pound of ricotta cheese. I'll take a bag of sugar and coffee, too."

    "How come you don't take the sugar from the bakery?" the grocer asked.

    "This is what Rose put on the list."

    "You got cash money?"

    "I have the money, Mr. Morgagni. Thank you."

    When Nunzio returned home, he put the groceries on the table, kissed Aunt Nora, and returned downstairs to the bakery to help unload the trucks.

    I have got to get out of this place, he thought. He never told anyone about the thousand dollars he saved. He was thinking he might start his own business. A new life for Rose and me, he thought. Of course, I will always look out for Aunt Nora. What kind of business could I go into now? There's a depression. Who has money? Rich people, that's who. There are still lots of rich people. Why, Rose tells me every day that Bonet still sells expensive dresses. Not as many as before, but they're still in business.

And poor people still have to eat. If they can't come to the bakery for bread, I will deliver the bread to them at home, just like the milkman does. The more Nunzio thought of the idea of starting his own home delivery bread route, the more he liked it. He would have to talk it over with Vito. Nobody does anything without his okay. And Rose, he would have to see how she felt about it. He tried out a few names: 'Nunzio Cappolla's Baked Goods', 'Nunzio's Baked Goods', 'Cappolla's Baked Goods', 'Boston Baked Bread', Inc.

"Nunzio, Nunzio." Aunt Nora called from the front of the bakery. "Quit daydreaming and come upstairs. Rose is home, and dinner is on the table."

Nunzio sat at the table, playing with the long strands of spaghetti. "How were things at the shop, dear?" he asked Rose.

"Slow. Mrs. Donato came in to buy a dress. She had a young, nice looking man with her. You would never believe she lost a husband so recently. Oh, I almost forgot to tell you. Loretta is leaving for California in the morning. Her train leaves at nine-thirty. She said she would call tonight to say goodbye. Poor Paul will be alone for a whole month."

"Nunzio, how come you're playing with your pasta and not eating?" Aunt Nora asked.

"I'm just thinking," Nunzio replied.

"Were you listening to what I said, darling?" Rose asked.

"Yes, of course," he answered.

"Then what time does Loretta's train leave in the

morning?"

"What train?"

"And, what were you daydreaming about this time?" Rose asked, grinning.

"That pasta is going to get ice cold," Aunt Nora interrupted.

"I'm sorry, Aunt Nora, I'm just not hungry," Nunzio said. "I've been thinking. I want to start my own bread route, home delivery, door to door. I know I can do well. I'll bake everything downstairs, and then load the truck and deliver. And maybe hire helpers as the business grows. I can pay Vito a percentage, and he can hire someone to replace me. I don't want to be involved in the wine operation anymore."

"It's too bad Uncle Alberto had to... You could be the boss of Cappolla's Bakery," Aunt Nora sighed.

"I like the idea," Rose said.

"I have some money saved," Nunzio said. "And if you keep working a little while, I can do it."

"Nunzio," Rose said smiling as she took his hand, "I love you so very much. I know you will be successful."

The following day, Nunzio waited for Vito at the warehouse.

"What are you doing here?" Vito asked. "Why ain't you at the bakery?"

"I need to talk to you, Mr. Natali. I want to start my own bakery route and use Cappolla's to bake the breads. You can do fine without me, and I will pay you a percentage for your help. It would mean a lot to me."

"You got balls, kid. That Irish broad must be shaking it good for you. Cappolla's got bread routes now. People are out of work and starving, you got a good job making good bucks, and you want to start a fucking business?"

Frankie, overhearing, looked at Nunzio, "Hey, stunod, there's a depression going on. Where you going to get money for a business?"

"I have a few dollars saved," Nunzio said.

"You know something, kid?" said Vito. "I like you. I liked you from the first time I met you. You got style. Do what you're going to do, and if you need help... go see a doctor," he laughed. "Oh, by the way, how close are you to your father-in-law?"

"We tolerate each other," Nunzio replied. "We don't go on camping trips together. Why do you ask?"

"Him and your brother-in-law, both on the payroll along with most of the precinct. But, I may need some special favors in the near future. Keep in touch."

Nunzio did not like the idea too much, but thought better than to say anything after Vito just gave him the green light. The thought of having to ever discuss underworld activities with the Kellys gave him the shivers.

"Thank you, Mr. Natali," Nunzio said as he walked out of the warehouse.

"By the way, Nunzio, you can call me Vito."

"Thank you, Vito. Arrivederci."

Nunzio went downtown to Bonet's. Paul was in the front talking to two ladies. Nunzio just remembered Loretta left for Hollywood that morning.

"Hello, Nunzio," Paul said. "How are you?"

"I was hoping to see my Bella Rosa."

"Bella Rosa. That's Beautiful Rose, right Nunzio?"

"Right."

"She's in the back."

"Can I go back there?"

"Sure."

In the back room, Nunzio gave Rose a kiss on her forehead, and took her in his arms.

"Vito said okay," said Nunzio

"Oh, that's wonderful. Now all you need is customers, and a truck, and if..."

"Let me worry about what I need, my precious Bella

Rosa," he interrupted her, then thought of what he said. "That's it! That's what I'm going to call the bakery. La Bella Rosa Bakery. The Beautiful Rose. You are my beautiful Rose, so why shouldn't that be the name?"

"Nunzio, that's so romantic, naming the business after me, and it sounds so catchy, so poetic. La Bella Rosa. I love it!"

"I'm going to get started right away," Nunzio said.

"Well, I'd better get back to work, now. With Loretta gone and me the only one here... I'm even modeling a little."

"Oh yeah? Nobody better get fresh with you," he laughed.

"You have nothing to worry about, my love. Not now, not ever."

"See you tonight, Bella Rosa."

Nunzio walked home singing La Bella Rosa all the way, and smiling. People looked at him as if he were crazy. Boston is a great city, he thought. The depression will not last forever. Anyway, soon everyone will be buying bread from La Bella Rosa Bakery, owned and operated by Nunzio Cappolla and his wife, Rose. I think I will give David a call.

He passed the Foscolo place on the way home. He could still picture the ambulances and police cars in his imagination. God, what a terrible night.

The sign on the bakery was fading. 'Cappolla's'. It's all that was left of Uncle Alberto's life; a faded sign and a widow. Life is a mixture, just like bread is flour and water. Life is joy and sorrow.

CHAPTER ELEVEN
Hollywood, California

The man at the Los Angeles train station was holding up a sign which read 'Loretta Bonet'. Loretta waved at him as she stepped on the platform.

"I'm Loretta Bonet," she called, walking toward the man, who had a chauffeur with a Rolls Royce standing behind him.

"Elias Manuel, your host and escort. Welcome to California, heaven on earth," the man smiled.

Loretta looked around at the mountains in the background, the green grass - for her the green grass was odd for February - and felt the warm air. And she studied Elias Manuel's tall muscular body, his boyish looks and deep rich tan. What a handsome man, she thought. "I think I like this place," she said.

"You will have a whole day to yourself to go sightseeing before the fashion show, and we won't be filming until the day after tomorrow," Elias said. He took her suitcase, put it in the trunk of the car, and they were off to her hotel. "You will be having dinner with the other girls, and several stars will be there. I will pick you up at seven o'clock."

"I'll be ready with bells on," Loretta said.

"Oh, and incidentally," Elias added, "when you get to your room, a lady by the name of Grace will be there to help you with your makeup, hair and dressing. She is yours for your entire stay in Hollywood. Anything you need, just tell her."

"Thank you. That's wonderful. This must be a dream."

The bellboy took Loretta to her room. It was a suite fit for a princess, with a large double bed with a canopy, a white and gold couch, and a dressing room.

Grace introduced herself, took the suitcase and started to unpack. "Is there anything you need right now, Madam?" she asked.

Loretta looked at her. What an attractive black lady, she thought. "I would like to send some telegrams to Boston," she responded. "And I would love to have a bath."

"Write down what you want in the telegrams, and I will have them sent immediately. I will draw your bath as soon as I hang up your clothes."

Loretta wrote one telegram to Paul. *"Arrived safely. Stop. It's wonderful here. Stop. Wish you could be here. Stop. I love you, Loretta. Stop.'*

The other she sent to Nunzio. *'California is a lot like Italy. Stop. Love to Rose and Nora, Stop. See you next week. Stop. Loretta.*

She sat in the bathtub singing in Italian, with a glass of champagne on the side of the tub, while Grace scrubbed her back. She couldn't help thinking about Paul. Yes, I love him, but why was I so attracted to that Elias Manuel?

I suppose that is normal for a girl to be attracted to other men. Especially when they're so good-looking. But I'm here to do the fashion show and I'm going to behave like a married woman should, she told herself.

"Are you married, Grace?" she asked.

"Yes, Madam. I have two boys, two girls and a fine husband. He's an actor."

"Oh, really? In movies?" Loretta asked.

"Movies and on the stage," she answered.

"That's wonderful. Who has he played?"

"Plays a nigger, Madam. Everything he's in he plays a nigger. And when they need a lady for the nigger, I get the part. In the movie called Plantation, they used Ivan,

75

me, and the kids. All six of us they used. Paid us two hundred dollars."

"It must be exciting making a movie," said Loretta. "I would love to be an actress, if I could."

"You sure are pretty enough, Madam."

"Thank you, Grace. I think I'll get dressed, now. Mr. Manuel is picking me up at seven o'clock."

"That Mr. Manuel loves the ladies," Grace said. "He was in Plantation with us. Played a slave dealer. He would like to be a star. Meanwhile, he does this escort work to get close to the ladies. Be careful. He can charm the pants off a Nun," she laughed.

"I'm a married woman," Loretta answered. "I'm just here to do the show, and then I'm going back to Boston."

Elias arrived at seven o'clock sharp, dressed in a tuxedo, a corsage in his hand for Loretta. "You look absolutely magnificent," he told her.

"Thank you," she blushed. "So do you."

She didn't know why she said that, but too late to take it back, she thought. Loretta was a little nervous. When Elias took her hand she felt like Paul was there watching. They arrived at the restaurant on Sunset Boulevard in less than ten minutes.

"Champagne's. What a beautiful name for a restaurant," Loretta said.

The canopy in the front of the restaurant was milky white and there were four uniformed gentlemen parking cars. A man in a black tuxedo opened the double glass doors.

"If I didn't know better, I would swear that was Mary Pickford going in," she said to Elias.

"That was Mary Pickford," he replied.

"This is so exciting," she said.

She was seated at the table with the other models and their escorts. There was a fruit cup in front of each setting and more silverware and glasses than she had ever seen on one table. There was a full orchestra playing, and at the front table were not only Mary Pickford, but Warner Baxter, Lionel Barrymore and several studio heads.

"This is a night I will never forget," she whispered to Elias.

She kept sipping champagne until she couldn't stop giggling. When she danced with Elias, Paul and Boston seemed like they never happened. She did not resist when he kissed her with his open mouth. She knew he wanted her and she wanted him. They left the restaurant without saying anything to each other. They knew what they were going to do. Elias took her to his apartment. He made love to her with the skill of a carpenter building a house. Detailing each move, not neglecting any part of her body. She answered each of his moves with one of her own as if she was born only to please Elias Manuel. When they were done she laid in his arms admiring his Greek-god features.

"This was the greatest night of my life," she said.

Elias was sound asleep. She kissed him on the nose and dozed off.

Morning came a little too fast for Loretta. Elias woke her with a kiss and they made love until he realized what time it was.

"We'd better get up," he said. "Today is the big day for you. I'll drive you back to your hotel, and meet you at the studio."

"I want to come back here and make love with you tonight," she said, hardly believing her own ears.

"That would be nice, sweetheart," he said.

Loretta could not get over the weather in Hollywood. It was February and it felt like June. "I wish I could stay, go to the beach all day, Elias."

"Perhaps after you're through with the fashion show you could stay an extra few days and we could go to the beach together and I could really show you Southern

California."

"I couldn't do that. What would I tell my husband? I really enjoy being here with you, Elias, and I'll never forget it, but I couldn't."

"You only have one life, Loretta. If you don't do what makes you happy in this life, then when? In the next life you may be a boa constrictor or a Welsh Terrier carrying someone's shoes in your mouth. Better enjoy life now."

"That is very well put," she laughed. "We will see. Besides I know you have many, many girlfriends and I can understand how they can all adore you. You are marvelous."

"You may not believe this but I would trade every girl I have ever been with, every worldly possession and I would abdicate my throne for you."

"What throne?"

"Why, the King of Studs, of course."

"I should have known," she laughed.

Grace greeted Loretta at the hotel room. "Well, I see Mr. Manuel put another notch on the old six shooter," she said. "Better start getting ready, Madam. The fashion show ain't gonna wait for you no way."

Loretta took a bath, applied her makeup and rushed downstairs to the waiting Rolls Royce. When she arrived at the back lot of Hometown Studios, Elias was waiting, and opened the door to the car.

"You're just on time. Mr. Levine, the head of the studio, is talking to the audience. Today is just a preliminary show to get you all used to the procedures. Tomorrow, the news people will be filming and, next week at this time, you will be in every theater in the world."

"Yes. And I'll be showing Paul Bonet's latest creations, won't I? I feel so terribly guilty."

"Remember the Welsh Terrier," he said.

She didn't bother to answer.

The New Patriots

Loretta was the fourth model to be presented and she nervously moved about the platform as the Master of Ceremonies explained the style and mentioned the designer, Paul Bonet. Each time he said Paul's name Loretta flinched remembering last night. And what she would be doing again tonight. "Only one life," Elias had said.

"That was very good ladies," the M.C. said. "Tomorrow, we will be doing it over in a shorter version for the newsreel. Have a good night."

Loretta stepped down from the platform and walked over to Elias. "How was I?" she asked.

"In his heyday, DaVinci could not have created a more beautiful picture. Oh, Mr. Levine wants to talk to you for a few minutes in his office. I'll walk you over."

"Isaac Levine, the head of Hometown? What would he want to see me for?"

"I don't know. I told him what a good lay you were. Maybe... Don't look so mad, I'm only kidding. He couldn't take his eyes off of you, though. Who knows what he wants, he's the boss."

Isaac Levine's office was very unpretentious. It could have passed for the office of a new accountant - a love seat and a desk, a telephone and a few books. The carpet looked as if more then one cup of coffee had spilled on it and there was a bottle of Canadian Whiskey on the desk. Mr. Levine obviously doesn't care much for the Volstead Act, Loretta thought.

"Miss Bonet, how do you do? I'm Isaac Levine."

"It is a pleasure to meet you, sir. And it's Mrs. Bonet."

"Yes, of course, Mrs. Bonet," he replied. "Loretta, if I may call you that, you are a very beautiful girl and a most gracious model. You are exactly what I am looking for. There's a new picture we are going to be filming about an Italian girl romantically involved with a French count. Can you act?"

Loretta just stared at him. Was she hearing him right? "I don't know," she said. "I never tried."

"I would like you to take a screen test. If you pass, we will train you. Would you be willing to play the part?"

"What is the name of the movie?" was the first thing she could think to ask.

"The Count of Lyon," he answered.

"I don't know what to say.... my husband," Loretta was fumbling her words.

"It is a decision you will have to make. First thing tomorrow, after the filming of the newsreel, you will take the screen test. We'll see how photogenic you are and how you sound on tape. Then we will talk."

Loretta just stood there in shock. "Good day, Loretta." Mr. Levine said.

"Thank you, Mr. Levine," she said as she got up and left his office.

"Well?" Elias asked, meeting her outside the office. "What did he want?"

"He wants me to take a screen test. He has a part in a movie for me," she said, still stunned. "It's unreal, too unbelievable."

"That's wonderful, sweetheart. Let's go out and celebrate. Wait, first let's go make love and then we will celebrate. Then we can make love again, then celebrate again."

"You're crazy, do you know that, Elias Manuel? But it sounds like the second best offer I've had today."

"Oh, yeah. When I get through with you this time you won't think it was the second best. Nothing will ever be first again."

She knew he was right, and that scared her even more. She could not stop what was happening to her life and didn't know if she wanted to try. "Welsh Terrier," she said.

"I see my little analogy made an impact."

"Everything about you makes an impact on me," she

said, and licked his ear.

They made love in the back of the Rolls even with the chauffeur listening and sneaking peaks.

"I left my dignity in Boston," she said. "Along with my self respect."

"You were reborn, sweetheart, that's all. Born to be who you really are, a degenerate like the rest of us."

The next day Loretta was the first one at the Fashion Show. She knew her screen test was to follow the newsreel filming and she was extremely nervous. Elias was there trying to keep her calm but it was no use. She did not want to drink any alcohol for fear of wrecking the whole show. Finally the crews were in place and all the models had arrived. The director was calling everyone to their places.

"Good luck, sweetheart," Elias said, smiling as he kissed her bare shoulder.

Loretta took her place on the platform. Although the M.C. repeated everything he said the day before, it didn't matter because the voice part of the film would have to be dubbed in at the studio. The entire fashion portion of the newsreel would be about 85 seconds at the most.

When it was over, Loretta reported to the screen testing director, Eddie Wilson. She was to read a small scene from O'Henry's The Lady Higher Up. She would be reading the part of Miss Diana, and she had fifteen minutes to study the one page script.

"Oh, la, la," Loretta said, reading the part of Diana. "Notice that la, la, la, Aunt Liberty? Got that from Paris by night on the roof garden under me. You'll hear that la, la, la, at the Cafe McCann now, along with garçon. The bohemian crowd there has become tired of garçon since O'Rafferty, the headwaiter, punched three of them for calling him that. Oh, no, the town's strictly on the bum these nights. Everybody's away."

"Cut," the director yelled. "Cut, cut, cut, cut, cut, that's a take. Mr. Levine will be in shortly to watch the film."

"Elias, I don't know what-in-hell I was saying, and with my Italian accent, it's going to be a joke," Loretta said, not knowing whether she wanted to laugh or cry.

"Don't worry, sweetheart," he reassured her. "The purpose of the screen test is to see how you look, as well as the sound on the film, and to see if you can act. God knows, I took enough screen tests to land two-liners in second-rate films. You looked pretty good up there, and you didn't sound half bad, either.

"Ha, I'll bet I did. Oh, la, la, la. Who the hell is O'Henry, anyway?" she asked

"That's not important," Elias started to explain. "Here comes Levine."

"Ah, Loretta," Mr. Levine greeted her. "Time to review your screen test. I love to use O'Henry stories for our screen tests. They're so, you know, poetic and so emotional."

"Oh, of course," Loretta answered.

Everyone was silent while Levine reviewed the film. After the 90-second scene, he remained silent. At length he turned to Loretta and said, "What you lack in acting ability you make up for in beauty. It will take some work, but I see you as a future star. I'm going to sign you on a one picture deal to do The Count of Lyon." He glanced at Elias. "And I may even have a part for you, Elias." He returned his attention to Loretta, "Report to my office nine o'clock in the morning. Good day, everybody."

"That's it?" Loretta asked, looking at Elias. "I'm going to be in a movie, and that's all there is to it? What do I do now? Do I dance, do I jump up and sing, yell, what?"

"You do whatever you like, sweetheart. Let's go out and celebrate. You're going to be a movie star."

"Oh, my God, what do I tell Paul? I should be leaving for Boston tonight. What do I tell Paul?"

"That is something you are going to have to decide for yourself. If you want to be Loretta Bonet, Boston housewife or Loretta Bonet, if you use that name, star of the silver screen. The darling of America."

"I know one thing, Elias. I can never get enough of you. I don't want to ever be away from you. I just can't stand to hurt Paul. I just don't know what to do. Please take me to my hotel and let me be alone for a while. I want to think."

"Of course, sweetheart. I understand."

Loretta didn't say anything all the way back to the hotel. She went to her room without saying a word to Elias, or to Grace. She lay on the bed, staring at the ceiling, wondering what to tell Paul, until she fell into a deep sleep.

CHAPTER TWELVE
June 1930, Boston

Nunzio had invited more than one hundred people to the unveiling of his new truck. He and Rose stood proudly in front of the white panel truck with the bold black lettering that read: 'LA BELLA ROSA' - Fresh baked goods. No. 80 Commercial Street', with the telephone number right under the address.

Father Vincent was there to christen the truck, and Vito, who had helped Nunzio get started, was there. David and Sally, Aunt Nora, the Kellys and everyone who knew Nunzio came, except, of course, Loretta and Paul.

"I wish Loretta was here to share this moment with me," Nunzio said.

"I can't believe she's still in California and divorcing Paul," Rose answered. "I mean, her being a Catholic, and all."

"She's living with some actor by the name of Elias," Nunzio answered.

"I got a letter from her yesterday," David intervened. "Her movie, The Count of Lyon, will be finished in October, and I guess we will all go to see it."

"I can't believe the whole thing," Rose added.

"Loretta, our friend, Loretta, a movie star. It's incredible."

"She's not a star yet, only making one movie. It may never even be released," Sally said.

"And what about her husband?" Nora asked. "He's still alive, is he not?"

"Nobody sees or hears from him," Rose answered. "He closed up the shop and moved. I think to New York.

I know he loved Loretta very much. Well, so much for that. We're here to celebrate the new, not to dwell on the old."

"Hey, one more year and you graduate, David," Nunzio said, changing the subject.

"That's correct," David replied. "That will be the next party. By the way, Nunzio, my wife and I are finally going on our honeymoon. We are leaving Monday morning for Vienna. That is where Sally's grandparents live. We've decided to spend the summer there."

"Wow, Vienna. I guess you will see your family while you're in Europe."

"Of course," David said. "Sally's grandfather is a professor at the University in Vienna, and I have a cousin who is also a Professor at the same University."

"Do they know each other?" Nunzio asked.

"If not, they will after we visit them. I better brush up on my German," David said.

"I'll teach you some Yiddish, love," Sally said. "That's what my grandfather speaks at home. But he speaks German outside the community. I was only three years old when my parents left Vienna and came to the United States."

"What the hell is a red-blooded American boy like me doing here anyway?" Jim Kelly asked.

"Free beer," Vito said. "Free beer, my Mick friend. I'm more red-blooded American then you, for Christ sake. I was a captain in the big war. Fucking hero I am."

"Brought the war home with you, right to the streets of Boston," Jim answered.

"Fongoul," Vito laughed.

"Tomorrow," Nunzio shouted over all the talking. "Tomorrow at five o'clock in the morning, Victor's Luncheonette will get the first delivery of bread from the La Bella Rosa Bakery."

"Long live La Bella Rosa," Vito yelled. The whole

crowd, most of them drunk, started yelling, "Viva La Bella Rosa, Viva Nunzio." They carried on well into the night.

Rose and Nunzio left the party way before it was over. Nunzio had to get up at three-thirty to load the truck. He would begin his new route by soliciting customers, and making deliveries himself. Rose would stay in the office, answering phones and doing all of the paperwork. He could hardly get to sleep for the excitement.

All over the country there were hunger marches and demonstrations being staged by the unemployed workers. The Great Depression had spread everywhere. Even in Europe there was havoc. Germany, especially, was feeling the depression, having to make reparations for the war.

And yet, here in my world, Nunzio thought, the three of us who met on the way to this country have it all. Loretta is making a movie, Torquato is going to Vienna on his honeymoon, and I am the proud owner of La Bella Rosa Bakery. Thank you Jesus.

And with that, Nunzio fell asleep.

CHAPTER THIRTEEN
November 1930, New York City

The marquee at the Paramount Theater could be seen as far away as Mars and Jupiter, at least it seemed that way to the 53 Bostonians stepping off the charted bus. They had come for the New York premier of The Count of Lyon, starring Claude Wentworth, with Elias Manuel as Napoleon Bonaparte, and introducing Loretta Bonet.

Loretta and Elias were outside the theater signing autographs and greeting the crowd as they had done at the premier in Los Angeles. She could not hold back her emotion when she saw the Boston busload.

"Nunzio, darling. Rose, David, and Father Vincent," she called out. She looked for her own father, but he was not on the bus. She dealt with her disappointment, and then hugged each of the passengers as they got in line.

"Do I get an autograph?" Nunzio asked.

Loretta hugged him. "I've missed you so much," she whispered. "Oh, everyone," she said aloud. "I would like you to meet Elias Manuel, or for tonight, you will know him as Emperor Napoleon. I hope you all enjoy the movie. There will be a champagne party after. I hope those pains in the you-know-what Feds leave us alone tonight. I hate to think they might destroy all that lovely French champagne we brought."

The newsreel came on first, showing the Great Depression around the world. A scene in Germany showed the rise of a political party called the Nationalist Socialist Workers Party, with a little mustached, loudmouth as their leader.

"That's the guy I told you about," David whispered to

Nunzio and the others in his row. "Adolph Hitler, the Austrian who is spreading all those anti-Jewish lies in Germany and causing a lot of trouble. I would hope the German people will see through his bullshit and put him in his place. However, we saw a lot of his supporters when we were in Vienna."

"Shhh! The movie is beginning," a voice in the next row whispered loudly.

"Look how beautiful Loretta is, David," Nunzio said.

"Quiet, please," another voice was heard.

"Do you think the director meant for Claude what's-his-name to keep looking at Loretta's chest?" Rose asked.

"Looks like Napoleon wants to count out the Count," Sally said.

"Quiet, damn it!" the voice screeched. "I didn't come all the damned way from Boston to listen to you people yak away during the movie." It was Jim Kelly, Jr.

"Loretta, you were sensational," Sally told her in the lobby, afterward. The compliments came from all sides. Loretta was overwhelmed.

Elias smiled and said sarcastically, "She's starting to believe her own publicity. It's getting impossible to live with her."

"You can leave anytime, sweetie pie," Loretta shot back.

Elias, obviously embarrassed, said nothing.

"That Claude Wentworth is quite handsome, Loretta," Rose said.

"That's the makeup and padding. Actually, he's a little shit who thinks he's one of the Gods from Mount Olympia. He kept playing grab-ass with me off the set, and since he's a star, nobody said anything, and my darling Napoleon thought it was funny. I'll bet he would have liked to play with Claude himself."

"We've come a long way from 'I can't get enough of you', haven't we?" Elias hissed. "Maybe this movie should have been called the Count and the Cunt."

"Oh, come now, Elias. Napoleon was a great man, why would they call him a cunt just because it's you playing the part? On second thought, it makes sense," she laughed and then said, "Enough of this, my friends are here. Let's be civil."

After the champagne and hors d'oeuvres, Loretta, obviously intoxicated, yelled out, "Well everyone, we have to fly back to Hollywood. Thank you all for coming. I love you all." Then leaning into Nunzio, she said, "Tell my father I love him, and to please understand my life. Give him this envelope. There's one thousand dollars in it. Ciao, amico."

"Loretta. I wish you all the good luck in the world," Nunzio said, as he kissed her goodbye.

"Loretta went down the line and hugged everyone. My next picture is called Sister Angel. I hope to see you all at that premier as well."

On the bus ride back, almost everyone fell asleep, except Nunzio and David. "I won't be able to sleep tonight," said Nunzio. "Got to get to work as soon as we get back to Boston. Got 35 new customers in the last month. Things are really rolling."

"I'm happy for you. You deserve to be successful, Nunzio, you've worked hard. Oh, by the way, we didn't mention it before, but we have good news. Sally is pregnant."

"What? You're going to be a daddy, and didn't tell anyone? Congratulations, David. When is the big event to take place?"

"Well, I didn't want to ruin Loretta's night. We expect the baby in May."

Nunzio elbowed Rose, asleep at his side, "Rosy, you awake?"

"Yes," Rose said, "I heard. It's wonderful. I'm so happy for you both, David."

"And how about you two? Don't you think it's time you started a family?"

"First, I must bring my parents and Maria to America," said Nunzio. "Then we can plan for children."

"Well, at the rate you're getting customers, it shouldn't be too long."

"No, not too long," replied Nunzio, as he laid his head back and closed his eyes.

"Too bad Aunt Nora didn't come tonight," Rose said.

"And, too bad Loretta's father didn't show up," David added.

"Did I tell you this was the first time I ever rode on a bus," Nunzio said, opening one eye.

"There will be many first times and many last times. That's what life is, darling," Rose said. "Now, try to get some sleep before we get home."

The New Patriots

CHAPTER FOURTEEN
March 4, 1933, Boston

"First of all, let me assert my firm belief that the only thing we have to fear is fear itself." The voice on the radio, the voice of the 'New Deal', was the thirty-second President of the United States, Franklin Delano Roosevelt, former Governor of New York and the hope of the future for America.

"The man has his work cut out for him," David said. "What with millions still unemployed, countless farmers with mortgages foreclosing, bank after bank in bankruptcy, unrest in Europe, and so on and so forth, the New Deal better be a royal flush."

"He's a fine speaker. I wish him all the luck in the world," Nunzio said as he took little Alberto from Rose and fed him his bottle. "One year old next week, my Alberto," he said to David. "You and Sally will be here for the birthday party, yes?" Nunzio asked.

"Wouldn't miss it for the world. Edmond and Joel will be here with us. Imagine, they are almost two years old. How time flies," David said.

"So much is happening so fast. There you are, living in New Hampshire, already a Vice President at Continental Electric, a big house, twin boys and you're only out of college two years and..."

"What about you, Nunzio," David cut in. "You're the largest baked goods supplier in Massachusetts, with a new house and a beautiful son. And now that your family is here from Italy, living right next door, you have all you could have hoped for not that long ago. All except, of course, for Bruno, but he's doing well in Bari. You have come a long way Nunzio. We have come a long way. By the way, how is Maria doing?"

"Maria is in night school. She is dating a very nice boy, Stefano Martinelli, a contractor. She met him in church. I'm thrilled that she, and Mama and Papa too, want to help out at La Bella Rosa. We are a real family again."

Rose took Alberto from Nunzio. "I'm going to put the bambino to sleep, and then I'll serve the coffee and guess what? Rum cake from the bakeries of La Bella Rosa." She sang as she left the room.

"You're a lucky man, Nunzio. You scored a thousand when you married that one," David said. "I see she speaks a little Italian."

"Very little," Nunzio replied. "She loves to call the baby bambino, and when my mother is here, it's mangiare Mama and buon giorno. Get the picture?"

"I love it," David said.

Reaching into his pocket, Nunzio said, "I got a letter from Loretta. She asked me to read it to you, David, so she wouldn't have to write twice. I'll read it out loud."

"Go a head, read it Nunzio."

"Dear Nunzio,

Oh, how I miss you and David. And how happy I am that you both are doing so well, especially in these times when poverty and despair are the order of the day. After four films, I finally am referred to as a 'star'. Yes, a full-fledged star. Since I got rid of that terrible person, Elias, I have been living with Oliver Hanson Young. You saw him in my last film Portrait of Julian. He played my father. I hope that's not incest. He wants me to marry him. In England he was a great Shakespearian stage actor. Here in Hollywood he's just an old shit character actor, but he's so nice to me and makes me feel so awfully good. I envy you and David, so happily married, you a

son, and David twins. I love you both so much... the soil
marks on this letter are my tears.

Love, Loretta

P.S. If this letter winds up in Marsi Marrow's column
I will tear you apart."

"What can I say, Nunzio, what can I say? It's time to
leave. The last train to New Hampshire leaves in an hour
and Sally worries. Thank you for a great dinner, Rosy."

"Come on," Nunzio said. "I'll drive you to the
station."

As they dove down Fleet Street, the traffic was
backed up for miles. Block parties celebrated F.D.R.'s
inauguration, a Democratic city and a Democratic
President. Pictures of the President were everywhere. "I
hope you make the train," Nunzio said.

"Turn off and take North," David replied.

Nunzio turned onto North where the traffic was
moving a little better.

"I'd like you to come to the plant and see what we're
doing," David said.

"Oh?" Nunzio responded, as the two got out of the car
to walk to the station. "And what are you doing that I
should come all the way to Manchester, New Hampshire,
to see?"

David looked at Nunzio with the excitement of a little
boy who just got his first new bike. "Communications,
Nunzio. Communications. It's unbelievable what we are
working on. We'll let General Electric and the rest of
them build toasters and gadgets. We're working on mind-
boggling projects like sending pictures through the air
and ..."

"And what? How can you send pictures through the
air? What the hell are you talking about?" Nunzio asked.

"Nunzio, my friend, you know how we sat listening
to the President's speech on the radio? A miracle, right?

Voices in the air. Well, someday you will be able to sit in your living room and watch the President live, as he speaks, on a screen in your house. You will be able to watch one of Loretta's films at home on a station just like you do when you turn on your radio. Communications. It has endless possibilities and I'm part of it, helping to engineer it."

"I think you're dreaming, David. How can you send a picture through the air?"

"Electronics, Nunzio. How do you think they send voices through the air, and the telephone? Electronics. It's fascinating. Well, here's the train station. I'll see you next week at Alberto's birthday party. Ciao, amico."

Nunzio replied, still thinking about what David said, "Pictures through the air? Next you'll be telling me about sending people to the moon."

"And you, my good friend, may you be the first one to go. Arrivederci."

Nunzio felt something wet on his forehead. A snowflake, he thought. Suddenly there were more snowflakes, although they were very light. Still, he thought, it could stick, and a blizzard could be coming. He decided to pick Maria up at the school. She would be getting out in about half an hour. He called Rose to let her know, and drove over to Hanover Street. He noticed a familiar figure, a man walking with his hands in his pocket. It was Vito Natali. "Hey, Vito," Nunzio cried out of the car window.

"Nunzio. Hey, bigshot, what are you doing out on a cold night like this?"

"Picking up my sister at the night school."

"Nunzio, you heard they repealed the Volstead. You'll be able to drink legally pretty soon."

"So what are you going to do now, Vito?" Nunzio asked.

"Well, let me think. I have some money saved, and I

have some investments. I could stay in crime until I get caught or shot. But then again, I am interested in a very successful business. Let me think of the name of it again," he said sarcastically. "Oh, now I remember, La Bella Rosa Bakery, or is it Bakeries, partner? Better go pick up your sister. I'll see you in our office tomorrow."

"You're awfully quiet Nunzio," Maria said, sitting next to him in the car on the way home.

The snow was coming down harder, and Nunzio was driving too fast. He didn't say anything but he nodded. Vito never bothered him before, he was thinking. The booze business had occupied all his time, but now with the Volstead Act repealed and a new administration in Washington. Oh, fuck it, he thought, there's plenty for everybody. Besides, where would I be if Vito didn't help me. "Come on, sweet Maria, we're home."

He walked her to the door. Mama and Papa were outside on the porch. Nunzio stayed for only a minute, kissed them all Good night, and went home. Rose was asleep when he arrived home. The meeting with Vito and the events of the day didn't occupy Nunzio's thoughts, only the pictures through the air. Pictures through the air, was all he could think about as he lay in bed.

Vito couldn't stop him from thinking about what David had told him. How? He tried to visualize it. Strangely, he was getting aroused. He felt like making love. Why did she have to be asleep. "Rose, Rose are you sleeping?" Nunzio whispered in her ear.

"Mmmmm," was all she said.

Nunzio kissed her breast softly and ran his hand over her stomach, gently, the way it always excited her.

"I was fast asleep, darling," she said. "I finally got Alberto to sleep. I'm so very tired."

"I love you, Rosy. More then anything I want you. I want you now."

Rose embraced him, and he entered her without fully

95

undressing, without the usual foreplay. Half asleep, they made love, then drifted into a deep sleep in each others arms.

Alberto started to cry, and woke Nunzio. He started to wake Rose, but decided to let her sleep.

Nunzio started laughing as he changed Alberto's diaper. Life is so funny, so beautiful, so amazing, so strange and wonderful, he thought. He crept back into bed after putting Alberto down, looked up at the ceiling and whispered, "God, you amaze me. There is nothing you cannot do." Pictures through the air was his last thought before he drifted to sleep.

CHAPTER FIFTEEN
March 5, 1933   Manchester, New Hampshire

The third floor of Continental Electric was David Fairchild's baby. He designed it and nurtured it and convinced the Board of Directors to invest millions of dollars in television research. David walked around the third floor, admiring the many television screens and scanners, chatting with the engineers, and thinking of how his friend, Nunzio, was in such awe of the idea of pictures being transmitted through the air waves.

After all, television had been around for a long time, he mused. There was regularly scheduled broadcasting on station WABC in New York City, and NBC had begun experimental broadcasting from the top of the Empire State Building in 1931. There were already many names in television; Charles Francis Jenkins, the American scientist who conceived the idea of transmitting a picture by combining photography, optics and radio, and using the scanning disc with vacuum-tube amplifiers and photo electric cells. And other scientists: Hilo T. Farnsworth and John Logie Bard, who were applying the works of Nipkow, Hertz, Fleming, de Forest and Edison to perfect the receiving of images on screen.

David wanted to perfect the engineering of television for the mass market. He envisioned his CEC as the leader of a new industry. In the near future there would be a television set in nearly every home in the world. And why shouldn't CEC be the largest of all the companies? He took such pride in what had been accomplished in such a short time, and he loved his work.

One of his scientists, Harly MacIntire, was working

on an electric gun which breaks up the images. David looked over his shoulder as Harly explained, "The gun shoots a beam of electrons onto the electric image on the back of the target."

David took some notes on Harly's experiments, and watched Michael Regal work on the scanning beam. He took some more notes and went to his office to do some research for a while. He was so engrossed he almost forgot that State Senator, Eric Hampton, was coming from Concord to have lunch. He decided to call Sally to invite her along.

"Yes, darling, I would love to have lunch with you and Senator Hampton. Martha will watch the twins. I'll meet you at the Emerson Club. I want to stop and get a birthday gift for little Alberto."

"I love you," David told her as he put down the phone.

David and Senator Hampton rode over to the Emerson Club together in David's Cadillac.

"I am happy to serve on the CEC Advisory Board, David. I just hope that as Chairman of the State Senate Financial Committee, I don't get involved in any conflict of interest decisions."

"I will see that you don't," David answered. "And when I speak to the Chairman of our Board, Manny Weiss, I will make him aware of that fact. We do need your expertise in getting around certain government regulations."

The car pulled up to the Emerson Club, and the valet took over the Cadillac. Sally was waiting in the plush lounge of the most elegant of all clubs in Manchester. The maître d' seated them in the bay room at David's regular table.

"We prefer the term, working through government regulations," Senator Hampton said. "Working around could be construed as illegal, and that would be out of the question, David. Right?"

"I don't want to do anything illegal, Senator, but there seems to be more and more red tape in doing business. Your position is important to us in making CEC the biggest television manufacturer in the world. It will mean thousands of new jobs, and we will put this state on the map for real. The Granite State can become the Broadcasting State, as well."

"Sounds good, David," was all Senator Hampton said. He was smiling at Sally, as she intently studied the menu. "We are going to watch the new administration in Washington very closely. FDR has many outrageous ideas for his New Deal, and if he can get the nation back to work to end this depression, it will be a lot easier for companies like CEC to expand. I'm glad the rumor that you were thinking of moving CEC to Boston was just a rumor. New Hampshire cannot afford to lose major employers."

"We don't want to leave the state, Senator. We love New Hampshire, and we feel this state has a lot to offer now and in the future, but we need some breathers and tax credits so we can go on with our research. Our product line is moving slowly, and we hope to just break even in the next quarter. We have tried, unsuccessfully, to lobby the Senate for changes in the corporate tax structure, and we need a man like yourself to help us, without any conflict of interest, of course. In order to spend the amount of money I have convinced the board to spend, we must be able to cut our overhead in other areas, as well as our tax bite."

"I'll do what I can," Senator Hampton said. "Now then, let's order lunch. I'm starved, and I must get back to Concord."

After lunch, Sally went home. David and Senator Hampton went back to CEC where the Senator's car was waiting. A newspaper boy was standing outside the entrance to CEC. David bought a paper.

Barry C. Lefferts

"It's been two months since Hitler took over in Germany, and every time you look at a paper, there's his face somewhere," David said.

"That maniac is going to be trouble, David. Trouble for the world, and trouble for Jews in Germany."

"Let's hope not," David said. "Maybe he'll be good for Germany. Except for his anti-Semitism, I kind of admire his energy. It's too soon to tell what kind of leader he will be. Have a pleasant day, Senator. I will meet with you again before our next Board of Directors meeting. Oh, and as an advisory board member, you'll be paid a consultant fee of $5,000 a year. Is that fair?"

"More then fair," The Senator answered.

That night, David and Sally lay in bed reading the New Hampshire Daily News.

"That Senator Hampton seemed very nice, David, but I heard from some of the ladies at the Temple that Eric Hampton has been known to make anti-Semitic remarks. It's said that he gave up his law practice because his main clients were clothing manufacturers and he didn't want to go against unscrupulous Jews with Jewish lawyers, only to lose cases. So he ran for the Senate. They say he also recommended the reading of The Protocol of the Elders of Zion, a trashy anti-Semitic book full of lies."

"Don't listen to everything you hear and accept it as fact, darling. Senator Hampton is a brilliant legislator and lawyer, and he had some problems with Jewish businessmen. They could have been gentile, as well, and the results would have been the same. He has not shown any ill feeling toward me as a Jew, and I need him."

Sally leaned over to kiss David, and pointed to the story on Hitler in the paper. "That man is blaming the Jews for all of Germany's problems, and the people are buying it. Even here in the United States there are people agreeing with the Nazis. Remember when we were visiting my grandparents, what was going on? Well, I believe it's getting worse there."

"Sally, when was it ever not getting worse? There is always something going on somewhere in the world. Hitler is just a little man with a big mouth, and maybe he will even do some good. The Jews have suffered everywhere, and dealt with hatred everywhere, and still survived. We will survive, no matter what."

"I love you, David. I can't even imagine what life would be like without you," she said, putting down the newspaper and climbing on top of David. "Now, let's forget Continental Electric and Senator what's his name and Hitler and..." she whispered in his ear, "Let's try for a girl this time."

CHAPTER SIXTEEN
July, 1934   Hollywood, California

Loretta sat by the mirror in her dressing room, nursing the half empty bottle of Chivas Regal she had opened that morning. The new studio head, Anthony Roman, had scolded her for drinking on the job, and she was noticeably upset. Richard, her hairdresser, had come in to do her hair and had to listen to the wrath of Loretta's anger.

"Who does that fuck think he's talking to?" she demanded "Aren't I entitled to drink if I want to? I made this studio. Without me they would be up shit creek."

"Yes, Miss Bonet, you are a great star, and The Lady from Venice should win you an Oscar," replied Richard.

"That's right. Did you see that Claudette Colbert accept the Oscar? I'm ten times better then she is, and more beautiful. Don't you agree?"

"Of course, Miss Bonet. Much better and more beautiful. Mr. Young is a very lucky man."

"Mr. Young doesn't know it yet, but he's yesterday's wine. He's a goddamned alcoholic and a leach. I can't support him anymore, and tonight he goes. But right now I am hot to trot, and if I am to be convincing in my love scene this afternoon, I need to get in the mood, so how about getting me in the mood, Richard."

"Well, eh, I can't Miss Bonet. And besides, you know, well, the way I am."

"Tell me, Richard. How are you?"

"I don't want to discuss it. Please, let me do your hair, and let's leave it at that."

"I know you're a queer, darling, but you're so

gorgeous. Perhaps I could cure you. I know all the right moves, and I could do the same things that some of your boyfriends do for you," she laughed.

"Your hair is done, Miss Bonet, and you're on in five minutes," he said, as he sighed with relief and left the dressing room.

Loretta cursed under her breath, and took another drink.

"We're ready to shoot the next scene, Miss Bonet," a voice called outside the dressing room.

"I will not do any scenes if I have to smell that crap on your breath," Andre Darvi yelled at her when she got on set.

"The hell with you then. I'll get another leading man. I'm the fucking star of this picture," Loretta yelled back.

"I want to see you in my office now, Loretta," Anthony Roman shouted from behind the cameraman. Loretta followed Roman into his office.

"Look, you're our brightest star, and we are grateful to have such a box office draw working for the studio, but this drinking is ruining you. And I will not allow you to ruin the studio. Cut it out, Loretta, or you will be washed up. Understand?"

"Nobody talks to me like that! I could go to any studio, and they would give me anything I want. RKO offered me double my salary to work for them."

"Sweetheart, you're under contract, and you're costing this studio a lot of money by stalling this picture with your drinking and your attitude. Please, just shape up. I'm asking you, nicely, sweetheart. A lot of people are depending on you."

"Now, that's better. Talk to me with respect and I won't be mad. I'll behave myself."

"Thank you. Now can we get back to work?"

Loretta began to see Anthony Roman in a different light. He was, after all, the youngest and best looking studio head in Hollywood, and he was single. She watched how the girls all made plays for him, but until now she wasn't interested in him. Isaac Levine was still the owner of Hometown Pictures, but he needed a studio head that could project an image. And Anthony Roman certainly did that.

Loretta apologized to Andre, and promised to lay off the booze when she was working. The scene went well, and it was a take.

Loretta did not hesitate to say yes when Anthony Roman invited her to dinner. First, of course, was the matter of telling Oliver Hanson Young to take a hike. Having done this, she waited anxiously for Anthony Roman to pick her up.

Loretta looked at the pictures of David's and Nunzio's children in her photo album, the twins and little Alberto. Boston and her friends were a far cry from her mansion in Hollywood, she was thinking when her maid, Cabriella, announced that Mr. Roman was in the waiting area.

"I'm taking you out for a simple dinner. I hope you like Chinese food." Anthony said.

Loretta could not believe he was telling her and not asking. Men had always asked her where she would like to dine, and this guy was telling her.

"I never had Chinese food," Loretta said.

"Well, there's always a first time. I know you will love it," he said.

And she did. Loretta never enjoyed a dinner more. Anthony was a delightful companion. He kept her entertained throughout dinner with his little stories and jokes. He didn't try to flatter her or come on to her, as other men in her life had.

After dinner, Anthony said, "Come on, let's go see It Happened One Night. It's playing at Grauman's. Let's see what the competition has to offer."

The New Patriots

The newsreel was just beginning. Nazi Germany. Hitler was recruiting millions of Germans into his army. There was open contempt of order and justice, and the people seemed to be going along with it. They were marching in the streets. Soldiers marching, school children mimicking soldiers, as they marched to school, singing. 'Heil Hitler' was the new salutation replacing hello, goodbye, good day, good luck, etc.

Loretta couldn't wait for the newsreel to end. She didn't like what was happening in the world. After all, wasn't that the reason people went to the movies? To escape all of that? Finally, the movie began. It was worth the wait. She and Anthony enjoyed it, and she said she agreed that it did deserve the Best Picture Oscar.

"Politics," Anthony replied. "It's all politics. You are a remarkable woman, Loretta. If you stay off the bottle and take care of yourself, you'll remain so. I am quite fond of you, and have been since I met you. I didn't mean to scream at you this morning, but it was necessary.

"Yes, I know," Loretta said.

CHAPTER SEVENTEEN
January 1935 Boston

Nunzio walked around the testing room at the bakery like a new father. After all, the new rye bread was his baby. La Bella Rosa Italian bread, pumpernickel and white bread had a new brother, La Bella Rosa Rye. "By February, we will have the rye on all our customer's shelves, with and without seeds," he bragged to his bakers.

"Hey, Mr. Cappolla!" Santo the foreman, yelled. "Mr. Natali wanted me to remind you about the meeting with the Union officials at noon. I called your driver to bring the car around to the main gate."

"Thank you, Santo," Nunzio replied.

Since Vito Natali had been actively involved at La Bella Rosa, they had spread out to service most of Massachusetts, including Cape Cod, and had three bread routes operating in Rhode Island. Besides the breads and rolls, they had a pastry division.

Nunzio was thinking about the eighteen hours a day he spent at the office, and how little time he gave to Rose, Little Alberto and Patrick. Patrick, always coughing, such a sick baby, he thought. And poor Rose, always alone in that big house. She has a maid, a nurse and two children, but she is alone because her husband is married to the business.

Nunzio was still thinking about how he could spend more time with his family, as he got in the car. He asked the driver to take the long route. He certainly was not in any hurry to visit with Vito. He needed some time to take his mind off of the business for a while. He was remembering how he had enjoyed everyone being together at the New Year's Eve party. Everyone was there, Father DiSalvi, Mama and Papa, Maria and Stefano announcing their engagement; Vito, David and Sally, and half the employees of La Bella Rosa, as well as half the elite of Boston. Unfortunately, Aunt Nora had died only one month before. I loved that woman, he mused. Everyone loved her.

He was still daydreaming when he heard, "Mr. Cappolla, Mr. Cappolla," as the driver nudged him.

"Oh, are we here already? I'm sorry. I was nodding off. With these eighteen hour days, I sleep where and when I can," Nunzio laughed.

He walked into the meeting room and was greeted by his lawyer, Dan Walker, Vito, and the President of the local, Joseph Allen. Mr. Allen nodded, "Mr. Cappolla, nice to see you again. Please have a seat," he said, as Vito handed Nunzio a sheet of paper.

"This is the agenda," Vito said. "I worked a little deal with Mr. Allen before the meeting. I hope it is acceptable to you. We give a little, we get a little."

"What do we give and what do we get?" Nunzio asked.

"We give the route men a commission on sales, an incentive to increase their sales. We give the plant employees a pension program. That way, we take care of them when they get old and they don't bother us with strikes. And they leave us alone about holidays and all that horse shit for awhile."

"Gentlemen, can we begin?" Joe Allen asked in his commanding voice, with the twenty-five cent Havana cigar tucked securely in the corner of his mouth. "I showed Mr. Natali and Mr. Walker our requirements. They seem to go along, so this should be an easy contract to write up and present to the employees for the vote. What do you think, Mr. Cappolla? You do read English?

Barry C. Lefferts

Or you need a copy in Italian?" Allen smiled sarcastically.

Nunzio didn't like him at all, but smiled and said, "I read English fine, Mr. President of the Union. This commission is a great idea, but the percentage you got written here must have been an error by your secretary, an easy one to correct, I'm sure. And the pension funds? Who will administer his funds? And what does an employee who quits before he retires get?

"Very simple," Allen replied. "As far as the commission, that could work on a scale based on how long the man has worked, how much new business he is writing and how fast his route is growing. If he quits before he retires, then he only gets a small portion of his pension, based on how much he has contributed. Capisce paesano?" Allen again smiled, the smoke coming out of the other side of his mouth.

"And who administers the pension fund, Sir?" Nunzio asked.

"Well, if you like, we could ask Mussolini to administer the fund," Allen replied with a giggle. "But, if he's too busy chewing garlic, the union will administer the pension fund. We will invest the contributions and handle all the cases."

"Out of the dues the members pay?" Nunzio asked.

"Hey, Vito," Allen said. "What's the Italian word for schmuck? Never mind. The dues pay union officials' salaries, and for all the paperwork to run the union. You pay half, the employee pays the other fifty percent."

"That could run into a lot of money, Mr. Allen, money we don't have. We're still growing, and our capital is committed. How can we pay into a pension fund?"

"You got to take care of your people, Cappolla. If you don't have a contract, your customers are going to be toasting somebody else's bread next month, while your employees walk the picket line."

"Look here, fuckface," Nunzio shot back, finally

tired of the sarcasm. "I started this business, and no fat ass union punk is going to tell me how to run it. There are millions of unemployed men in this country, and like FDR, I'll give them a new deal. I'm willing to negotiate a reasonable wage, Christmas and New Years off, and we can talk about pensions when La Bella Rosa is ready and able to pay for pensions. You don't like my proposition, you can stick it up your smart, arrogant ass."

"Listen here, Cappolla," Allen said, as he rose to stand and point at Nunzio. "You damned ginnies think you can get off the boat in this country and take over like that Capone creep. Well not here, not in Boston. Not now, not ever. You don't sign a contract, we strike. You hire scabs, you better buy a lot of sponges, 'cause there's gonna be a lot of blood in the gutter. Now, you will have to excuse me as I got other things to do." Allen walked out of the meeting.

"You fucked up, Nunzio," Vito said

"He's right," Walker agreed.

"We will see," Nunzio said. "We will see."

That night Nunzio lay in bed staring at the ceiling. He did not eat dinner. He kissed the baby, and went right to bed.

"What's the matter, darling?" Rose asked.

"Power," Nunzio replied. "Power is what it's all about. Italy, the United States, it's all the same. Who can have the power, who can control who. You work, you slave, you build, and there is always someone, something, standing behind you ready to eat you up."

"What are you talking about, sweetheart?" Rose asked.

"I'll tell you tomorrow. I'm going to sleep."

No sooner had Nunzio fallen asleep, than a knock on the bedroom door woke him. "Mrs. Cappolla, it's Patrick. He's coughing again, I can't get him to stop."

"Quick, Janet, call Dr. Goldman," Rose nervously

replied.

"You sure it's not Whooping Cough?" Nunzio asked.

"Dr. Goldman said it's not. He doesn't know what it is, it comes and goes. Oh dear Lord, my poor Patrick, my poor baby," Rose said, heading for Patrick's room.

An hour later, Dr. Goldman came rushing into the room. "Let's take a look. It's just like the other times, Rose. I ran tests, but can't find any reason for the coughing. I'm going to admit him to the hospital. We need to do extensive tests and have some other doctors look at him. This medicine should stop the coughing for now. Take him over to St. Gregory's, and I'll meet you there in twenty minutes."

"I'll bring the car around front," Nunzio said as he rushed to get dressed.

"Oh, God, please let him be all right," Rose prayed.

"At least Alberto is sleeping," Janet mumbled. "I'll stay in the other room with him until you get home."

The next morning Nunzio sat in his office drinking coffee and reading his newspaper, waiting for Vito. With a sleepless night and a head full of problems, he was a nervous wreck. On the front page of the paper was a story on FDR's National Industrial Recovery Act, an attempt by the administration to regulate business. There was also a story on how Hitler was rearming Germany, and the Allies were not enforcing the Versailles Treaty. There was also an article announcing Loretta Bonet's engagement to Anthony Roman, President of Hometown Pictures.

Nunzio picked up the phone and spoke to his secretary, "Alice, call Mrs. Cappolla and see if she got any word on Patrick's condition. And have an engagement gift sent to Loretta Bonet in care of Hometown Studios, Hollywood, California."

"Charge it to Nunzio Cappolla," Vito whispered as he walked into the office. "What the hell happened to you, Nunzio? You look like you've been beat, kicked and run over," Vito said.

"Bad night, no sleep. Patrick's been coughing again, and with the union business on my mind, well, you know how it is."

"I'm really sorry about Patrick. What did Dr. Goldman say?"

He put Patrick in St. Gregory's. I'm waiting to find out. Anyway, what's gonna be with that Allen asshole?"

"You know, Nunzio, when you first went to work with your uncle back when I was bootlegging, I thought you were just a little shit from the old country, not even a Sicilian. I figured you would either get yourself killed or become another working stiff, but you're a sharp guy and I've grown to like and admire you, but you got a lot to learn about dealing with people. Guys like Joe Allen, assholes as they may be, run the show, and you gotta play ball with them or you wind up sucking wind. I had a breakfast meeting with Steve Marshall, he's Allen's assistant. He said that Allen's nephew is running for councilman in Braintree. If we were to make a thirty-thousand dollar donation to his nephew's campaign fund, well, he would see to it that we got a two year contract. Two percent commission for the route man plus a three dollar a week raise in base salary and five cents an hour raise for the plant employees. He'll put the pension plan on hold. Besides, the new deal is working on something called social security that's supposed to take care of people when they retire."

"That's great," Nunzio replied. "But first of all, the campaign contribution is a payoff. That's illegal as all hell, isn't it? And thirty-thousand dollars? Christ, he could run for President."

"Nunzio, you got a lot to learn. Compared to what that pension fund would have cost, and better yet, what we would lose in a strike, thirty-thousand is a drop in the bucket. And illegal? What is that? You learn that word in night school, or maybe stuffing bottles of wine in bread?"

"Do what you have to do, Vito. Go get a contract. Alice, you get any information from Rose?" Nunzio shouted.

"Mrs. Cappolla is on the phone now," Alice shouted back.

"Nunzio, come quick. It's Patrick," she was crying hysterically. "He's, he's dead. Patrick, my baby, is dead."

"I'll be right there," Nunzio started to cry, and dropped the phone. "Vito, Patrick died. I've got to go to Rose."

"I'll drive you," Vito said.

"No, you take care of things. Tony will drive me."

Father DiSalvi was already at the hospital giving last rites when Nunzio arrived. Nunzio took Rose in his arms. They held each other and cried.

"I loved that baby, Nunzio. I loved him so much. I can't believe this has happened. I can't believe he is gone."

"I loved him, too, sweetheart. The lord works in ways we can't understand."

CHAPTER EIGHTEEN
June 1935

Rose Cappolla sat on the leather couch in Dr. Goldman's office, nervously thumbing through the magazines. Each time she heard footsteps or a door close, she would look up, hoping it was Dr. Goldman. The walls of the office were decorated with diplomas and pictures of all the babies Dr. Goldman had delivered. The picture of Patrick brought the sadness back and a tear ran down Rose's cheek. Finally, the door opened and Dr. Goldman walked into the office. He sat in his swivel chair behind the large mahogany desk.

"Congratulations, Rose, you're pregnant," he said looking at Rose without making direct eye contact.

"Thank you, Doctor," she replied with a half smile.

"Don't thank me," he said walking over to her and taking her hand in his gently. "Thank your husband. And let's pray that this child will be healthy, and you will have many more if you desire. Ruth will make you an appointment for next month. If you have any problems at all, don't hesitate to call me."

"Thank you for everything, Dr. Goldman. I'll see you next month," Rose said, as she got up and walked out of the office.

It was warm outside, and the sun felt good. She walked over to the plant to tell Nunzio the news.

"That's wonderful, darling," Nunzio said, embracing her. "Let's go to the club for lunch and celebrate."

After the second glass of champagne, Nunzio said, "Oh, my love is like the red, red rose in June, or something like that. It's a poem that always reminds me of you Rose.

I'm so happy you're, I mean, we're having another child. I love you."

"And I love you," she answered.

"Guess what?" he asked.

"What?"

"Loretta and Anthony are going to be married right here in Boston, at the end of the month. Of course, we're invited, and David and Sally will be there. It will be great to be together again."

"Oh, Nunzio, that's great news. I'll go over to Renee's and buy a dress today."

"Time to go back to work, darling. I'll have Franco take you to your car. See you tonight," Nunzio said as he helped Rose out of her chair.

Rose called her father and her brother to tell them the news, and went shopping.

The tragedy of losing a child hurts so much, she thought to herself. But life must go on, and a new baby will be a joy. And Alberto, my beautiful, precious little Alberto, how big he's getting. Looks just like Nunzio, that nose, and those eyes, almost black like Nunzio's. Why do you keep calling him Alby? Nunzio always asked. His name is Alberto.

And she always answered teasingly, because he's, well he's my Alby, that's why, she said in her mind. Alberto's just a little too, you know, too Italian.' She laughed out loud, then looked around the store to see if anyone was watching her. She picked out a dress for the wedding, paid for it and left.

Back in his office, Nunzio reviewed the union contract and smiled to himself as he put it back in the folder.

In November, Joe Allen's nephew would be running for councilman in Braintree, a small town outside of Boston. Of course, if he wins it will give Joe Allen even more inside political clout, and future headaches for

The New Patriots

Nunzio. Nunzio toyed with the idea of Joe Allen having more and more power in future negotiations on contracts. But what can I do? With FDR devising all these new programs, and the country supposedly on its way to recovery, I'll just have to give Caesar what is Caesar's, keep the rest, and that's that.

Nunzio liked to listen to FDR's fireside chats and all the new deal programs. Everything is initials in Washington, he thought, there's the TV, and so on and so forth. Roosevelt has restored diplomatic relations with Russia, so maybe they'll serve caviar at the club. Hey, maybe I'll bake caviar cake for our uptown customers. Daydreaming is so much fun, Nunzio said to himself, before the phone rang, breaking his trance.

"Nunzio." It was Vito's voice. "It's me. I just made a deal on flour saving us three cents a bag, and I won't be in 'til Thursday."

"Good going, Vito. I'll see you on Thursday. Oh, by the way, Rose is pregnant," Nunzio laughed.

"Congratulations," Vito said and hung up.

That night, Nunzio and Rose went to the movies to see Loretta's new picture, The Lady from Venice. It was a double feature playing with Mutiny on the Bounty.

"I enjoyed Loretta's picture," Rose said after they left the theater. "But Mutiny on the Bounty was really good. Bet it wins the Oscar."

"Could be," Nunzio replied. "Loretta was okay, but the picture was slow."

"Nice shots of Italy though." Rose said.

"That was the Hollywood Hills and that gondola ride was as phony as could be," replied Nunzio. "Someday Loretta will get a great part and win the Academy Award. That's if they ever vote for foreigners."

"Nunzio, darling, that poem you were talking about this afternoon, I looked it up. It's 'A Red, Red Rose' by Robert Burns and it goes like this. 'Oh, my love's like a red, red rose that's newly sprung in June. Oh, my love's like the melody that's sweetly played in tune, etc. etc. He spells love, l-u-v-e."

"That will be our poem, darling," Nunzio teased. "You are my red, red Rose."

"And you are my shining knight, darling," Rose giggled.

"I saw Loretta's father today, Rose. I asked him if he was excited about Loretta marrying an Italian man and having the wedding in Boston. And I won't repeat what he said."

"I don't think he's too thrilled about Loretta's life. And the money she sends him, well, he always sends it back." Rose replied.

"Maybe this time it will work," he said.

As they entered the house and got ready for bed, Nunzio asked, "Anything else you want to tell me before I go to sleep?"

"Alby has learned the alphabet," she said.

Nunzio took her in his arms and reached over to turn off the lamp.

CHAPTER NINETEEN
September 1935

The crowd at the ball field was on its feet. Not one person could be seen sitting down, and the applause was so loud you would have thought it was a bombardment. At the plate for the Boston Braves was the immortal George Herman 'Babe' Ruth. He had started his amazing career with the Boston Red Sox, and spent fifteen years with the New York Yankees to become a legend. And here he was back in Boston with the Braves. Neither Nunzio nor David was that familiar with baseball, but this was, after all, the great American pastime. And who in New England, of any importance at all, would not give their right hand for a ticket to see Babe Ruth in a Boston uniform? So there they were, on their feet, with both hands in the air, applauding the Babe. Ruth struck out. Everyone sat down, and the Braves, down two-nothing, took the field.

"I thought he only hit home runs," David said.

"In New York he hits home runs. The air is thinner here and he's getting older," Nunzio replied.

"I got mustard all over my pants and shoes," David complained.

"It'll come out," Nunzio said. "This is fun, paesano. Glad you could come to Boston. It was nice of Vito to give up his tickets. I'm going to owe him for this one."

"Well, you made sure he got invited to Loretta's wedding. Especially when she can't stand him."

"Yeah. That was a nice wedding. Maybe she finally married someone who could make her really happy. I never saw her like that, the look in her eyes when she looked at him. I hope this time it's for keeps," Nunzio said.

"You know, Sally is pregnant, and with Rose due in December, we're going to have plenty to keep us busy. No time to worry about Loretta. She always manages."

"I'll tell you what, David. This place must use a lot of hot dog buns. Why couldn't La Bella Rosa bake hot dog buns and sell them to the stadium?"

"Never stop with business, kid, do you? Anyway, find out who does the buying and make yourself a deal. Someday people will stay home and watch the games on television, you know."

"Right," Nunzio said. "The pictures through the air."

The Braves were back at the plate trying to get something going. Three quick outs and still two-nothing. They took the field. The Babe tipped his hat as he ran out to center field, and the crowd went wild in acknowledgment. That was the only thing keeping the people there in an otherwise boring game, especially with Boston losing.

David took out his flask and took a gulp of Canadian Whisky. He passed the flask to Nunzio. "Takes the nip out," David said. "It's cold out today, and damp."

The batter for the Giants hit a line drive and was rounding to second. Ruth fielded the ball and threw him out at third. The crowd went crazy.

"He still can throw that ball," David said. "Oh, I meant to tell you, Nunzio. Continental signed a contract with the Italian government to supply them with communication equipment, and, since I'm the only engineer who can speak Italian, I'll be going over to help train their communication officers. The order came from Count Galeazzo Ciano, Benito's son-in-law himself."

"Good for you, David. I think Mussolini is going to start a war. I saw in the newsreel his army was on the Ethiopian border, and it wouldn't be any surprise if he invaded Ethiopia with the help of your equipment."

"This deal could lead to a big promotion for me. Continental could be a major world supplier of communication equipment. And if Italy invades Ethiopia, so what? I'm more concerned with the monster regime in Germany. That's where the next war is coming from. I got a copy of Hitler's book. Care to read it?"

"No, thank you. I have enough with running the bakery and taking care of a family to bother with politics. That reminds me, speaking of politics, Joe Allen's nephew's campaign in Braintree is going full blast, now, and Vito and I are involved. I'm going to be pretty busy with that until after election day, so if you don't hear from me, you'll know why."

"Gotcha. I'll be leaving for Italy on the 22nd," David said. "That's only two weeks away. I'll speak to you before then, and we'll get together when I get back."

It was the bottom of the seventh inning, three to nothing in favor of the Giants. The Braves had two men on and one out, and Babe Ruth was up. Two balls, one strike, a fastball and he hits it out of the field. Three to three. The crowd jumped out of their seats. The Braves went on to win five to three.

"I've never seen anything like this," David shouted over the crowd.

The Babe bowed to the fans as he returned to the dugout. There was madness in the streets when David and Nunzio left the stadium. Nunzio dropped David at the train station, and went back to the bakery.

CHAPTER TWENTY
October 4, 1935

Joe Allen's nephew, Richard Gary, sat at his Campaign Headquarters, located behind the town hall in Braintree, with a telephone in one hand and a pencil in the other. He loved to call everyone 'Baby'. Man, woman or child, to Richard Gary no one had a name other than 'Baby'.

"Hey, Baby," he yelled at Nunzio sitting in front of him, the telephone still at his ear even though nobody was on the line. "Find out what grease ball's got citizenship in Braintree and make sure they're gonna vote for me."

Nunzio didn't answer. He walked outside and took the letter out of his pocket. It was from Bari, Italy, his brother Bruno.

> *Dear Brother,*
> *I am sorry to have to tell you that dear Father Bettino died in his sleep this morning. The whole town is in mourning and I know how you cared for him. I wanted to let you know as soon as possible. I will write again very soon. Love to Mama, Papa, Maria, and to your family too.*
> *Love, Bruno*

Nunzio wiped the tears away and walked around the little park by town hall. He thought about his childhood. Father Bettino, always there when he needed him. David was in Italy. He'd be coming home at the end of the week, Nunzio thought to himself.

As he passed the newsstand, there it was, the

headline: *ITALIAN AIR FORCE LED BY COUNT CIANO BOMBS ETHIOPIA. EMPEROR HAILE SELASSIE PROTESTS TO LEAGUE OF NATIONS.*

Nunzio went back to campaign headquarters. He had no sooner walked inside when Richard Gary, still on the telephone, shouted at him, "Baby, you taking care of that assignment or what? My uncle said you were on the team."

"Listen, little shit," Nunzio said, "you talk to me, you show respect, or I'm going to step all over your face, understand, Baby?" Nunzio pulled the telephone out of the wall and went home.

CHAPTER TWENTY-ONE
Election day, 1935

David Fairchild listened to the returns at home. He only cared about Senator Eric Hampton's re-election. The Senator had been an enormous help in getting legislation passed that was critical to Continental's growth. The Senator had not been pleased with the sale of supplies to the warring Fascist government in Italy, but business was business. And, with the size of the contribution to his campaign's fund, the Senator would do better keeping his mouth shut, David thought. Besides, he thought again, if war breaks out in Europe again, Continental Electric will be ready to make billions.

Sally opened the door to the study. She was four months pregnant and still no sign of a belly.

"Can I make you something to eat, darling?" She asked.

"Thanks, I'm not hungry," David answered. "But you can pour me a drink if you like."

"I'm sending out invitations to Edmond's and Joel's birthday party. Can you believe, four years old already," Sally said as she poured the brandy into the little glass on the desk.

"It looks like Hampton will win by a landslide."

"I'm happy for you that he's winning, but I'm more concerned with what is happening in Europe. The Nazi's are passing laws in Germany to deny Jews their rights. You hear such horror stories and the United States is doing nothing. Next year Roosevelt is up for re-election and the Supreme Court has been calling a lot of his New Deal unconstitutional. Roosevelt wants to change the court.

He's got balls but he's doing nothing for the Jews," Sally muttered angrily.

"I can't worry about the whole world, darling," David replied. "Only my little corner. And right now that is Continental Electric and the election. Besides, the justices are in for life and the President had better get his act together if he wants to be re-elected."

"I joined the women's auxiliary, darling," she said. "If we get enough memberships perhaps we could do some lobbying and help the people who need help the most."

"When do you have time, between taking care of the two boys and running this house?"

"I make the time just like you do," she answered.

"Women should not be involved in politics," he replied sternly.

"That's what everyone told Catherine the Great and Queen Victoria but they wouldn't listen either," she laughed.

CHAPTER TWENTY-TWO
The next day

"Fourteen votes. I won by fourteen lousy votes, Uncle Joe," Richard Gary moaned.

"Well it is better than losing by fourteen votes, stupid. Er... correction. I mean Councilman Gary," Joe Allen laughed. "Congratulations."

"I need to make an acceptance speech."

"Fuck the speech, your honorable Councilman. You're lucky they don't ask for a recount on the votes, and without the Union, you couldn't win dogcatcher. Keep a low profile for a while and then we'll have plenty of shit to keep you busy. This is only a stepping stone to the Governor's mansion."

"Or beyond, like the White House in Washington," Gary proffered.

"Must be the shithouse you're talking about, nephew. For the White House, I'll have to get somebody with a brain. Where the fuck is that Cappolla? He was supposed to meet me here an hour ago."

"I don't like that guy, Uncle Joe. He's a smartass."

"Who gives a rat shit what you like? We need the Dago. Through him we can control the bakery industry and perhaps the food industry. This is only the beginning. You get along with him. Understand?"

"Sure, Uncle Joe," he relented.

Nunzio walked into campaign headquarters about ten minutes later. "Congratulations, Councilman Gary," he said.

"Thank you, Baby," Richard Gary replied, offering his hand.

Nunzio took the hand loosely and shook it. "That's a handshake?" Gary asked. "Come on, Baby, gimme a handshake." He grabbed Nunzio's hand in a vise like grip. "Thanks for the help, Baby," he said.

"Now that this bullshit is over with, let me run my business the way I see fit, okay?" Nunzio said.

"Sure, Nunzio. You run your business, but I run the Union. Things are changing in this world. The working man wants his share of the pie and we are here to see that he gets it. Nothing more, nothing less."

"I'm all for that, but I think you want more for Joe Allen than you do for the workingman," Nunzio replied.

"You're a young snot nose, Cappolla," Allen yelled. "You got a lot to learn. And you will learn! You've been very lucky so far and, no doubt, you are going to go far in this world, but this Union is going with you as long as you intend to stay in business."

"Hey, Uncle Joe," Gary interrupted. "This is a joyous occasion. All these people are here to celebrate. Nunzio, your paesano, Vito, is here. Come on, Baby. Have a drink and let's cut out this bickering. We're one big happy family. Hey, everybody, I want to make a toast to the new councilman... me."

CHAPTER TWENTY-THREE
July 20, 1936

The voice of Walter Winchel described the action on the screen. Loretta Bonet's new motion picture, Victoria was playing second fiddle to General Francisco Franco.

Winchell was describing how Franco led the military revolt against the Spanish Republic two days earlier, and the Fascist leader promptly joined the Rome-Berlin Axis. Britain, France and the United States maintained strict neutrality. Roosevelt was campaigning for a second term with a promise that American men will not die on foreign soil. In Ethiopia the war was over and was marked with terrible atrocities. Mussolini's son, Vittorio, talked of Italy's victory. Not one nation raised a voice in defense of Ethiopia. Haile Selassie, the Emperor, who many considered a prophet, had fled the country.

As the movie Victoria began, the patrons of the Boston Regent Theater were still spellbound from the newsreel. Loretta, radiant as ever, played the part of the wife of an Italian general during the Napoleonic Wars. Victoria was having a love affair with a Russian Prince, a cousin of the Czar, while her husband, the General, was preparing his army to meet Napoleon against the invasion of Russia.

"Loretta's best picture to date," Nunzio said as he and Rose left the theater.

"I agree whole-heartedly," she answered. "And Patricia didn't cry once, did she?" she asked the baby in her arms as she cuddled her. "I love you. Yes, I love you," she continued in baby talk.

Nunzio was giving Alberto a piggy back ride as they walked to the car. "I'm glad we took the children with us," Rose said. "It seems we always leave them with the babysitter and the nurse, and I don't like to leave them with anyone, especially my little Patricia. She's only a baby," once again she cuddled the baby.

"I can't get over how much the baby looks like you, Rosy, with those blue eyes and freckles. Who would believe her father is Italian.

"Speaking of Italian, Nunzio, it looks like your old country and that awful Adolph Hitler are really stirring up trouble," Rose said.

"Don't believe everything you see in newsreels. They love sensationalism. Let's get home, it's hot out tonight."

"You know, its been a while since we heard from Loretta," Rose said as Nunzio started the car.

"Well, according to the movie magazines, she and Anthony are very happy. They bought a mansion someplace outside of Los Angeles called Ojai Valley, away from the glitter and glamour. Maybe we'll go out there and visit them."

"Oh, could we? When? Oh, Nunzio, you're not just kidding are you?"

"Well, I can't get away now, business and all. But maybe after the summer. I hear California is very hot in the summer."

"I bet David and Sally would love to go with us. And Edmond and Joel and little Joshua. And you, me and Alberto and Patricia. We could really keep Loretta busy," Rose laughed.

"Do you realize we have never taken a vacation, Rose. Except for a couple of weekends in New Hampshire, and Cape Cod, of course. California...what a great idea. Like Al Jolson sings, California, here I come."

"I think you better leave the singing to Al Jolson, you're a hell of a baker, but a singer? 'Fraid not."

Nunzio pulled the car into the driveway and helped

Rose and Patricia out of the car. Alberto was groggy and started to whine.

The nurse answered the door and told Nunzio to call Vito right away, it was urgent.

"Hello, Vito," Nunzio said into the phone. "It's Nunzio."

"Well. While you were having fun at the movies," Vito said, "I scored the General Market account."

"That's great! I'll see you at the office in the morning," Nunzio replied.

"Can't wait until the morning. It's a union deal, thirty-five outlets in five states and growing. Supermarkets are the thing of the future. A&P, General and others. Got Joe Allen and the Vice President from General at the office. Get right down here for a meeting, please."

"Okay, I'm on my way," Nunzio replied. He hung up the phone, kissed Rose and the children, and left the house.

When he got to the office there was a fresh pot of coffee and strips of La Bella Rosa coffee cake on the table. Vito was seated between Joe Allen and Earl Tannenbaum of General Markets.

"Mr. Tannenbaum," Nunzio said shaking his hand. "So good to see you. I'm happy we're going to be doing business together. It's just that, well it's eleven-thirty at night."

"I do business twenty-four hours a day. And I like to work when everyone else is sleeping," Tannenbaum said.

"General is a union shop," Joe Allen added. "Union trucks, union help."

"And no doubt the hand of the union boss will be dipping into the union till, Joe," Nunzio said smiling.

Joe Allen just grinned and winked at Vito.

"Mr. Cappolla," Tannenbaum said, "your partner, Vito, and I have entered into an agreement for La Bella Rosa to supply us with sandwich bread and rolls under our label, and you can have shelf space for your specialty items. We have thirty-two outlets now and we're opening four more next year. We operate in five states and plan on moving into the southern states in the near future. Do you think you can gear your operation to handle our account?"

"To be honest with you, Mr. Tannenbaum, I don't know," Nunzio replied. "I would have to buy more ovens and trucks, and hire a lot more help. And to serve five states? I don't know if we can do it."

Vito interrupted. "We can truck everything into the other states until we build new bakeries."

"What five states are we taking about?" Nunzio asked.

"New England," Tannenbaum answered.

"You won't have to buy trucks, Nunzio," Joe Allen added. "You can make a deal with one of the union trucking outfits. They will carry the bread at night to be delivered when the stores open each morning."

"Golden opportunity, Nunzio," Vito said, an anxious look on his face.

"How do we make a profit, Vito?" Nunzio asked.

"The overhead of new help and trucking contracts. General has agreed to pay all our costs in private labeling bread products plus five percent for our profit. We make the real money on cake and cookies. We can expand our line. You know, prune Danish, Italian cookies, etc. We pay them a fair profit on those items, just like we do our other customers. If it works out with General, Nunzio, the sky's the limit."

"And you, Joe Allen, what is it you want out of this?" Nunzio asked.

"For one thing, I'll handle the trucking contract, and when your contract is up in December, you will be able to easily afford a pension fund. You're going to be a very, very rich man, Nunzio. You have obligations to take care of those who helped make you rich."

"We're a corporation, Nunzio. A big corporation," Vito said. "Someday, maybe every family in America will be putting their butter on La Bella Rosa bread, drinking their coffee and eating La Bella Rosa coffee cake. We'll have so much money we can buy Boston. Every inch of it."

"I don't know what I would do with every inch of Boston," Nunzio laughed. "But, we have a deal, Mr. Tannenbaum. When would you like to begin?"

"Start off with our Boston stores. As soon as you have the manpower and equipment, and, of course, the trucking contract, we can begin selling your products in all our stores. Oh, and we pay all bills these days less two percent, to be deposited in an account under the name of T and R Trucking, Inc., Bank of Boston, of course."

"Of course," Nunzio replied. "And the 'T' in T and R trucking..... Tannenbaum?"

"You catch on quick, Mr. Cappolla. Until our next meeting, as you Italians say, salute." Tannenbaum made a gesture to toast Nunzio.

"Well, now we can go home and get some sleep, Nunzio," Vito said, patting Nunzio on the back.

"I have to be back here in three hours Vito. I might as well sleep on the couch in the office. I'm going to call Rose."

"Good night," Joe Allen said as he walked out the door with Tannenbaum.

Nunzio walked around the plant, watching the bakers work in the quiet of the night. Nine years since I first walked into Uncle Alberto's bakery, he thought. I can still see Moses and Uncle Alberto sifting the flour. In December I'll be twenty-seven years old and look at me, a giant businessman. America gave me everything. The business, Rose, the children. No, change that... God, you gave me everything in America. He called Rose and went to sleep on the office sofa.

CHAPTER TWENTY-FOUR
August 16, 1936

Hometown Studios sent a limo to the train station to pick up the Fairchilds and the Cappollas.

"Oh, Anthony, I adore you," Loretta said as she nervously inspected the mansion for any last minute details.

Fuji and Tomo, her Japanese maid and Hawaiian born Japanese butler, were dusting and straightening up. The kitchen staff was preparing a seafood feast, garnished with just about every vegetable known.

"You never go to this much trouble for any of my friends, Loretta" Anthony complained.

"Oh, darling. Nunzio and David are more then friends. They're, well, like family. I love them."

"As much as you love me?" he asked.

"Don't be silly. I could never love anyone as much as I love you, Anthony Roman."

"How long are your friends staying? We begin shooting Girl with a Gun next week."

"They're both busy men. They'll be leaving next week, but I want to show them how movies are made and take them on a tour of the studio. Do be a darling and narrate the tour for them."

"Anything to make you happy, Loretta Bonet."

"They should be here any minute. I suppose I should have gone to Los Angeles to greet them, but there was so much to do to get ready."

"Did you ever go to bed with either of them, Loretta? Not that it matters now, of course, but I'm just curious."

"Only in my fantasies, Anthony, darling. Only in my

fantasies."

The limo pulled up to the gate and the chauffeur stopped to clear security. Both Nunzio and David were in awe, as were Rose and Sally.

"Even in my wildest imagination I could not picture the estate would look like this," David said.

They got out of the car to look around. Ojai, a town in Ventura County, about sixty miles north of Los Angeles and thirty miles south of Santa Barbara, was breathtaking. The forty-acre estate was surrounded by mountains.

"Reminds me of Italy," David said.

"Only a Baron could live in an estate like this in Italy, David," Nunzio answered.

"Yes, and remember, my father was a Baron."

"That's right, you are a Baron. I forgot for a minute, your highness," Nunzio laughed. "And I'm just a poor baker, so what am I doing here?"

"Well," David said, "I hereby dub you Knight of the Order of the Oven, so now you are royalty. Look, there's Loretta and Anthony."

Loretta came running out to greet them. "David, Sally, Nunzio, Rose," she hugged them. "Oh, it's so good to see you all. And the children, they're all so precious."

"Let's go into the house, shall we?" Anthony asked, helping with the luggage.

The ladies walked together. Rose and Sally, carrying the babies, followed Loretta into the house.

"We saw your last movie, Victoria," Rose said. "A definite academy award winner."

"Thank you for being so sweet, Rose. But The Great Zigfield has a lock on it. Politics. Besides, Hometown Studios never wins anything," Loretta answered.

"You should at least get a nomination for best actress," Nunzio added.

"Even if I do, talk is Louise Rainer has that sewn up. I don't care anyway, as long as I get the check."

"In this town it's not who you know that counts, but who you blow," Anthony said laughing. "And my wife? Well, she is my wife. Hey, everybody, plenty to eat and drink. No shop talk for a while, okay?"

Loretta, obviously uncomfortable, looked at her friends. "Sally, Rose, come on. I'll show you the house. Tomo, please look after the children." She smiled at her friends. "Would you believe we even have an upstairs maid, just like in the movies?" She laughed.

The bedroom Loretta and Anthony shared was on the second floor. The bed was covered with a gold-laced bedspread, and the white carpeting covering the floor looked like snow.

"There are seven bedrooms in the house," Loretta said, "including the guest rooms you will be using. The servants sleep in the house across the field. They go back and forth with a horse and buggy. I love it. The kitchen has two entrances, one leading into the dining room and one into the breakfast room where Anthony and I eat when we are alone. We seldom use the living room. We do much of our entertaining in the ballroom, and when we relax we use the study."

"The house is magnificent, Loretta," Rose said as they joined up with the others. "I'm so happy for you."

Fuji passed brandy around on a silver tray and Loretta announced she wanted to make a toast. "To nine wonderful years of friendship, and to a million more."

The following morning they had a real country breakfast, and Anthony arranged for the Hometown limo to take everyone on a tour of Los Angeles and Hometown Studios.

After five days in California, they were all exhausted.

"Sightseeing all day and parties at night. I can't keep up this pace," Rose said.

"We're leaving in the morning, Loretta, so let tonight be the party of parties," Nunzio said.

"I'm going to miss all of you very much," Loretta said. "Tonight we are going to have some special guests. Clark Gable and Bette Davis. And maybe Spencer Tracy and Katharine Hepburn, if they decide to come here after the party at Bill Hearst's place."

"Unfortunately, none of the big, big stars are under contract to Hometown," Anthony complained.

"Except Loretta," Sally replied.

"Of course," Anthony answered. "We do have a lot of big stars, including Loretta, but no Gables or Tracys or Munis. You know what I mean?"

"Well, anyway, this has been one of the nicest weeks of my life and I'll be talking about it for a long time," Rose said.

"If you will excuse me, I have work to do in the study," Anthony said, as he put down his drink and left the room.

Andrea, the upstairs maid, was waiting in the study. She was already undressed down to her bra and panties when Anthony walked into the room.

"This will have to be a quickie," he said. "Don't want my wife to get suspicious."

Andrea smiled and pulled him toward her. Her wide red lips pressed gently on his mouth. She was thin, and her black curly hair covered half her face. She had been in this country three weeks when Anthony hired her as an extra for the film Victoria, then gave her the job as upstairs maid and mistress.

She fulfilled his need for constant sex. He still loved Loretta, but Loretta never seemed to be in the mood, always acting as if she was doing him a favor. He was completely naked and sitting on the rocker. Andrea was on his lap and they were rocking back and forth as she cried out in ecstasy.

Anthony was afraid someone would hear and kept putting his hand over her mouth to quiet her.

"Oh, Mr. Roman, it's so good, I can't help myself."

Tomo was by the door listening. He shook his head. Better to mind my own business, he thought.

Rose, Sally and Loretta were having coffee in the breakfast room. David was asleep on the couch.

"I think I'll go to the study and see if Anthony wants company while he's working on whatever it is he's working on," Nunzio announced.

"I would rather you wouldn't," Loretta said. The look on her face made Nunzio uncomfortable.

"What's wrong, Loretta?" Nunzio asked.

"I, I just don't bother Anthony when he's busy in the study," she replied.

A while later, Anthony appeared in the room. He had a nervous smile on his face. "Well, that was that, and I'm all finished," he said.

Nunzio could see the tear in the corner of Loretta's eye. He knew something was going on, but didn't say anything.

The next morning, the ride back to the train station seemed longer than when they arrived.

"Great vacation," David said. "And what a great party last night."

"Yes, it was very nice," Nunzio replied as he gazed out the window thinking about Loretta. He couldn't forget the look on her face the prior afternoon.

CHAPTER TWENTY-FIVE
January 20, 1937

The day was one neither Nunzio nor David would ever forget. They were part of the audience listening and witnessing the second inaugural address of Franklin Delano Roosevelt, the President of the United States of America.

"What greater honor can be bestowed on us two immigrants?" Nunzio asked.

Senator Hampton had arranged for the invitations, and Joe Allen had tried to pressure Nunzio into giving up his invitation but Nunzio stood his ground and here he was with David in Washington.

Having defeated Alfred Landon by a landslide, the President was more confident of his popularity. And that was evidenced by the nature of his speech and the overwhelming enthusiasm of the members of Congress present.

"I bet they won't mess with the New Deal this trip, Senator. Not if they want FDR's support in their own re-elections," David said.

"He still has a long way to go, and the country has a long way to go. And with what's going on with the Axis powers of Germany, Japan and Italy, who knows? We might be involved in a war again, David. Anyway, politics is his business," Senator Hampton said. "You just enjoy being here and take care of Continental Electric."

"I am sorry to say that the nation has not reached the happy valley I have envisioned, but we are working on it," the President said. "I pledge to continue to work to relieve the poverty that engulfs one-third of the people of this nation. Yes, one-third of the people of this nation are today ill-housed, ill-clad and ill-nourished. This administration will work toward erasing that figure."

The crowd was on it's feet, applauding.

"With Sally and Rose both pregnant, I'm glad to hear that," Nunzio laughed to David.

Senator Hampton leaned over and whispered, "Ninety percent of the wealth is in the hands of five percent of the people in this country. Always was and always will be, FDR or otherwise. In fact, his home in New York could feed half of Boston for a year."

"It's the way it has always been, Senator," David said. "If a man owned half the world, would he share it with everyone else? Or would he let everyone else fight over their share of the other half and keep his half all to himself? Greed, I guess you would call it."

"On the other hand, David," the Senator replied, "look at the way the damned Bolsheviks do things. They divide the wealth, supposedly evenly, but a small percentage retain the power and with that power they can control. They don't need anything else, because they can take what they want."

"That's what the Nazis are doing in Germany," David said. "They have the power, and they are increasing that power by elimination of the opposition. A few have it all, and the masses get the shaft."

"Our relationship, yours and mine, is built on the same principal, David," the Senator said. "You want special consideration for your company, and I want your help. I scratch your back, you scratch mine. Some people might say it's illegal, others would argue it was capitalism at its finest. We're all motivated by one thing or another; to be in control and to have the world by the balls."

"That's some heavy stuff you two are discussing," Nunzio interrupted. "I have to leave now, got to get back to Boston. Thank you for the ticket, Senator. David, I'll call you. Ciao."

Nunzio left the hall and took a cab to the train station. He caught the 3:10 back to Boston and headed right for his dinner meeting with Earl Tannenbaum.

"How was the Inauguration?" Tannenbaum asked.

"An experience of a lifetime," Nunzio replied. "I feel like a real American, like I was born here. If you know what I mean?"

"I think I know what you mean," Tannenbaum answered. "What happens if there's a war, and Italy is the enemy? It looks like that could be a real possibility. Where would your allegiance be Nunzio?"

"I hope it doesn't come to that, Earl."

"We're real happy with your products, Nunzio. We're opening fifteen more outlets this year. You're going to have to open another plant. Joe Allen is going to be negotiating a new contract, but what the hell, eh? You're going to be making so much money it won't matter."

"The only problem is that the contract is usually geared so that the Union and Joe Allen get more than the workers, and that's not right. Sure, I'm going to make lots of money, but I got a conscience."

"That's what I like best about you, Nunzio. And I admire you for the way you are. But, business is business, and we're playing in Joe Allen's ballpark, so we have to play by his rules or not at all. Also, that nephew of his, the Mayor, he's talking about running for Congress now. Who knows, maybe someday that little shit will be in the White House."

"God help us all," Nunzio replied. "That will be the day Mussolini will be throwing a welcome home party for his new personal baker, Nunzio Cappolla."

They both laughed, and Nunzio picked up the check. "Got to get home to Rose now, Earl. I'll get to work on the plans for the new plant in the morning. Take care of yourself."

They shook hands and Nunzio left the restaurant. He

drove by the Bijou Theater on the way home. He pulled over to look at the poster. Harold Weeks and Loretta Bonet in What After the Conquest?, about Italy's war with Ethiopia. How lovely she looked on the poster, he mused. Under the poster, it read, 'Coming next week, The life of Emile Zola.' They would have to see that one, too. Rose loves the movies. Ever since they returned from California, Rose has been on a movie kick. Driving away from the theater he couldn't help thinking about Loretta. She was still with Anthony Roman, but she'd been drinking again, and that was too bad.

"All the money and all the comforts and all the power Senator Hampton was talking about doesn't change the basic aspects of being a human animal. We still have to live with our thoughts and our feelings," Nunzio said, talking to himself.

Rose was asleep when he walked into the bedroom. He kissed her gently on the forehead, checked on the kids and went to bed. There was a note on his pillow: "Darling, call your father asap. A letter from Italy came today. Your brother Bruno was arrested by the Fascists."

CHAPTER TWENTY-SIX
The next day

Enzio and Anna Cappolla waited nervously outside the Italian Embassy while Nunzio spoke to the Liaison Officer. The tired look on their faces from the long night's drive to New York was clearly visible. The only thing they knew was that several Italian Nationals were arrested for actively protesting the Rome-Berlin Pact and the Ethiopian invasion.

"My brother has never been political," Nunzio cried. "Why would he be arrested? And what are they doing with him?"

"I'm sorry," the officer replied. "I have no information, and Rome is not commenting. Please go home. If I have any information, I will forward it to you."

Nunzio put his arms around his mother and father, and walked them out of the Embassy. He had the bible Bruno had given him when he left Bari, and for some reason, he brought it along.

"What will we do?" Enzio asked his son. "What will Cara do? I must go back to Bari and help. Bruno needs me."

"I'm going with you," Anna cried.

"And what are you going to do when you get there?" Nunzio asked. "Perhaps make matters worse? Let's wait for more information. They may be just questioning him. I have some connections. Maybe it's time to bring Cara and the children to America and see if we can get Bruno released, and bring him here, too. Besides, the children are not children anymore. Antonio is seventeen and Theresa is sixteen. I can use them all in the business. Everything will work out, you'll see. Let's go home."

"God blessed us when he gave us you, Nunzio," Enzio replied. "As sure as he blessed the Virgin with the Holy One."

"Are you sure, Nunzio?" his mother asked. "Are you sure you can do this?"

"Have I ever let you down?" Nunzio asked.

They drove back to Boston with a look of hope on their faces. It was a mission to be accomplished. Nunzio dropped them off at the house and went to the office to place a call to David.

"David," he said, explaining the situation, "can you get your friend, the Senator, to arrange a meeting with the State Department? I got to pull a deal, whatever it takes to get Bruno and his wife and children out of Italy. I will pay whatever is necessary. I have never asked anything of you before, but this must be done, please."

"What are friends for?" David replied. "I can't make any promises, but I will do my best. Those Fascists are tough to deal with, but where there's corruption, there's more corruption. I'll get right on it."

Nunzio sat in his office staring at the phone. The contracts, the Union, Tannenbaum, were all on hold. Two hours later the phone rang.

"It's Mr. Waters from the State Department, Mr. Cappolla," the secretary said.

Nunzio quickly grabbed the phone. "This is Nunzio Cappolla, Mr. Waters," he said. "Do you have any news?"

"Mr. Cappolla, your brother has been charged with treason and proclaimed an enemy of the state. At the request of a mutual acquaintance, our embassy in Rome has detailed all the information and has spoken to the prosecuting official for the Italian Government. The indication is that for a rather large sum of money they could arrange a pardon, providing he leaves Italy for good. Can you handle the payoff?

"How much?" Nunzio asked?

"One hundred thousand, American," Waters replied.

"How do I go about it?"

"I don't know, but I will have the right people in touch with you. It's highly irregular for me to be involved in anything like this, Mr. Cappolla. But I owe favors to those that helped me get my job, so I'm sticking my neck out. You'll be contacted. Have a good day." The phone went silent.

Again the phone rang. "Your wife, Mr. Cappolla."

"Rose, what is it? I'm very tired," Nunzio said into the telephone.

"I can imagine. And I'm sorry to bother you. Your parents are here, and Maria, too. Even my father and brother are here. The phone hasn't stopped ringing, and we were wondering if you had any news. Are you coming home soon?"

"I'm working on getting a release. Things look good. Tell Mama and Papa I'll be home soon. I've got to get some sleep."

No sooner did Nunzio hang up the phone, then it rang again.

"Mr. Fairchild for you, Mr. Cappolla."

"David?" Nunzio whispered into the phone.

"You sound terrible, Nunzio. Better get some rest, or you'll have a breakdown. Things are being arranged. You spoke to the State Department, right?"

"Yes, some guy named Waters. I need a hundred grand in a hurry."

"No problem," David said. "I have it in the vault. I'll transfer it to your bank, or better yet, to a bank in Zurich."

"I love you, David. I really love you."

"Likewise, paesano. You know, it's interesting. Mussolini wants to restore Italy to its ancient greatness when Rome ruled the world and, of course, he would be Caesar. Yet, he takes no lesson from the results of the fall of the Empire, and makes the same mistakes as the ancient Caesar."

"I really don't give a fuck about all that. I just want my brother to be all right. I'm sorry if I sound angry, David. I'm exhausted."

"I understand. Call you tomorrow. Let me handle things. We Jews are good at negotiating releases. We've had thousands of years of practice."

"Thank you, David. From the bottom of my heart, I thank you."

Nunzio put the phone down and closed his eyes. He fell into a half sleep. Three hours passed, and again the phone rang.

"Mr. Cappolla. Mr. Cappolla." His secretary was shaking him.

Nunzio opened his eyes.

"It's your wife."

He picked up the phone. "Rose, I..I ... was sleeping. What is it?"

"You better come home. Please, right away."

"What is it? Tell me? I hear crying in the background, what is it?"

"We got a telegram. Your sister-in-law is in London with her children," Rose said.

"And Bruno? Is Bruno in London?"

"Please come home now," she replied.

"Tell me now! What did the telegram say?" he demanded.

"I'm sorry, darling," she said. "Bruno is dead, beaten to death. That's all it says. Cara and the children are arranging passage to Boston."

"I'm on my way home," Nunzio said, as tears formed in his eyes.

He put down the receiver and stared out the window. He took a shot of whiskey from the bottle in his desk.

"I don't understand you, God," he said aloud. "The

things you do, the good and the bad."

"Is anything wrong?" his secretary asked, as he came into the waiting room, with the shot glass absentmindedly held in his hand.

Nunzio looked at her. Tears streamed down his face. "I'm going home now, Janet," he said quietly. "I'm going home." He went into Vito's office to give him the news, and to ask him to run things for a couple of days.

"I'm sorry about your brother," Vito said. "If there is anything..."

"Thank you, Vito," Nunzio interrupted. "Just hold down the fort."

His arrival at the house was one of the most painful experiences Nunzio had ever encountered; more so, even, than the death of Patrick. As a child, Bruno had been his mentor. He was the older brother. He worshiped Bruno; big and athletic and always there for everyone. Bruno loved life and everyone loved Bruno. Even though Nunzio had not seen him for ten years, it seemed like yesterday they were together. So much has happened, he thought.

Nunzio stood in the foyer holding his crying mother, embracing her without saying a word. The room was filled with family and friends. Everyone was silent.

"Why Bruno, Nunzio?" Mama asked. "He never hurt anyone. Everyone loved Bruno."

"I don't understand it either, Mama," he replied. "I don't understand what's going on."

"Arrangements are made for Bruno's wife and children to come to Boston," Rose said.

"Good," was all Nunzio could say.

"We will have a funeral service here," Maria said.

"How can we possibly get the body?" Nunzio asked. "And besides, Bruno would want to be buried on his native soil, not in a country he has never seen. I need some air. I'm going for a drive."

He drove over to Hanover Street, and parked the car.

He walked by the old bakery and looked at the house upstairs. He could imagine Uncle Alberto looking out the window.

He continued walking down the street as old familiar faces smiled at him, unaware of his sorrow, thinking to himself. I can see where I have come from, he thought. But, where am I going from here?

I would trade everything to have Uncle Alberto, Patrick and Bruno back. But you don't make deals, do you God? Only the devil makes deals, right?

The cold was making him shiver. He put his hands in his pockets and continued walking. A few snow flurries were visible, and he could feel the wetness on his face. Time to go home, he said to himself.

He stopped at St. John's church on the way home. "Give me five minutes alone with my brother," he said, kneeling. When he was through, he left the church, walked over to where he parked the car, and cried hysterically. Finally, when it got dark, he went home.

CHAPTER TWENTY-SEVEN
March 12, 1938

The snow on the ground had turned to ice.

Rose Cappolla, six months pregnant and trying to keep warm, stood outside the mansion with her father. He insisted on driving her, along with the real estate agent.

Nunzio wanted the whole family to live in one compound, and this three-acre site with the fourteen room mansion was perfect. A house for Papa Cappolla and his family, she said to herself. And after the wedding in June, Maria and Stefano could build a house in the wooded area on the north side of the property. Plenty of room for all the children to play.

"I don't know if Lexington is ready for all these grease balls yet," Jim Kelly remarked to his daughter.

"Daddy, you know how I feel about that kind of talk. Besides, you will be living here too," she said.

"In a pig's ass I will," he replied. "I'm glad your husband is doing so well and that you have money to burn, but I'll stay in Boston and take care of myself, thank you."

"If you'll come back to the office, I'll get the paperwork started, Mrs. Cappolla," the realtor said.

"Fine," Rose said. "I can't take this cold. It's going right through me. I sure can use a cup of coffee."

"I can use about two shots of Irish whiskey myself," Jim Kelly added.

"I'll make sure you each have what you want at the office," the realtor replied.

When they arrived at the office, Rose immediately called Nunzio. "Darling," she said. "You were right, as usual. The place is perfect. Mr. Thompson is preparing all the papers, and I gave him a check for the deposit."

"That's wonderful, Rose. I'm busy with new contracts. Vito is at the dedication ceremony for the new plant. Things are happening so fast my head is spinning. I just spoke to David, and he said Sally is in hysterics. Hitler took Austria yesterday, and with her grandparents living in Vienna, she's beside herself. I understand they are trying to move them into Poland in a hurry. You know Hitler's policy toward the Jews. Anyway, I've got to run. Loretta and Anthony will be here for Maria's wedding, and I have a million things to do. You can handle everything with the realtor and bring home whatever I need to sign."

"Okay. I love you," she said, hanging up the phone.

Rose looked at the newspaper on the realtor's desk. It showed a picture of Mussolini doing the goose step. Only he called it the Roman step. Austria is on Italy's border, and Mussolini did not appear too happy with Hitler's action.

"Poor Sally," she whispered to herself.

"Not a pretty picture, what's going on in Europe," Mr. Thompson said, noticing her distraught look.

Jim Kelly had to put his two cents in. "Them Krauts and Dagos could kill each other off and the Commies and Jews, too. What do we care? This is the U.S. We're safe here. And for that matter, I know a bunch I would send over there in a ..."

"Please, father. Enough," Rose interrupted.

"You're entitled to your opinion, Officer Kelly," Mr. Thompson smiled. "I'll have the papers ready in the morning, Mrs. Cappolla. Here's a receipt for your deposit. Good luck in your new estate, shall we say. And, Lexington is quite historical, as you know. You'll be walking in the shadows of the founding fathers."

"Yes," Jim Kelly laughed. "Surrounded by WOP gangsters and Jewish money grabbers. The good people of Lexington are probably out buying guns right now."

"Sometimes, I hate you father," Rose said. "Take me home now, please."

When she arrived home, Rose was surprised to see Maria sitting on the porch. "Aren't you working today, Maria?" she asked.

"Nunzio let me go home early. Stefano and I are going shopping. Nunzio said to tell you he will be home late. He and Vito have some contracts to go over. Why don't you come shopping with us?"

"I'm exhausted and cold, dear. I think I'll just go to bed early. I want to have dinner with the children though. Oh, and we've decided to buy that place in Lexington. You will love it Maria."

"What is important is that you love it, Rose. You're going to be living there," Maria answered.

"Nunzio wants us all to be living there. He has a lot for you and Stefano already picked out.

"Maybe me and Stefano don't want to live next to the family in Lexington. Stefano is his own person, and he's doing good without Nunzio. Believe it or not, there are some people that can get along without my brother's help. I appreciate what he has done for me, and Mama and Papa, but he can't just run my whole life forever. Maybe me and Stefano want to live on Mars."

"Maria, please don't discuss that with Nunzio just yet, he has enough on his mind," Rose said.

"I don't want to work in the bakery, anymore. All I am is the boss' dumb sister who is just there to spy. Nobody is friendly toward me, because they think I'm going to tell my brother that they are not working hard enough. And I don't even know what I am supposed to do, and all Nunzio tells me is just look pretty and don't do anything to embarrass him. I want to go back to Bari. I didn't want to come to America in the first place. It was Nunzio's idea. If I stayed there, maybe Bruno would still be alive."

"Please, Maria, I'm tired. Some other time."

"Tired from what? Carrying the baby? Or maybe from looking at houses? You've got a maid and cook and nanny. All you got to do is wake up, give a few instructions here and there, and go back to sleep. Easy enough life. How come you're tired?"

"First my father, and now you?" Rose answered angrily. "I told him to go to hell and I'm telling you the same thing. Only please don't aggravate Nunzio until after your wedding. He's looking forward to the wedding like a child looks forward to Christmas."

Maria relented. "I didn't mean to get you upset, Rose. You're wonderful. But how do you like living with my whole family and Cara and Antonio and Theresa? They're enough to drive anyone crazy, always yelling. How do you put up with it, Rose?" Maria asked.

"I love your brother more then I can say. His family is my family. And it's not so bad."

"Nunzio is lucky to have you Rose, even if you're not Italian. Forgive me for being rude to you. You don't deserve it. Please come shopping with us. We're looking for things to wear on our honeymoon, and you would be a big help. Oh, here comes Stefano, now."

"I'd love to go, Maria, if I won't be in the way. Let me check on the children first. But, please promise you won't say anything to upset Nunzio until after the wedding."

"I promise," she said.

The two women embraced, and Rose went into the house.

"What's that all about?" Stefano asked as he walked up to the porch and kissed Maria.

"Nothing. Come inside. Rose is going shopping with us. She has better taste than both of us put together."

"Both of us put together. That is a most pleasing thought. I dream of us put together," he smiled.

"Well, just think, my dear. Three more months and your dream will come true." She hugged him, and they went into the house."

CHAPTER TWENTY-EIGHT
June 1938

Rose inspected the grounds of the huge house as if she were an army sergeant inspecting the troops. She looked over every inch of the new white paint on the walls for dirt or chips, checked the plumbing in the toilets and looked carefully at the lawn. If as much as a leaf was on the ground she would instruct Lester, her maintenance man, to pick it up. It had been two weeks since they moved into the house and that day they would be entertaining over three hundred guests for Maria's wedding. There were going to be many important people here, she thought to herself. Senators, city officials and bankers who could not care less about Maria and Stefano, but cared only about being at Nunzio Cappolla's mansion for a party.

The crew hired by the caterer was busy setting up tables and chairs on the lawn. The bandstand was already assembled with the chairs lined up for the fifteen piece orchestra.

Nunzio was dressed in his magnificent tuxedo. "This wedding will not be forgotten for a long time," he said to Rose.

The Martinellis, Stefano's parents, Guido and Theresa, who had arrived early to help set things up, approached Nunzio and Rose. "Nunzio." Guido called out. "One would think Maria was your daughter instead of your sister, the way you are making this wedding. You amaze me."

"Maria's happiness is important to me, Guido. I want her and Stefano to have a good start in life, and this celebration will be a happy occasion for us all, I hope,"

Nunzio answered.

"I hear that your friend, the famous movie star Loretta Bonet, will be here," Theresa Martinelli added.

"Yes," Rose answered with a smile aimed at Nunzio.

"And so many other important people," Nunzio shot back.

"They make such a beautiful couple," Theresa said.

"See that lot over there, Theresa, Guido? That's where the beautiful couple will build their home and Stefano can come to La Bella Rosa and have a fabulous future. As we prosper, so shall he," Nunzio bragged.

Rose smiled at the Martinellis, but didn't say a word. Not the time, she thought.

As the guests arrived, the orchestra played something from The Marriage of Figaro, and Nunzio was on his second bottle of wine. He greeted Father Vincent, who was being considered for Bishop of Boston.

"Bon Giorno," he said hugging the priest. "Welcome to the Cappolla Estate. We call it Casa de La Rosa. Like that Father? I just made it up."

"Looks like you're feeling no pain, Nunzio," the priest said. "Congratulations for your sister, and for your new home, and your success. God has chosen to shine on you, and bless you. Always remember, the Lord giveth and he also taketh."

"And he helps those who help themselves, Father," Nunzio added. "Now, have something to drink. I have to greet my guests." He walked over to Joe Allen and his wife, and Councilman Gary, who arrived with Mr. and Mrs. Tannenbaum.

David and Sally were at the door with Senator Hampton and his wife. Nunzio and Rose were so busy shaking hands and hugging the guests it was difficult to keep in mind that this was Maria's wedding and not some political shindig. Enzio Cappolla, nudging Nunzio every five minutes, "Why isn't the bride and groom greeting the guests, Nunzio."

"They don't know these people, Papa," Nunzio snapped.

"This looks more like a party for your new house, than a wedding celebration," Enzio remarked.

"Papa, Papa. Go have some vino, manga, there's much for you to do. Dance with Mama, dance with Maria and let me run the party. You know who is paying for the party?" He continued without the obvious answer. "Me, that's who. So go have fun. Here comes Loretta and Anthony. You want to meet a movie star, Papa?"

Rose was hugging Loretta as Nunzio strode over to them. "You look wonderful, Loretta," he said, while hugging and kissing her as one would embrace his lover.

"Hello, Nunzio, darling," she said, pushing him gently. "You must be a little sacked," she laughed. "Getting my bad habits, are you?"

Rose took Loretta by the hand, "Come on. Let me show you the house," she said.

"First, I want to see David and Sally, and meet Maria's beau," Loretta answered while grabbing a glass of champagne from one of the many waiters walking the grounds with trays of food and champagne.

Nunzio, catching up to David asked, "How are things at Continental Electric?"

"If you really want to know," David smiled putting his arm around Nunzio, "things are going very well. We're getting a lot of government contracts, thanks to Eric Hampton's help. And the television research is going remarkably well."

"Oh, yes," Nunzio said. "Pictures through the air into the living room. How much money is your company spending on that? Wait, don't tell me. I shouldn't ask you things like that. You're second in command at the company now, aren't you?"

"I suppose," David answered.

"You suppose?" Nunzio smirked.

"Looks like you're doing well yourself, Nunzio. Extremely well, in fact."

"At La Bella Rosa Bakery, David, we make lots and lots of dough. Get it? Dough." Nunzio laughed, proud of his little play on words. "Not to change the subject David, but Sally looks so sad. I've never seen her without a smile before. Is something wrong between you two?" Nunzio asked.

"It's her grandparents. They left Austria and are living with relatives in Krakow, Poland. Sally is so worried about them. Hitler is growing stronger and stronger, and talks of Germany taking over the world. His hatred of Jews has her very upset. You're not a Jew, Nunzio, you wouldn't understand.

"And what of Mussolini, David? He killed my brother. I understand Hitler and Mussolini. Pollutions, are what they are. They're all the same, dubots and greedy," Nunzio responded with emphasis. "But this is a wedding, David. My sister Maria's wedding. Let's be joyous, eat, drink, dance. Hey, musicians," Nunzio yelled, "play Funiculi Funicula." He started singing, "Sometimes the world is made of fun and frolic, and so do I, and so do I." He grabbed Maria and started spinning her around the lawn. "Today, you are the loveliest girl on the planet, my sister," he said.

"And you are the drunkest, my brother," she laughed as she hugged him. "I love you, Nunzio. You are the most wonderful brother in the world."

Anthony Roman was in deep conversation with Senator Hampton as Rose walked over to Loretta, who was signing autographs for some of the guests.

"Are you working on any pictures right now, Loretta?" Rose asked trying to get her attention.

"Well," she laughed, "because of my Italian accent, Vivian Leigh beat me out of the part for Scarlet O'Hara in

Gone with the Wind, but I am about to start a movie based on the life of Napoleon Bonaparte's wife, Josephine. The title is 'Til Death Do We Wait. I'm looking forward to it. It is the best role I've ever read. And you know what else, Rose? I'm pregnant. I'm going to be a mommy."

"That's wonderful, Loretta. I'll bet Anthony is ecstatic. How come neither of you have said anything? When are you expecting? I thought you put on some weight, but I didn't want to say anything."

"I'm in the fourth month, Rose, and the baby isn't Anthony's. He knows it, but we're staying together. You wouldn't understand, and I don't think this is a good time to explain. Somehow, we care for each other a lot, and we have our careers to think about. Anyway, I wanted to tell someone, and you are the only person in the world I feel comfortable talking to. You have that gift, Rose, that rare gift." The two hugged, and Rose walked over to Sally, who was talking to Mrs. Tannenbaum about her grandparents.

"I also have relatives in Krakow," Mrs. Tannenbaum said. "But Hitler would never dare to invade Poland. That would bring the British Empire into the war, and they would burn his little Nazi ass."

"I hope you're right, Etta," Sally said.

"Are you two enjoying yourselves? Can I get you anything?" Rose asked.

"It's a wonderful party," Sally answered.

"Everything's fine," Etta Tannenbaum assured her.

"Can I talk to you a minute, Rose?" Nunzio interrupted.

"What is it, darling?" she asked.

"I just had a chat with my sister. She does not want to live here. Stefano wants to build tall buildings in New York. They are moving to goddamn New York. How come I'm the last to find out this bullshit? I feel like a fool."

"They have their life to live, darling," Rose said. "You are anything but a fool. Wish them well and let them go. Instead of building them a house, let's give them the money so they can get started in New York."

"But I want my family to share in the business. I had plans for Stefano," he said.

"You're not God, Nunzio," she said. "You are a wonderful man, and I love you more each day. Let people live their own lives. Our children will grow up and they may want to be something other than what you had in mind. Now is the time for you to begin to realize it."

"You're a smart broad, Rose Cappolla, you know that?"

"Yes, I know," she laughed.

"And you're not half bad looking either. How about coming upstairs with me. I'll bet these people wouldn't even miss us."

"You're right. Let's go."

With the orchestra playing Sentimental Journey, Nunzio lead Rose into the house and up to the bedroom. They did not see any of the guests off. They left that to Maria and Stefano.

CHAPTER TWENTY-NINE
Christmas, 1938, Hollywood, California

Loretta Bonet put the script on the nightstand and went into the nursery to check on Judy. Two months old, and she never stops crying, she thought to herself. Such a beautiful little girl, though.

"I just changed her diaper, madam," the maid said.

"Thank you, Fuji. I'm just looking in on her. Isn't she beautiful?" Loretta said

"Like her mother, if I may say so," Fuji said blushing.

"Thank you, Fuji. By the way, has Mr. Anthony been home at all today? He mentioned he would be home Christmas Day, but I haven't seen him yet."

"Sorry, Madam," Fuji answered, folding the baby's blanket. "I haven't seen Mister for three days."

"I see. If he comes home, I'll be in the study working on my script. I'm so sick of Napoleon movies Fuji, I would love to play Juliet, or perhaps Joan of Arc."

"Yes," Fuji answered with a puzzled expression.

Loretta took another look at the baby. Her father's eyes, she thought. Why does she have to have her father's eyes to goddamn haunt me? She thought back to the night she conceived Judy. Anthony was out screwing one of his starlets, or whomever, that night. Loretta had been drinking, so she called Reggie Dell, Hometown's new find. She had sensed he had the hots for her, and she was right. They went over to Reggie's house in the Hollywood Hills, and after two drinks and a little necking, they were naked in the pool. They made wild, passionate love in the pool, on the diving board, in the living room. She did not come home for two days. Reggie had the most incredible eyes. You could not stop looking at them. And now Judy has those same eyes.

Loretta poured herself a drink and picked up the script. Look at me, she thought again, unable to concentrate on her lines. Here I am, a movie star, men throw themselves at my feet. I make more money then I ever dreamed I could. I'm married to Anthony Roman, and I have this house. So why am I so fucking miserable? I was happy back in Boston with Paul. Oh, no, I wasn't. I was never happy, and I will never be happy.

She continued talking to herself. Remember, you have a baby now. You're going to be a good mother. Better than mine was. Papa never talks about my Mama. Buton he calls her under his breath. Well, Judy's not going to call me a buton. Will she ever find out that her daddy is Reggie Dell? How could she? Nobody knows but me. Even Reggie doesn't know. Shit, I was only with him that one night. We avoid each other at the studio. All these years I don't get pregnant, and one night with superstud Reggie Dell, and what do you know? But I do have such a beautiful baby. I do love her so. She poured another drink and tried studying the script.

"Missus, want anything before I retire for night?" Tomo asked. He was standing in the doorway and startled Loretta.

"Ah, no thank you, Tomo. Good night. Oh, is Fuji still in with Judy?"

"Judy is asleep, Missus. Fuji go to bed."

"Thank you, Tomo," Loretta said as she poured another drink and continued looking at the script. What a way to spend Christmas, again daydreaming, her mind wandering away from the script. The brandy was making her numb. She reached for the telephone. Who can I call? Everyone's with their families. It's Christmas Eve. Why isn't Anthony here? Even on Christmas Eve he's got to be out with one of his floozies. He must hate me. Why doesn't he just leave? We haven't slept together in a year.

Why do I have such bad luck?

Loretta realized she was holding the phone in her hand, and put it back on the receiver. She poured another drink, stared at the glass, threw it against the wall and began to cry. After a few minutes, she fell into a deep sleep on the floor. When she awoke she could hear Judy crying in the nursery. She looked at the clock on the mantle. It was almost seven in the morning, Christmas Day. Still groggy, she stumbled into the nursery. Fuji was holding the baby and had the bottle ready.

"Everything under control, Madam," she said.

"I ... I....don't know what I would do without you Fuji," Loretta said.

"Mister Anthony home, Madam. Him upstairs in bedroom."

Loretta ran into the bathroom, washed her face and rinsed her mouth. As gracefully as she could, she walked into the bedroom. Anthony was packing.

"Going on a trip, darling?" she asked.

"It's no use, Loretta," he said. "You and I. We have nothing anymore. I gave your baby my name, she won't be a bastard. But her father will be."

"I..." Loretta tried to interrupt.

Anthony continued right over her words. "I'm not her father, but she is Judith Heather Roman, according to her birth certificate, and she's all yours Loretta. Good luck."

"Please don't leave Anthony, I need you. Please, let's try again. Please," Loretta cried.

"Loretta, I do care about you, and I probably will always love you, but it's just not meant to be. I can't stay with you, and I can't stay in this situation. I'm involved with someone else. My lawyer will work out the details of our property settlement. You can have the house."

Anthony finished packing and walked toward the door. He turned to Loretta and said, "I forgot to wish you a Merry Christmas. Goodbye, Loretta."

Loretta wanted to cry, but started laughing hysterically, instead. Merry Christmas! She laughed. He actually wished me a Merry Christmas and walked out of my life. "Tomo! Tomo!" she yelled.

"Yes, Missus?" Tomo came rushing over.

"Pour me a drink, a double."

"But Missus, it's only seven-thirty in the morning, Tomo answered.

"Pour me a drink, damn it, Tomo. I know what time it is," she shot back.

"Maybe you like to hold your baby a while, Missus," Fuji asked attempting to give the baby to Loretta.

"No, that's all right, Fuji. I've got things to do. You do a good job with her," Loretta said as she gulped down another brandy and went back to her room. She fell on the bed and started to cry. "I'll make it, I'll be all right." The bottle of brandy still with her, she drank until she finally passed out.

CHAPTER THIRTY
January 2, 1939

Little Alberto and Patricia watched Rose as she cuddled one-month old Vitorio as if they weren't even in the room. Nunzio, aware of the familiar jealous look on their faces, took the little ball from the toy box and began to play with them.

"Vito still thinks we named Vitorio after him, doesn't he, Nunzio?" Rose asked.

"Yes," Nunzio said. "But who cares? I wouldn't name our dog after Vito. But without him we never would have reached the success we have. And besides, the man is a genius. Even as a bootlegger he was the best and the smartest. Give credit where credit is due. Hey, look how Alby throws the ball. Babe Ruth, your replacement has arrived."

"Babe Ruth has retired, darling," Rose said.

"I knew that. Wow, listen to those winds outside. And all that snow. It's a real blizzard. I hope none of my trucks get stuck today. Damn, I should go to the office. Vito called. He made it in all right.

"I'm glad to have you home today," Rose said. "We haven't been alone all weekend with the New Year's Eve party and all the company."

"Since we moved into this place, we haven't even visited anybody, Rose. They either come here, or we don't see anyone. Let's go up to New Hampshire and visit David and Sally. What do you say?"

"Too much trouble to take the kids, and I won't leave V alone," Rose answered.

"I understand that, but why do you insist on calling him V, why not at least Vito?"

"V is fine." Rose answered. "You insisted on Vitorio. No more Italian names for our children, if we have anymore, which I doubt. Three is enough."

"I love kids, Rose. I want three dozen. We can afford it."

"No problem, darling. As long as you get pregnant and carry them for nine months, have as many as you want. Oops, hand me a diaper, darling, or better still, I'll play ball with Alby and Patty and you change V's diaper."

"Okay, you can't scare me. Oh, there's the telephone. I'll get it," Nunzio laughed.

"What is it?" Nunzio asked into the receiver. "Say that again, David," Nunzio grabbed the chair from behind the table to sit down. He took a pencil and paper and started writing as he continued his conversation with David. "That's Mercy Hospital, Western Avenue, Los Angeles, Room 302. But she will be all right you said? Thank God."

"What is it? Los Angeles, Loretta? Loretta is in the hospital?" Rose asked. "What's wrong?"

"I'll tell you when I hang up, Rose. Go on, David. Uh, yes, I see. That poor girl. Today's paper? No, I didn't read it. There's a blizzard here and I haven't been out all day. He's a son-of-a-bitch. Somebody will stop him and his gang of bums. Okay, David, I'll put through a call to the hospital and call you back tonight. You too. Ciao."

"What was that all about? What's wrong with Loretta? And who's a son of a bitch? What gang of bums? What?" Rose asked, holding the half diapered baby in her arms.

"Loretta tried to kill herself. Some kind of poison. Only, thank God, she didn't try hard enough, and she's recovering at Mercy Hospital in Los Angeles. Anthony left her. She is very distraught, and it's in today's paper. David was also telling me that in Vienna, the Nazis are throwing garbage on the streets and making Jews clean it up on their hands and knees. Sally's grandparents are in Poland, but she still has many relatives left in Austria. She's very upset. David said his company is screening all orders for any communication equipment to make sure nothing goes to Germany or Italy. He's already cancelled all contracts with the Italian government because of Mussolini's friendship with Hitler."

"Do you think there will be a war?" Rose asked.

"I think things will get worst before they get better. But I think the Italians and the Germans will see what bastards are leading them, and restore the Royalty to power and get rid of the gangsters once and for all. Nobody wants a war. I'm going to see if I can get a call through to Loretta."

"Let me speak to her if you do," Rose said.

CHAPTER THIRTY-ONE
The next day, January 3, 1939, Los Angeles

Dr. Fryman didn't get excited anymore about having movie stars as patients. In his 15 years on the staff of Mercy Hospital he had taken care of such greats as Fredrich March and Helen Hayes, so it was no big deal to him having Loretta Bonet as a patient. He found her to be beautiful, even though she was suffering from alcohol and poisonous substance overdose. Her color was coming back. She ate a full breakfast, and was talking.

"Good morning, Dr. Fryman," the nurse smiled.

"Good morning, Edna," the doctor mumbled entering Loretta's room. "I have never seen so many plants and flowers in one room since I've been at Mercy. You must have a lot of fans and admirers, Loretta. Is it okay to call you Loretta, or do you prefer Miss Bonet?"

"Loretta is fine, doctor. That's my name. Bonet is my first husband's name. Paul Bonet, the fashion designer. He made up that name for me, Anyway, what's the difference?"

"You're looking rather well this morning. How do you feel?" he asked.

"I feel like that stuff food turns into after traveling through the intestinal tubes and the other organs on its way to the rectum," she laughed.

"I see you have a good sense of humor," the doctor laughed. "That was a pretty dumb thing you did, trying to take your own life, a young beautiful movie star with a lovely daughter, and everything in the world to live for. But I won't get into that with you now. I'm glad you're recovering nicely. In a few days you can leave here. Oh, and there are teams of reporters all over the hospital. We told them you are doing well and that they couldn't interview you. Would you like to make a statement? Something like this could ruin your career you know? But it doesn't have to if the press likes you and prints favorable stories."

"You're very kind to be so concerned, Dr. Fryman."

"You can call me Stanley."

"Well, Stanley, you can tell the press I was very depressed and accidentally took the poison thinking it was medicine. And I'm sorry, and that I just want to go home to my child and continue working on my new movie. That should make the studio happy."

"Well, I'll tell the reporters. I'll be in to check on you again this afternoon."

"Thanks again, doctor. You're very nice. Are you married?" Loretta asked, blushing, not believing she had asked him that.

"No. I was married once, no children. My wife died in an accident. It's been ten years now."

"I'm sorry doctor. I hope I didn't bring up an unpleasant memory for you."

"That's all right, Loretta. I'll see you later."

"See you later, Stanley," she smiled.

"You made my day," the doctor laughed as he left the private room.

Loretta looked through the cards from well wishers and fans. There was nothing from Anthony. Three phone calls from Nunzio and Rose, two from David, a telegram from Paul Bonet. *"Loretta, Stop. Speedy Recovery, Stop. No matter what I will always adore you, Stop. Love, Paul."*

The telegram was wet with Loretta's tears. Why couldn't I be satisfied with what I had, she thought to herself. The next telegram was from her father. *"I am on the next train to Los Angeles, Stop. You have strayed far from the nest, Stop. I'll bring the nest to you, Stop. All the love I have, Stop. Your Papa."*

"Your maid called, Mrs. Bonet," the nurse said. "Are you taking calls yet?"

"Yes, I am. Did she leave a message?" Loretta asked.

"Yes, she did. But it was hard to understand her foreign accent. No offense to you, I have no trouble understanding you, Miss Bonet, seen all your pictures."

"I'm happy to hear that, thank you. What was the message?"

"Just not to worry. The baby is fine and everything is under control. What kind of accent was it anyway? Where is she from?"

"Japanese. She's from Japan. But she's lived in Los Angeles since she was twelve years old, and her husband is Hawaiian born Japanese, so she considers herself an American."

"Well, anyway, can I get you anything, Miss Bonet?" the nurse asked.

"How would you like to make ten dollars, easy money, nurse.... What is your name?"

"Becky. Becky Andrews," the nurse answered. "Who do I have to kill?" she said jokingly.

"You don't have to kill anyone. Just run an errand for me. I need you to go to the store."

"Okay. What store would you like me to go to?"

"The nearest liquor store, please. A small bottle of brandy, for my nerves. It would really help," Loretta pleaded.

"If I get you a bottle of brandy, I'll lose my job and be up the creek. My husband is in medical school and we have two kids. I... I just couldn't," the nurse replied nervously.

"Look," Loretta pleaded. "I'll give you fifty dollars and a part in my next movie. If you get fired, which you won't, I'll get you a job at a better salary, or I'll put your husband through medical school. Damn it, please get me the bottle."

"Well, if you're that damned desperate, I'll take a chance. One bottle of brandy coming up. Give me the money and I'm on my way."

"Ah, could you lay out the money? I don't have a thing with me in this hospital. Not even my toothbrush. I'll have my maid's husband bring it later."

"Okay. I don't know why I'm agreeing to this, but I'm on my way, Miss Bonet."

'Stunod,' Loretta thought to herself as the nurse walked out. She doesn't know why she's doing this. Look at what the hell I offered her for a lousy drink. Jesus, another minute and I would have signed the fucking house and car over to her. What the hell is wrong with me?"

She got out of bed and looked at the flower arrangements around the room, especially the one from Isaac Levine, the head of Hometown Studios. The card said, Please don't do this ever again. You're my favorite paesana. Loretta smiled as she read all the other cards. She went back to bed and was dozing off when the nurse returned with the brandy.

"Just leave it in the big plant, Becky. Dig it in good so no one will find it and I will straighten out with you later."

"Yes, Miss Bonet. Fifty dollars and a part in your next movie, right?" the nurse said.

"Right, right, right and double right. Close the door and pour me one drink before you bury the bottle love, thank you."

Loretta took a quick gulp of brandy and closed her eyes. The brandy still in her mouth as she again dozed off.

It was three-thirty in the afternoon when Doctor Fryman returned to the hospital. He stood over the sleeping Loretta Bonet and admired her beautiful face. As his eyes wandered to the exposed breasts he felt his blood rush with excitement.

He then noticed the glass on the nightstand, picked it up and put it to his nose. "Brandy," he said to himself. Gazing around the room he noticed the top of a bottle through the red and yellow roses of the Hometown Studios' flower arrangement. "Strange, these movie people," he said to himself. "They smuggle in booze to one of their own that is in the hospital for the very reason of alcohol abuse." He stared at the bottle and called for the nurse. "Miss Andrews," the doctor said sharply. "Do you have any idea how this bottle of brandy got into this flower arrangement?"

The nurse stood there, not knowing what to say.

Loretta, eyes half opened, remembering her generous offer, said, "I had it smuggled in."

"You can leave us, Miss Andrews," the doctor ordered. "I want to talk to Miss Bonet, alone."

"Stanley, sweetheart," Loretta said sarcastically, "we have only known each other a short while and you are already angry with me."

"I'm not going to ask you who or how the brandy arrived in your room, but I am going to ask you not to let it happen again. Please, Loretta, you have a new chance to get well, and you don't need to depend on alcohol."

"What do I need to depend on? I'm getting dressed and checking out of your lovely hospital, Stanley." Loretta stood up and let the hospital gown fall to the floor. The doctor stood there staring at her wonderful body.

"Want to make me better, Stanley, darling? Make love to me. I know you want to, and I was watching you watch me when you thought I was asleep. I could see you had a hard on. You had one since you came into the room," Loretta put her hand gently on the doctor's bulge.

"Please, Loretta," the doctor whispered. "I'm a doctor at this hospital, and this isn't right. I can't. You're right, I want to and I am excited, but I can't."

Loretta unzipped his pants and fell to the floor on her

knees.

"Oh, God," the doctor sighed as he fell backward on the bed. "It's been so long since I've had a woman, Loretta..."

They were going strong, unaware that Becky Andrews was standing in the doorway watching.

No need to worry about them, Becky thought to herself, as she slipped back out of the room. Better be a real good part in that movie, and I hope I never again walk in to find Doctor Fryman taking such personal care of his patients.

CHAPTER THIRTY-TWO
September 3, 1939. Manchester, New Hampshire

The twin brothers, eight years old, were fighting over the stamp on the letter from Poland. Sally was holding the baby in one arm and the letter in the other hand. "This was written August 15th, David," she cried. "Everything is fine, Grandma says. What am I going to do, David? Edmond, Joel, stop it, damn it," she yelled at the twins who had just torn the stamp in half.

"I'm sure they will be all right," David assured her as he put his arms out to take the baby.

"David, when my parents died from the fever, my grandparents raised me until I came to America with my Uncle Shlomo when I was fourteen. With Hitler and his Nazis invading Poland, where will they go? Warsaw is a disaster, and they're heading to Krakow. What will become of them, God only knows. We must do something. You have friends in high office. Surely you can do something."

"Wait," David said. "The news is coming in on the radio. Maybe we'll hear something about the British demanding that Germany remove its forces from Poland."

"Ladies and Gentlemen of New Hampshire," the newscaster began. *"The United Kingdom and The Republic of France have one hour ago simultaneously declared war on Germany. German aggression in Poland and the merciless bombing of Warsaw is a clear indication that Hitler plans to take over Europe. Let us pray that the British can stop this madman soon. The United States government wants to assure the American people that we will not actively engage American forces in this fight. Here is President Roosevelt's speech of the other day.*

"I have said not once but many times, that I have seen war and that I hate war. I say that again and again. I hope that the Untied States will keep out of this war. I believe that it will. And I give you assurance and reassurance that every effort of your Government will be directed toward that end."

"David, I must go to Poland," Sally said. "I must help them. They're my grandparents. We have servants to watch the children until I return. You must understand."

"How can you go? For God's sake, there's a war on."

"I'll go through Russia. I have relatives in Kiev, which is not that far from Krakow. Will you help me, please?"

"This is pure madness, Sally. We have a family, the twins, the baby. How can..."

"You must understand, David. If I don't try to help them, and something happens to them..."

"What can happen to them? There are millions of Poles, and with England and France involved now, the whole thing will be over in no time, you'll see."

"David, the Nazis are persecuting Jews as a matter of official policy. I have this gut feeling this is going to be a bloody war and that the Jews, under Nazi guns, will suffer a horrific fate. Please let me do what I must do."

"Very well. What do I need to do?" David asked.

"In New York there is an organization called The United Workers. My Uncle Shlomo is a member. In fact, he is the treasurer. They have a direct contact with the Party in Moscow, and they can help me get papers."

"They're Communists! You want me to deal with Communists? I'm an immigrant in this country. I could jeopardize everything."

"Don't be ridiculous, you're not joining. You're only asking for help in getting me into Russia, and I'll take it from there. Please do it for me, please."

"Sally, I must be crazy, but very well," David said.

"I'll leave for New York in the morning. I have some business to conduct in New York anyway. I might as well kill two birds with one stone. What is the address of this Bolshevik organization?"

"It's on Canal Street, downstairs from K and K Delicatessen, in the cellar. They meet at 6:00 p.m. sharp, and they don't like to be called Bolsheviks. They are Americans who care about the workingman and are tired of being exploited by the big companies. It's part of a world revolution."

"That's a lot of horseshit, Sally. And if they're not Bolsheviks, why the direct line to Moscow?"

"Because that's where the home of the revolution is."

"Are you one of them? Maybe I don't know you as well as I thought."

"I believe in equality and a better life for the working man, and I want to help my grandparents."

The next morning, David got out of the taxi on the corner of Canal Street, a half a block from K and K Delicatessen and walked slowly to his destination. He could see the dim light through the cellar window as he walked down the four steps in front of the deli. There were about twenty men and four women seated in front of the podium where a speaker stood in front of an American flag. A short, fat man with red hair and beard approached the door.

"Can I help you?" the man asked David.

"I'm looking for Shlomo Marcus," David said.

"He's sitting in the first row. I'll get him."

"David, I haven't seen you since your wedding. You look wonderful," Shlomo said, shaking hands with David. "Sally told me you were coming. It's terrible what this Hitler is doing. And now a war in Poland. It's wonderful that you want to help."

"Listen, Shlomo. I think this is crazy. Sally wants to go to Russia, and once she makes up her mind there is no changing it, so what can I do?"

"Have a seat, boychik. The meeting is going on. After, we will talk. Oh, you have to sign the roster and print your name, address and occupation. It's policy."

The meeting lasted about two hours, and David sat daydreaming through most of it, not really interested in what these people had to say. After the meeting, Shlomo gave David a cup of coffee and discussed the strategy.

"Sally will travel to Russia with a special visa, proceed to Krakow with a Russian, and escort her grandparents back to Kiev. Arrangements will be made by the Party for them to emigrate to Toronto, Canada."

With the plans all made, David boarded the train back to Manchester. The trip back seemed like an eternity. The world moves too fast, he thought to himself.

CHAPTER THIRTY-THREE
September 23, 1939. Boston

Nunzio sat in his office at La Bella Rosa Bakery, reading the newspaper's account of the Russian Invasion of Eastern Poland six days before. He reached for the phone. "Get me David Fairchild in New Hampshire, please, and call me when he's on the line," he told his secretary. Again, Nunzio stared at the picture of the Russian Ambassador explaining that Russia only wanted to protect her own frontiers, and the Polish army offered little resistance.

"I have Mr. Fairchild on the line," the secretary announced, interrupting his thoughts.

"Hi," Nunzio greeted. "Have you heard from Sally? I'm really concerned."

"She's in Russia, Nunzio. I got a wire that the invasion hasn't affected her. She will be leaving for Krakow in the morning. Nunzio, I'm scared for her, for us. This thing is crazy. She has no business there. But, you know Sally."

"Keep me informed, will you David? If there is anything I can do to help, let me know."

"Thank you, Nunzio. Oh, and what is this about Richard Gary running for Mayor over in Braintree?"

"Yeah, Baby is trying to step up, and I'll tell you the truth, he's been a big help to me. So has his uncle. Business is great and we're growing. Vito takes care of all the Union business and the politics, and I take care of production. Works fine."

"Twelve years, you, me and Loretta have been in America, and look at us. You, a bakery tycoon, and me second in command at Continental. Loretta's a big star in

Hollywood. We could have still been in Europe. We are very lucky, Nunzio."

"David, speaking of Loretta, have you heard from her lately?"

"No, but her new picture is playing in downtown Manchester. The papers mention something about her being seen around Los Angeles with a big shot doctor."

"I saw her father the other day, David. He hasn't heard anything from her, and he looks terrible. I think I'll give her a call."

"Fine, give her my love. I have my hands full with the kids and with Sally being away... Well, I'll call you back when I have some news."

"Ciao, David."

"Ciao, Nunzio."

Nunzio put down the receiver and continued to stare at the newspaper. So many little wars going on, China, Japan, Italy, Poland, Russia, and countries he had never heard of, all involved in one hostility or another. And now England and France, he thought to himself.

How does all of this affect me, Nunzio Cappolla? It doesn't have to. I'm safe right here in the great state of Massachusetts. I have La Bella Rosa, my home, my Rose and my family. We are safe, thank God. Sally is foolish for going to Poland, she belongs home with David.

Nunzio walked into the plant and checked the order slips. Forty thousand loaves of white bread alone for General Markets, he mused. Vito is having lunch with Tannenbaum today, and if they increase the volume, we will have to build another plant, he added to his musing.

It was after ten that evening when he finally arrived home. The children were asleep, and Rose was in bed reading.

"Are you hungry, darling?" Rose called from the bedroom.

"I'll take something," he answered.

Nunzio took a slice of cheese and a glass of wine to the bedroom, put it down on the table next to the bed and undressed.

"I wish you wouldn't eat in bed," Rose said.

"It's only cheese and wine. It's the first thing I've had today, except for nibbling on bread. I spoke to David today. Nothing much new on Sally. She's going into Poland in the morning."

"I hope she will be all right, Nunzio. I wonder what Poland is like? I know a lady from Poland. She used to be a seamstress at Bonet's when I worked there. She had a real heavy accent, was fat and mannish looking, but very nice."

"I know nothing about Poland, Rose, and I don't care to find out. I just hope Sally will be all right."

"Do you think the United States will go to war with Germany or get involved in the war?"

"I'm sure the United States will sell supplies to England, but I don't think Roosevelt will send troops. Poland can handle those Nazis themselves. They've got a big Navy, I hear."

"What's the Navy going to do, Nunzio? Drown the German army?"

"Today I shipped forty thousand loaves of white bread to General Markets, alone," Nunzio bragged. "That's what's important to me. That's here and now. People have to eat. They eat no matter who is shooting at whom, no matter who is in control."

"That's not like you, Nunzio. You're a caring person."

"Dead people don't eat bread. If there is a war, there will be a lot of dead people. You and I have no control over what is happening, Rose. Nothing we can do but what we are doing. Live our life, take care of our family, and I must run my business."

"I know that, darling, but I am still concerned. Concerned for Sally and all those innocent people in

Poland that God only knows what will happen to them."
"It's in God's hands Rose. Let's go to sleep."

CHAPTER THIRTY-FOUR
December 15, 1939

Loretta Bonet and Dr. Stanley Fryman arrived at the premier of Gone With The Wind with little fanfare. The public was interested only in getting a glimpse of Clark Gable, Olivia DeHaviland, Vivian Leigh and even Leslie Howard. The arrival of Margaret Mitchell at the theater in Atlanta could only be outdone by the arrival of perhaps F.D.R. at a Democratic Convention.

The theater was decorated to resemble Scarlett O'Hara's plantation, named Tara. The war in Europe was of little concern to those present at this premier of what perhaps was the greatest motion picture of all time.

"Can you believe this Stanley, this crowd? Hardly anybody showed up for the premier of 'Til Death Do We Wait," Loretta complained. "Do you think my fans are angry with me?"

"I'm a doctor, not a show business analyst, darling. But you were invited to Atlanta for this premier, so I'm sure people still care about the beautiful Italian star, Loretta Bonet."

After the three hour, thirty-minute epic ended, there were speeches by Margaret Mitchell and Dorothy Lamar.

"I wish I could have been Scarlett O'Hara, Stanley. That Clark Gable is divine."

"Well if it makes you feel better, you can call me Rhett tonight," he laughed.

"I don't feel up to going to the party tonight, Rhett. Can we just go back to the hotel?"

"Frankly, Loretta, I don't give a damn. The hotel it is. Anyway, I have to leave for L.A. in the morning. I wish I could go on to Boston with you."

"So do I. I want you to meet my father and my friend Nunzio. And, I do want to see my friend, David Fairchild, the poor thing. No word from his wife, Sally, caught up in all that rhetoric in Europe, trying to help her grandparents."

"The stories that are coming out of Germany and Poland are beyond imagination," he said. "According to reports by the British government, credible witnesses have detailed the tortures and atrocities visited upon Jews and others considered by the Nazis to be enemies of the state."

"Floggings with barbed wire, official destruction of synagogues, brutal killings, prisoners in camps doing physical labor beyond capacity, horrible rapes, and men forced to do knee bends while carrying huge stone blocks. Nothing in history can even match what they say is happening."

"Do you believe those stories, Stanley? Can civilized men actually treat others that way?"

"I'm a Jew, Loretta, and I believe they can. I believe the reports. In October, Hitler, the crazy bastard, tried to make peace with England, and even had the balls to ask F.D.R. to help. Probably so it would be easier to take over Europe. Well, as you know, F.D.R. turned him down and the maniac told him, point blank, what he intended to do. And last month, that other nut, Stalin, invaded Finland. Between Mussolini's Fascists, Hitler's Nazis, Russia and Japan, God only knows what this world is in for. The President is telling us that the United States will remain officially neutral in the war."

"Do you think he's wrong, Stanley? Do you think we will fight," Loretta asked.

"Sooner or later we will. I know many people who are going to England to join the Royal Army and Air Force."

"Italy was my country. Why does Italy have to help Hitler? It's that son of a bitch, Il Duce. My people don't want war. I know they don't."

"My parents came from Germany, Loretta, or rather, my father came from Germany and my mother from Vienna in Austria. Are they German and Austrian? Not according to Hitler. They are Jews, period. In September, Sigmund Freud died in London. He was born and raised in Vienna, a great Austrian. Right? According to Hitler, he died as a racially inferior Jew, unworthy of Austrian citizenship. The Germans are following this madman as sure as the Italians are following Mussolini. Perhaps not all, but enough to keep him in power, and enough to make war."

"This conversation is so depressing. I just hope Sally comes home okay and I do hope you get to meet my friends in Boston."

CHAPTER THIRTY-FIVE
New Year's Eve, 1939. Braintree, Massachusetts

Dr. Fryman was not at all impressed with Mayor Elect Richard Gary, and he told Loretta several times he would like to leave.

"We are here as guests of Nunzio and Rose, darling. Let's wait until they leave, please. It's not even eleven o'clock yet," said Loretta.

"Miss Bonet, can I have your autograph? You are one of my favorite stars," Earl Tannenbaum said.

"But, of course," Loretta answered, taking pen and paper from him. "What is your name?"

"Tannenbaum, Earl Tannenbaum."

Hearing that, Stanley looked up from the glass of sherry he had been nursing. "Tannenbaum? Are you Jewish? That's a Jewish name, isn't it?"

"Actually, my father was born of the Jewish faith, but I've been raised a Christian. I have no connections with Judaism. Why do you ask?"

"I'm Jewish. I thought I had maybe a landsman here, so I got a little anxious. Sorry," Stanley replied.

Tannenbaum laughed and went over to where Joe Allen and Richard Gary were standing.

Loretta whispered to Stanley, "I think we should visit my friend, David, in New Hampshire, when we leave here. Who, by the way, is Jewish."

"We should get back to Los Angeles. You've been away from your daughter for almost three weeks, and I must get back to work."

"Fuji and Tomo are quite capable of taking care of Judy. And your hospital will still be there when we get back. Nunzio and Rose are over by the bar, let's join them. I would love another drink."

"You've have had enough to drink, Loretta."

"Don't be a bore, darling. It's New Year's Eve. Let's have a good time. Hey, Nunzio and Rose, only a few more minutes and it's the big four-0h."

"I'll tell you, Loretta," Rose answered, "the years are going too fast. Nineteen forty, my God."

"Not yet," Nunzio said. "Still two minutes to go."

"Get ready," Richard Gary yelled. "It's countdown. Ten, nine, eight, seven, six, five, four, three, two, one, Happy New Year, everyone!"

After the kissing and hugging was over, Stanley asked Nunzio if they would be leaving soon. Nunzio agreed that at twelve-thirty they would leave.

The following day, Nunzio took Dr. Fryman on a tour of La Bella Rosa Bakery.

"Even New Year's day the plant keeps going, twenty-four hours a day," Nunzio bragged.

"You should be real proud of yourself, Nunzio, for having built up a business like this in such a short time And this bread is delicious."

"It's always delicious, hot and fresh from the oven. We keep adding new things to the line, cookies, cakes and such."

"I don't want to sample anymore, Nunzio. I'll get too fat. Loretta might not like that."

"You and Loretta getting married, Doctor?"

"I don't know, Nunzio. We love each other, I suppose, but it's difficult, we are so different. And, besides, I'm Jewish, and in these troubled times, that's not so fashionable."

"Loretta's first husband, Paul Bonet, was Jewish. I don't think it matters to her."

"Yes, I know, and she divorced him," Doctor Fryman said.

"Loretta has never really known what she wants.

She's a mixed up and insecure person. When I first met her on the ship from Italy, I hoped she would go for me. Of course, I'm glad now that I have Rose. I don't know what to tell you. I want to see Loretta happy. She has fame and fortune, and still she seems to..."

"What will be will be, Nunzio," Doctor Fryman interrupted. "You know the circumstances of how we met in the hospital? What can I say? Anyway, are you and Rose going to New Hampshire with us tomorrow?"

"As much as I would like to see my friend, David, I can't. My partner, Vito, and I have several meetings. I must be here."

"Loretta has told me all about your friend David, a family of Barons, MIT graduate and an executive at Continental Electric. He still hasn't heard from his wife since she went into Poland."

"That's right. Since the Russians attacked Finland, and with the State Department's involvement in the war, it's difficult for David to communicate. He's involved with the Communists in trying to get information, but he doesn't fill me in on all the details. Anyway, we love Sally, and hope she will be all right."

"What are you doing here?" Vito's voice asked from across the factory. "I thought you were staying home today. Anyway, Happy New Year," Vito said.

"Happy New Year," Nunzio answered. "Vito. this is Doctor Stanley Fryman, a friend of Loretta's. Stanley, Vito Natali. And that shy Negro is Acey, our foreman. He's been with us since the old days."

"Nice to meet you Doctor," said Vito.

"How come you weren't at Gary's party, Vito?" Nunzio asked.

"Let's just say I had other plans. A whole lot better plans than going to that scoundrel's house in Braintree. Now that he's gonna be Mayor, they should call it Brainless," laughed Vito.

"I think I agree with you," Stanley laughed.

Vito, still laughing, added, "But business is business, and we know which side of the bread the butter is on, right, Nunz? Well, it was nice meeting you, Doc. Got shit to do. Let's go, Acey. See you tomorrow, Nunzio."

"Ciao," Nunzio replied. "Oh, that meeting with General? Eight sharp, right?"

"Right. See ya," Vito said.

That night, Nunzio's mother cooked a pasta and sausage dinner for everyone. "I'm just sorry Maria and Stefano couldn't be here," she complained.

"This is the most beautiful house," Loretta said. "Rose, your taste is remarkable. Nothing like it even in Hollywood. Why, if you came to California, you could make a fortune as an interior decorator."

"She's not doing so bad here as my interior decorator," Nunzio replied.

"Your home, as I remember, is magnificent," Rose lied. "What was the name of that place? I could never get it right O - J - A - I."

"It's pronounced 'Oh High'. Easy. Anyway, we're selling it and moving to Los Angeles. I'm going to buy a house in Beverly Hills just for me and Judy and Fuji and Tomo. I don't need all the other help."

"And what about me?" Dr. Fryman asked.

"What about you, darling?" Loretta smiled.

"Will I be living in your new house?"

"Are you trying to tell me something?" Loretta, asked, pouting, obviously embarrassed.

"Will you marry me, Loretta?"

"You're asking me in front of all these people?"

"What people?" Nunzio asked. "We're not people. We're family."

"Sure, I will marry you, Doctor Fryman. Now, pour me a drink please."

"You don't need a drink, sweetheart," Stanley replied.

"This is going to be an interesting relationship. Nunzio dear, would you call Screen Romance Magazine, ask for Dick Tater, the columnist, and tell him guess who is getting hitched," Loretta laughed.

Barry C. Lefferts

CHAPTER THIRTY-SIX
May 1, 1940. London, England

David Fairchild sat in the bar of the Royal Hotel, minutes away from number 10 Downing Street, where the prior morning, Winston Churchill replaced Nevel Chamberlain as Prime Minister of the British Empire; a British Empire in jeopardy of being destroyed by the Nazi menace storming Western Europe. "I have nothing to offer but blood, toil, tears and sweat," the stocky, cigar smoking, Churchill declared.

David waited patiently for the Minister of Wars representative to arrive at the hotel for their meeting. Continental Electric was to provide the British intelligence with communications equipment and the new television equipment it had developed.

The last word David had about Sally and her grandparents, was that they had moved into Russia somewhere around the Ukraine. But David had lost contact, and couldn't find an avenue of communication with her. The Russian alliance with Hitler, as well as the war with England and France, made it more difficult. Why did she have to go to Poland? He kept asking himself. It's been so long and I miss her so much.

Thinking of the possibility of Sally falling into the hands of the Nazis, David's head would shake, and he quickly put the thought out of his mind. He thought about last month's meeting with the FCC and Roosevelt's announcement that they would delay the start of television service so the FCC could develop rules preventing any group from monopolizing the new medium. The financial experts say that television will not have the impact of radio or automobiles on the nation's economy. What a

186

crock of shit that is, David thought, as he ordered another brandy. All the years of research and development. Television was my baby. They'll all eat their words. Television will have more impact on this world than any other thing ever has.

"Mr. Fairchild, sorry I'm late," the man said interrupting David's thoughts.

David looked up from his drink, "Mr. Nolan, how do you do, sir? It's quite all right. I've been sitting here gathering my thoughts. Would you care for a drink?"

I'm a teetotaler," he replied. "Never touch the stuff. Don't mean to rush you, but Mr. Churchill has called a meeting later in the afternoon. With the Germans in Norway, and now Belgium, the situation is grave, mighty grave. We need all the help your country can give us."

"I do not represent my country, only my company, Continental Electric."

"Smashing, sir. Can we go to your room and talk? A bit public, this place, don't you agree?"

"Of course," David replied.

In the room, David showed Sir James Nolan the portfolio on the type of surveillance equipment Continental had developed, and how the British could benefit. Nolan was obviously impressed.

"Could you modify the listening devices to our specs?" he asked.

"Most definitely." David answered.

The order came to over ten million pounds, the largest single order in Continental's history. "This will have to be approved by the War Ministry," Nolan said. "But I see no problem. Churchill has only been in office one day and he has to rely on the experts. We have to move very fast. You will arrange shipping with your government."

"I will. You understand this is cash, since the United States is determined to remain neutral in this conflict. All sales of defense material is subject to this policy."

"I understand your position, Mr. Fairchild. I'm sure your government will recognize the Nazis are a problem to them, as well, and will change their policy very shortly. We will, however, pay cash. This is only a small part of the war equipment we will be buying from the United States. Believe me, it is a very small part. Good day, sir."

"Good day to you, Mr. Nolan. You will be hearing from me shortly."

CHAPTER THIRTY-SEVEN
June 10, 1940

Rose Cappolla was busy feeding the children, a chore she reserved for herself, despite the eagerness of the household staff to relieve her of her maternal duty, when the newscaster announced the marriage of Loretta Bonet to Dr. Stanley Fryman as *'A small wedding attended by close friends and a few relatives took place in the chamber of Superior Court Judge Alan Westbury of Los Angeles.'*

"What friends and relatives?" Rose wondered. "I wish Nunzio and I could have been there to lend her whatever moral support she might have needed," she said to herself. "Anyway, Loretta should be getting to be old hat at marriage." She chuckled with the thought.

"Why are you laughing, Mommy?" Alberto asked.

"Just thinking about something funny, Alby. It concerns your Aunt Loretta."

"She's not really my aunt, is she Mommy? But I tell all the kids at school she is. They all want me to get her autograph. When is she going to be in Boston, Mommy?"

"I don't know, sweetheart. Eat your vegetables before they get cold. You too, Patty."

"I hate vegetables, Mommy," Patty answered.

"Never mind. Eat them, or no ice cream."

"Okay. I don't want any ice cream anyway," Patty replied.

"What am I going to do with you kids? At least Vitorio eats his food to the last drop. What a good boy."

"Mr. Cappolla's on the phone, Madam," the maid announced. "May I take over for you?"

"Yes, thank you," Rose replied.

"Nunzio, dear, I was just feeding the children. I was

expecting you home by now. Is anything wrong? Aren't we having dinner with the Martinellis and Stefano and Maria? They should have been here on the last train from New York."

"All that in one breath, Rose? You amaze me. Stefano just called me at the office. They're going to be late. They stopped at the church for a special Mass. Meet us there, and we will go for dinner afterwards."

"Special Mass for what? What is wrong?" Rose asked.

"Italians all over the United States are praying today, Rose. It's a sad day. Mussolini announced his decision to join hands with Hitler in the war against England and France, despite Roosevelt's efforts to persuade him to keep out of the war. Roosevelt called Il Duce a backstabber, amongst other things, and vowed to give the utmost in aid to France and Britain. As much I hate that fascist pig, the thought of the United States as an enemy of Italy lays heavy on me."

"I'm sorry, Nunzio. There is always something, isn't there?"

"Will you be able to meet us around nine, Rose?"

"I'll be there before nine. Did you speak to David today?"

"No, why do you ask?"

"He called the house earlier. Absolutely no word on Sally. It's like she disappeared from the earth. He sounds awfully distraught. He wanted you to know that Manny Weiss died of pneumonia after his surgery, and David is taking over as Chief Executive Officer at Continental Electric. I don't know how he does it."

"I'll get in touch with him in the morning, if I can. Kiss the children Good night for me. I'll see you at the church."

Rose blew a kiss into the phone and placed the receiver on the hook. No sooner did she go back into the kitchen, than the maid announced that her father was in the living room.

"Grandpa. Grandpa Kelly," Alby and Patricia called as they ran into the living room. Within minutes they were all over him.

Even as much of a pain-in-the-ass as my father is, Rose thought, the kids adore him. "And how is Boston's finest today, Papa?" she asked when she got to the living room. "I see you're still in uniform. How come?

"Well, daughter mine, I heard today that the top WOP joined with The Fuhrer over there, so I just figured today was a good day to arrest a few greasy ones, and what a better place to start then the Cappolla mansion. But, of course, these lovely jewels are only half breeds, so I guess I'll have to hug them to death instead."

"Good thing, Papa. Lexington is out of your jurisdiction anyway," she smiled. "You talk that way around Nunzio, Papa, and you're liable to wind up as a loaf of bread."

"Watch me shake. Where is your husband anyway? I need to talk to him, personal like, if you don't mind."

"I don't mind, Papa, but not tonight. He's at the church, and I'm meeting him later. We're going to dinner with his sister and brother-in-law."

"Don't it bother you, Rose, when them Dagos talk ginnie around you and you can't understand? Don't you think they're talking about you, or something?"

"They talk English when I'm around, and throw in a lot of Italian words that I understand because Nunzio taught me. Now, if you want, you can put the children to bed for me, and stay a while."

"Okay, sure. I would love to. Don't forget to tell Nunzio I need to talk to him."

"Can you tell me what it's about?"

"Personal police business, sort of," Jim answered.

"What kind of police business could you possibly

have with Nunzio? Did the Sergeant forget to collect from the bakery for leaving the garbage out?"

"Cute, real cute. From my daughter, yet. Well, if you must know, the D.A. is conducting his regular election year investigation into corruption in Boston, and Vito Natali's name came up. And since Vito is Nunzio's partner, and I have the great fortune to be Nunzio's father-in-law, they asked me to ask Nunzio some questions. That's all."

"Well, it will have to wait, Papa. Nunzio has a lot on his mind. Now, I must start getting ready."

"This is quite a place you live in Rose, all from bread. It's amazing. Even with the little extras here and there, no cop could ever afford this joint."

"I'm your daughter, Papa. You should be happy for me, and anything you want in this world you can have, if you ask."

"Okay. We got an Alberto here that I love. A Patricia I adore, and a Vitorio that I'm wild about. Now, give the next one a name I can pronounce, like Sean or Tilley," he laughed.

"You're my favorite bigot, Papa. Next one's for you, I promise."

CHAPTER THIRTY-EIGHT
October 24, 1940

Nunzio stood on the steps of the County courthouse in downtown Boston. His lawyer, Anthony Parrise, stood by his side, chain smoking Camel cigarettes. Nunzio thought about the words of the message Massachusetts' Republican Governor Leverett Saltonstall sent to the District Attorney urging him to get indictments or else, whatever that meant.

Nunzio could not believe what he heard in the courtroom. He knew Vito was involved with the underworld when he was bootlegging, but that was all behind us, he thought to himself.

"The deals we have with General, the Union contracts, the Braintree election, are all on the up and up, Tony," Nunzio said to his attorney. "I'm clean. I knew nothing of the payoffs, and all the other shit the D.A. is saying. And why does the Governor want Vito so bad?"

"All bullshit politics, Nunzio. Don't worry, they have absolutely nothing on you, Vito, Allen or Gary. After ten years of Democrats running the state, a Republican crusader comes along and thinks he is single-handedly going to clean up Boston corruption. Just let them drag this thing out a while. Maybe Vito can take a little heat for bribing a public official, and make a deal so the D.A. is happy and gets off your ass."

"I don't think Vito will do that. He's never had to answer to the law for anything in the past."

"Listen, Nunzio. This city has been corrupt for years. You know what I'm talking about, and you know how you began your business with the wine smuggling during prohibition. And you know that Vito must have been involved in some killings in the old days. So what if he takes a little heat, and then it blows over?"

"Okay, Tony, I'll talk to Vito tonight. But you know we have another problem right now. Today begins the new law, the forty-hour work week. That means all of La Bella Rosa employees work a forty-hour week and get paid time and a half for overtime. Of course, I still work a hundred hours a week. Anyway, that law is going to cost money, and we're going to have to raise prices at a bad time."

"You go back to work, Nunzio," Parrise said. "I'll file a motion for a continuance on the hearing. Vito's attorney will do the same. I'll arrange for a meeting with the D.A., and find out what he wants to let this thing die. Then we'll have a meeting and see what's what. Okay?"

"Okay," Nunzio answered. "Call me later. Oh, I have some contracts for you to look over. We're supplying another chain with bread and cakes. They have stores all over the Eastern seaboard."

"Good for you, Nunzio. I'll have Stella send someone over to pick up the contracts."

Nunzio drove over to the harbor on the way to the bakery. The city is really busy producing war supplies, he thought to himself. He stopped the car and watched the longshoremen leading the ships with all the supplies going to England. How many Italians will die? Old friends? relatives? He was thinking of his brother, Bruno.

The sound of the ship's engine reminded him of when he came to America fourteen years ago. This very harbor is sending bullets to Europe, to kill friends and relatives. Why did Mussolini, that pig, have to do this? Him and that... that Nazi devil.

Nunzio bought a fish sandwich and a bowl of chowder, and sat in the car eating, watching the ships for about an hour before he drove around downtown Boston. The cool October air felt good blowing on his sweating face. He passed the corner where Bonet's used to be, thinking of when he met Rose. Bonet's boutique. Now it's Billy's Pool Hall, he mused. Two tough looking hoodlums stood out front, looking at a racing form. The theater across the street was showing two Loretta Bonet movies and five cartoons, for two bits. Nunzio laughed to himself. Americans have more nicknames for things than anyone else in the world. Two bits, a quarter; not twenty-five cents, no one says twenty-five cents. A buck, a sawbuck. Girls are babes or dolls. How did I ever learn this language? Ten words for everything. This is a crazy country, but I love it.

He pulled into the bakery's parking lot, into the spot marked 'President - Mr. Cappolla'. He stared at the white sign over his parking spot. The spot was big enough for three cars, so nobody's car door could hit his. Fourteen years in America, he thought to himself, and I'm a President. Thirty-two years old. "Vito, Vito, Vito," he said aloud. "Why do you make waves? Who needs D.A.'s investigating us?"

He got out of the car and entered the plant, where he saw Acey inspecting the ovens. He asked him if Vito was around.

"In the mixing room," Acey answered.

Vito was standing at the door of the mixing room, a clipboard in his hand, talking to Dave Bellows, the salesman from the New England Flour Company.

Vito looked up and saw Nunzio. "Nunzio, give me a few minutes with Dave here. We're going over a rather large discrepancy, and I think I found it. Oh, yes, here it is, Dave. This should have been 3,000 pounds, not 13,000. Some idiot put a one where it didn't belong."

"I'll get it straightened out. Thank you, Vito. Nice seeing you, Mr. Cappolla. Gotta run. I'm way behind today."

"Yeah, take it easy, Dave," Nunzio replied. "Vito,

what the hell is going on?"

"What are you talking about, Nunzio?"

"You weren't in court today, Vito. The D.A. is trying to get indictments against us for bribing public officials and paying off Union officials."

"My lawyer was there. Somebody had to stay here and run the bakery. I volunteered."

"What about the D.A. and the charges? The Governor is even involved in this case."

"Nunzio, you know what? Fuck the Governor, fuck the D.A. and fuck the case. In '36, Governor Curley, the biggest crook of all, wanted to clean up Boston, to clean up the mess he helped create. And then Hurley, in '38, made a lot of noise playing with himself. And now Saltonstall is on a crusade. Who gives a shit? How you doing with the B and B Market account? That's what you should be working on. We got lawyers to go to court, five dollars an hour we pay them Harvard boys."

"Vito, what if they make the charges stick and the Grand Jury returns an indictment? You will have to stand trial."

"Stand trial, my hemorrhoid-loaded ass. Listen partner. It wasn't that long ago you were a greenhorn kid working in back of Uncle Alberto's bakery. A little shit you were. Came close to getting the shit kicked out of you. Now you're Mr. Cappolla, President of La Bella Rosa bakery, living in a fucking mansion, supporting more goddamn relatives than King George. You know who did it for you? Me, that's who. The only thing you did was make those kids of yours, and that I wonder about, too? You got it all, Nunzio. Money, family, power. All I got is money and brains. And, oh yes, I have the plug. And I can pull the plug anytime I want, and you will once again be Nunzio the greenhorn. This country is growing, Nunzio. Someday soon there will be great big supermarkets all over the United States. They will make General look like water stops. After all the bullshit in Europe is over, the homeless will be heading for the promised land, paved with gold, just like you did. They will come here and do their screwing here and all those kids will be saying, 'Mommy, Mommy make me another sandwich,' and mommy will say, 'Junior, run down to the market and get me a loaf of bread, make sure it's La Bella Rosa.' And the money will just keep rolling in, and you and I will be so powerful we will have our own Governor or President, maybe your son, Alberto Cappolla, President of the United States of America."

"Vito, I'm deeply moved, I really am," Nunzio said with no little amount of sarcasm. "Parrise said maybe if you make a deal with the D.A., give him something to tell the press so he can get a few points for the election..."

"Just a second, Nunzio," Vito interrupted. "I'll make a deal with the D.A. He can have two cents off on his next package of dinner rolls. And here's something he can tell the press, ba fungoul!" He added the appropriate physical movement to emphasize his meaning. "With the English translation in parenthesis. Oh, yes, and the elections. Whoever the democrats throw against Saltonstall, La Bella Rosa will pick up the tab for the Boston campaign. I'll even have a sign tattooed to my forehead," Vito began laughing, and Nunzio joined in.

"Now," Vito asked, "Is the board meeting over, Mr. President? May I go back to work?"

Nunzio smiled, and went back to his office. "Get me Anthony Parrise on the phone," he told his secretary.

"Tony," Nunzio said into the telephone when the connection was made. "Vito said no deals. Let them do what they want. Take care of it."

"I don't think I can buy the D.A. on this one, Nunzio," Parrise replied.

"Then buy the Judge. Go through the Irish law firm, Kennedy, Powell and McGuire. We used them before. Let me know how much money you need."

"I'll talk to you later, Nunzio," Parrise said before hanging up.

Nunzio poured a cup of water from the pitcher on his desk, and picked up the newspaper. The story about alleged Union corruption in Boston was drowned out by the large picture of the Secretary of War, Henry L. Stimson, preparing for the first draft number to be picked on Tuesday. *'The first peacetime draft'*, it read. Peacetime? That's a joke, Nunzio thought to himself. The Germans are in Rumania and half of Europe, the Japanese are taking over countries I never heard of, and the United States is holding a peacetime military draft lottery. Sally is somewhere in Poland or Russia, and nobody has heard from her.

"Get me David Fairchild on the phone, please," Nunzio called out to his secretary.

A few minutes passed, and the secretary walked into Nunzio's office. "Mr. Fairchild's office said Mr. Fairchild is on his way to New York, but will be stopping in Boston. I'm sure he will call you from there, Mr. Cappolla."

"Thank you, Grace," Nunzio answered.

To make use of his time, Nunzio went over the contracts on the B and B Market account. Mostly private label stuff, he thought. I want La Bella Rosa on the label. As he read further, he realized that he would be supplying them with bread under the B and B label and La Bella Rosa. The same product. He would be competing against himself, only the B and B bread would be selling retail for one cent less. That would mean a penny would be rebated to B and B markets. They would also have the right to return any bread that was not sold the day of delivery, so it would be up to La Bella Rosa route men to anticipate their daily needs and not overstock. Overstock? How do you not overstock? Nunzio asked himself. You can only not overstock by under stocking, but then you run out and the customer buys a competitive brand. So what do you do with returns and old breads? At Uncle Alberto's we gave it away to the poor. We could do that and lose a fortune. Or sell it for pig food, but that wouldn't bring in enough to pay for the dough. If General and our other customers hear about this, they'll want the same provision. So what's the answer? Not take the account?

"Grace. Ask Mr. Natali to come to my office."

Vito walked in about twenty minutes later. "If this is about that D.A. bullshit again, I'm going to be pissed to no end," Vito snapped.

"No, it's not about that. I'm going over the B and B contract. Did you know about the return of day-old bread clause?"

"Of course, Nunzio, I was there when we worked out that contract. What's the big deal?"

"How do we make a profit doing that, pray tell?"

"Simple, my friend with the miniature brain. Route men get commissions on total sales in their territory, right? So they move bread around, who is going to know? The B and B in Revere gets the day old from the B and B in Brookline, and visa versa."

"Vito, this ain't the old bootlegging days anymore. What if they find out? And what if a route man sues and goes to B and B. We would have hell to pay."

"Okay, Nunzio, do you have any ideas?"

"Well, what if we were to open a few day-old stores, have the route men bring all the returns here, and we truck them over to the day-old stores. Then we sell the stuff at a discount and still make a profit," Nunzio said.

"That's ridiculous, Nunzio. You don't know nothing. First, we would be competing against our own customers with our own product, and second we would have to sell enough to cover rents and clerks, etc."

"That's true, Vito, but what if we opened the stores in rural areas, low-rent neighborhoods? We hire people from those areas. And, we sell milk, cigarettes and a few other items to cover expenses. None of our customers have stores in those areas, and they wouldn't drive there to save a few pennies."

Vito thought about the plan. "You know, it's crazy enough to work," Vito said at length. "We would need someone to run it."

"Acey. He would be perfect," Nunzio said. "We could start a separate corporation, and sell him everything. It would just be another customer, only we would hold ninety percent of the stock, and give Acey ten percent. Worth a shot. What do you think?"

"Why not? Call Acey in here," Vito said.

After hearing the deal, Acey was so excited he couldn't sit still. "I would be President of the Corporation, Mr. Natali?" Acey asked with a gleam in his voice.

"Yes, Acey. And you will own ten percent of the company, and get to vote at board meetings as well," Vito answered.

"What are we going to call the stores?" Acey asked.

"How about Ace Milk and Bread Stops," Nunzio replied.

"Ace Milk and Bread Stops. Ace Milk and Bread Stops," Acey kept repeating.

"Mr. Fairchild on the phone, Mr. Cappolla," the Secretary interrupted.

Nunzio nodded and picked up the phone. "Hello, David. I called your office and they told me you were on your way to Boston."

"Nunzio, I'm in Boston on business. I'd like to have dinner with you tonight. I know it's the last minute, but..."

"It's all right, paesano. I'll call Rose and tell her you're
coming. Around seven okay?"

"Seven o'clock is fine. See you then."

Nunzio hung up the phone and continued his

conversation with Vito and Acey. "Well, Acey, it's all settled. We'll get the ball rolling. I think that's the expression."

"Thank you. Thank you, both of you, thank you," Acey replied and left the office."

"For a dumb shit, you're pretty smart, Nunzio," Vito said. "We can use the other corporation in many ways. Many, many ways. Just looking ahead, of course."

"A criminal mind is a criminal mind, Vito. I'm going home. I'm beat, and David is coming over for dinner. Would you like to join us?"

"Love to. It's not often you invite me over, partner. See you at seven," Vito replied as he closed the door behind him .

"Grace," Nunzio called out. "Would you get Mrs. Cappolla on the phone please."

"Rose or Anna?" the secretary asked.

"Rose," Nunzio responded, somewhat annoyed.

"Rose," he said when the connection was made. "I hope you don't mind, but David is in town and I've invited him for dinner. Vito is coming, too."

"Of course, dear. I'll have Daisy fix stew," Rose said.

"Stew? Why Irish stew, Rose?"

"Well, I went to see the doctor today."

" And?" Nunzio asked.

"I'm with child again," Rose said cheerfully.

"That's wonderful! I'm happy about it, but what does that have to do with making Irish stew?"

"Nunzio, we have three Italian children. This one's going to be Irish."

"I'm totally confused, Rose. Maybe you can explain when I get home."

CHAPTER THIRTY-NINE
July 1, 1941. Krakow, Poland

Sally Fairchild and her grandparents sat in silence staring at each other. Tears rolled down their cheeks as they were told of the Nazi invasion of Russia. They had traveled from Krakow to this city of twenty-six thousand people, hoping to be able to cross the nearby border into the Ukraine and to freedom. Now the Nazis were in front of them as well as behind.

Sally wondered if David had received the letters she had tried to smuggle out with bribes to sympathetic Poles. All of her jewels and money were gone, and she was trapped in Jaroslaw, hiding in the attic of the Sollovski family, knowing full well what would happen if they were caught.

"Why did I have to leave my husband and my beautiful sons?" she said to her grandparents. "I love you both, and what I did I did out of love, but I want to go home. I don't want to die here like the others."

"Mine shayna, shayna madele," her grandmother said in Yiddish, trying to console her. "What God dictates, that is what will be."

"The Germans," Grandpa said. "The mamzarim. They are in Poland, Denmark, Norway, Belgium, Holland Yugoslavia, Greece and now they are in Russia. Who can stop them, I ask you, who can stop them? They will not leave a Jew alive on this planet. We are here on borrowed time, the Sollovskis will not be able to hide us for much longer or they, too, will be killed. If this is what God dictates, we have some God."

"Sha! Don't talk like that, you must have faith. We must not give up hope," Grandma yelled at him.

"Sally, you are an American. America is not at war, you must save yourself."

"Grandma, if I walk out of this house, those SS troopers will do terrible things to me. They will not care if I am an American, only that I am a Jewess. You have seen what they do. You have seen the horrible shootings. You have seen them herding people off to the death camps or wherever they take them. You have seen the children getting thrown up in the air and caught with bayonets. They are animals. We must still try to get into Russia, the Nazis will not defeat the Russians so easily. We can find safety in Russia. We must try."

"The German army is marching through Jaroslaw, probably heading toward Lvov in the Ukraine," Mrs. Sollovski said, "If you leave at night with papers saying you are Polish Christian, and head through the woods into Lubelski, you might be able to make it across the border to Sokal. It will be dangerous, but it's a chance."

"Thank you, Mrs. Sollovski. You have been wonderful, and we will never forget you. We will leave tomorrow night," Sally said.

"If you make it, that will be thanks enough," Mrs. Sollovski replied. "I hate those Nazi pigs. You know how long the Sollovskis have lived in Jaroslaw? Would you believe since the year 900 - a thousand years. There were Slavic tribes living here, and my husband's ancestors, as the story goes, were of the Slavic tribe, the Polians, who united this country. After Poland became an independent kingdom, the world did not leave us alone. We have been invaded by the Mongolians, the Turks, the Russians and now the Nazis. Enough history. Sally, I'll get you the papers, and pack you food and water for the journey."

"If there is a heaven, Mrs. Sollovski, you will be the most beloved angel," Sally said as she embraced the stocky Polish woman.

CHAPTER FORTY
September 3, 1941. Boston

Nunzio held the four month old baby in his arms while Rose looked at the cute little outfits in the very exclusive children's store 'Adam and Eve'. Nunzio was fully aware of all the people staring at the baby, and he was as proud as a father could be. Kelly was as beautiful a baby you could ask for.

"Kelly Cappolla," Rose said as she came over to kiss the baby's forehead for the fourth time in five minutes. "What a great idea using my maiden name as a first name, Nunzio. You have even made my father happy. You're very smart, you know that?"

"Can you hurry up and buy what you're going to buy, and let's get out of here," Nunzio said. "It's Friday, and I have to get back to the office. There's payroll and I have to talk to Acey about the new store he's opening in Salem."

"All you care about, darling, is that business. I know it's important, but there other things you know."

"Yes, other things like my six dollar silk tie being wet, and guess what it's wet with. Please take Kelly for a while. Why don't you just take ten outfits, and decide which ones to keep when you get home?"

"Nunzio, always so practical. Okay, but why do you have to go back to the office? It's almost five o'clock. Can't your workers and your supervisors handle things? You should delegate authority."

"Yeah, watch the whole thing go down the drain. If you don't do it yourself, it don't get done. Just look at the headline today. Hitler's got Poland surrounded. Looks like he's trying to starve the country into surrendering.

Won't be long, they'll be eating wiener schnitzel in Moscow if he's not stopped.

As they were leaving the store, Rose asked, "Still nothing on Sally, Nunzio?"

"Nah. I spoke to David the other day. I told him to send the boys to Boston to stay with us for a while. We've got the room, and you know how Alberto loves it when they visit."

"That would be nice, but I have my hands full now, with our children. And with a four month old baby, I don't need Joel and Edmond to take care of, too," she replied.

"That's not like you, Rosy. Besides, you have servants and what not, you wouldn't even know they're around."

"I'm sorry, Nunzio, I didn't mean... It's just that I see you less and less because you're so busy all of the time, and David also has plenty of money to have servants taking care of his kids. It was a stupid thing Sally did, leaving her family to go to Poland."

"True. But she believed strongly in helping her grandparents, and she did what she had to do."

"I don't want to argue about it, Nunzio. Please don't go back to the office. Let Vito do some work. He's not married, and can stay all night at the office if he chooses. I want you home with me tonight, please."

"Tell you what," Nunzio said, "I'll put you and Kelly into a cab and send you home. I'll run over to the office, stay maybe an hour, then I'll be home. Then we will pack up and drive down to the Cape for the weekend."

"Sounds wonderful, but I don't want to drag a four month old baby on a trip in this heat."

"Okay, it was just a thought. The kids have to be back to school Monday, anyway, and we're not finished shopping for clothes yet."

"That's no problem, Nunzio. Just call up Adam and Eve and tell them to send one of everything. We can afford it," Rose said sarcastically.

"The thing is, yes we can, Rose. It's hard to believe sometimes, isn't it?"

"With you, nothing is hard to believe, my love," she replied. "You, Nunzio Cappolla, were destined to make it big no matter what. I only hope that the D.A.'s investigation into Vito and the Union officials doesn't wind up destroying you. I worry about it all the time."

"Well, don't worry so much. Mr. Henry M. Atterson hasn't much of a case, and all he's trying to do is further his own political ambitions. I can't figure out why a man of his wealth would want to be a District Attorney and work so damned hard at screwing a successful businessman. Anyway, there's a taxi now, Rose. I'll see you in an hour."

Nunzio put Rose and the baby into the taxi and gave the driver a five dollar bill and the address. He watched the taxi drive down the block and turn the corner, and he drove down Richmond Street on the way to the office. He stopped to look at the old Bugle speakeasy where he used to deliver the wines everyday. Its name was changed to Don and Mick's Royal Pub. The front entrance was painted a bright red, and the sign was black with a gold crown painted on it. Interesting looking place, Nunzio thought to himself. I could use a cold beer or two.

He parked the car and walked into the lounge. The place was dimly lit, with pictures of European royalty on the walls. Keeping with the theme of the Royal Pub, Nunzio surmised.

The bartender was leaning over the bar talking to one of the patrons. There were three other customers at the bar, and they were staring at Nunzio as he took a seat.

Without changing positions, the bartender asked Nunzio what he would like.

"Cold tap beer," Nunzio answered nervously.

"One draft coming up," the bartender answered,

pulling a glass off the shelf and filling it with a liquid that was more foam then anything else. "Hope you like a good head on it," the bartender said with a wicked smile.

Nunzio did not understand his sarcasm. He looked over at two men in the corner, and noticed they were holding hands. He saw the other man at the bar staring at him. He looked the other way to avoid eye contact. When he looked back, he realized he recognized the man, but couldn't remember from where. What the hell kind of place is this anyway? Nunzio asked himself. And where, damn it, do I know that guy from? Maybe from the bootlegging days? Nah, I doubt it.

"Want to run a tab," the bartender asked, his finger lying gently on the back of Nunzio's hand.

Nunzio pulled his hand off the bar and said, "I'll pay cash. Here's a dollar, keep the change."

He gulped down the beer and got up to leave. He took one more glance at the man he thought he knew, when suddenly the answer came to him. David's friend from MIT! What the hell was his name? Donovan! That's it! Donovan Atterson, as in Henry Moore Atterson. Maybe a relative, although I doubt it. Nunzio walked over to him and smiled, "Are you Donovan Atterson?"

"If you're Adonis, then yes, I am. If you're the tax collector, I'm afraid you've got the wrong guy."

"Don't you remember me? I'm Nunzio, David's friend."

"Oh, yes, the baker. How are you? I've been reading a lot about you in the newspapers. How is David? I never hear from any of my old schoolmates."

"David is the head of Continental Electric. He's married and has three boys. But unfortunately, his wife went to Poland to rescue her grandparents, and got caught up in the Nazi invasion. Nobody's heard from her." He smiled lightly before continuing. "What about you, Donovan, weren't you studying engineering?"

"Yes, I was, but I'm in the bar business now. This is my place. I'm Don. And the bartender is Mick, my partner."

"This used to be the Bugler," Nunzio replied. "I used to deliver bread here, with wine hidden in each loaf. Alfie Mendlino's Bugler Lounge."

"Well, there's still some blowing going on, but not bugles," Donovan laughed.

"What kind of a place is this, anyway?" Nunzio asked, noticing the way the bartending was watching them.

"What do you think, Nunzio?" Donovan asked.

"This is a queer joint, isn't it?" Nunzio said.

"Queers, faggots, sissies. Our clientele are predominantly homosexual like me and Mick. We make a living here. And as long as the police leave us alone, which they do, we are doing fine."

"I see," Nunzio replied. "Your last name is Atterson. Is that why they leave you alone? Your father is the District Attorney, right?"

"No one is supposed to know that. My last name is Adams now. I'm Don Adams. My father gave me the money to buy this bar when he found out I was a homo. He ordered me never to tell anyone who I was, and to keep the fuck away from him forever, to quote him. It was an accident, you coming in here, Bakery Man. I'm asking you please... No, I'm begging you, keep this confidential. My father is a very powerful and rich man. I can't help what I am. Don't say anything to anyone about this."

"Donovan, nice seeing you again. I'll tell David I ran into you. Gotta leave." Nunzio saluted the bartender and walked out the door.

When he left the bar, he headed up to the end of Richmond and Lexington looking for a phone booth along the way. Finding one, he dialed the bakery and tapped the door of the phone booth nervously as he waited for an answer.

"Jim, this is Mr. Cappolla. Is Vito there?"

"Yes, I'll go get him."

When Vito picked up he said, "Where the hell are you, Nunzio? I've been waiting for you."

"I'm going home, Vito. Please stop by my house later, or in the morning, for coffee. I have some very interesting news for you."

"What kind of news, Goomba? You moving back to the old country?" Vito laughed.

"Yeah, right. I'm leaving Sunday. Taking all the money with me, too. Hey, listen, Vito, I ran into a fag today."

"Oh, I see. You want me to break the news to Rose. Her father always suspected, didn't he? Maybe you better tell her yourself. Those poor kids of yours...."

"Very funny, asshole. Listen, the queer's an old school chum of David's at MIT. His name is Atterson, as in Henry M. Atterson, who just happens to be his father."

"You saying the D.A.'s son is a sissy, Nunzio?"

"That's what I'm saying."

"Nunzio, the hell with coffee. You call your wife and tell her that her favorite pervert is coming over for dinner. And, by the way, I hate corned beef and cabbage, capisce? See ya later."

All Nunzio could think about on the way home were the jokes Vito would be telling the D.A. on Monday, as he moved to have all charges against him shit-canned.

CHAPTER FORTY-ONE
October 21, 1941. Los Angeles

Loretta Bonet put the dark glasses on before the lights went on in the theater so no one would recognize her.

"I'm just not in the mood to sign autographs and answer questions, darling," she said, taking Stanley's arm as they left the Hollywood Hills movie house. "Bogey had me believing he was Sam Spade, and that Peter Lorre, I must do a movie with him. I wish my agent would have gotten me a role in the Maltese Falcon."

"Come now. You're four months pregnant and you're playing the best part you ever played, Mrs. Stanley Fryman."

"Yes, love, you are so right. I am happy," she replied. She was thinking to herself, if not the happiest I have ever been, then certainly the most contented. "Hollywood Boulevard," she said aloud. "It's always so magical to me."

"And you, my darling, add to the magic," said Stanley.

"That newsreel got me a little depressed, Stanley. Did you see those German soldiers? They're right outside Moscow. All I could think about is that my friend David's wife, Sally, is still in that area somewhere, and the Germans are taking over the world."

"That's Kuibyshiev, darling, and I'm frightened myself. My parents were from a village right outside Kuibyshiev, on the Volga River. They came to America, New York, to be exact, two years before I was born. I still have relatives in Russia and in Poland. Gold only knows what will become of them and all the Jews over there.

"Stanley, this child I'm carrying, will this child be

considered a Jew?"

"Does it matter, Loretta?"

"Well, not to me, you know that. But, if the Nazis take over the world, they will kill all the Jews, won't they? You, me and our child."

"That's not going to happen, darling. The United States will whip the shit out of those Germans, just like they did in the First World War. Besides, we're not even in the war. And how would Hitler cross the Atlantic to attack us? He can't even cross the channel to invade England."

"Fuji is afraid the Japanese will get involved in the war, and he thinks they might even attack the United States," Loretta said.

"Loretta, that's preposterous. Why, the Japanese Ambassador, Nomura, is said to be preparing talks with Washington on respecting the United States as a neutral country and..."

"Stanley, I heard that thousands of Japanese Americans are being evacuated from the West Coast. What does that mean?"

"You are really keeping up on current events, Loretta. I don't know. I just can't imagine the Japanese attacking the United States. It would be suicide for them. We're a giant country. They wouldn't have a prayer. Forget it. I'm starved. Let's get some dinner. What do you feel like eating?" he asked.

"I would like a good, old-fashioned Italian dinner, like my mama used to make. Let's go to Villa Napoli."

"Good choice, darling. I just want to call the hospital and let them know where I'll be."

CHAPTER FORTY-TWO
December 11, 1941   Boston

Nunzio sat in his office staring at the headlines on the afternoon paper: 'US DECLARES WAR ON GERMANY AND ITALY.' The word Italy kept jumping off the page and smacking him in the face.

Vito was standing behind him looking over his shoulder. "I knew it was coming, Nunzio. A long time I knew it. Sunday morning, when the Japs bombed Pearl Harbor, I knew it was just the beginning," he said.

"You know, Vito," Nunzio said putting down the newspaper, "I never even heard of Pearl Harbor before Sunday. I didn't even know where Hawaii was. Jeez, I thought it was a separate country. And the only Japs I ever met were in California, working for Loretta. But Italy I know real well, and the United States going to war with Italy is like, how can I say it, it's like my hand fighting my leg."

"The President said to prepare for a long war, and he assured us the United States and its allies were going to win," Vito said. "I was born in this country, Nunzio. I was a captain in the last war, and I'm going to go back into the army, if they will take me."

"Oh, and what about me? Why can't I go into the army?" Nunzio asked.

"Because, we want to win and you got a million mouths to feed. You are needed right here running the business. Me? I got no one, and I want to go back into combat. I loved it, to tell you the truth."

"Somehow, I can believe that, Vito. I could believe you were born to kill. How would you feel if you had to shoot Italians?"

"Nunzio, during the bootlegging days, Italians killed Italians. Mussolini had your brother, Bruno, killed, indirectly. Anyway, what the hell's the difference? War is war. I only shoot at the enemy, whoever the enemy happens to be at the moment. Right now, the enemy is Germans, Italians and Japs. That is who I shoot at when I put on the uniform and get into the war."

"I'm scared of this war, Vito. The Nazis look pretty tough and mean. I don't know."

"Nunzio, next year there won't be any more Nazis. We're going to kick their asses. Tomorrow I'm going to the induction center to see if my commission is still good. Maybe they will even take me back as a Major. I'll call you tomorrow night. Take care Nunzio. You will have to carry the whole load. This will be a wartime economy. Things will be different, you'll see."

"People still eat bread in war time. I'll be okay," Nunzio smiled.

They shook hands, and Vito left the office. Nunzio put the newspaper under his arm and followed him out of the building. The cold December air felt refreshing, as he walked toward his car. How many of my employees would be called to arms, he asked himself. He looked around at the men leaving the building; bakers, drivers, packers. How many would be killed, he wondered. Most of them are Italian, probably with relatives in Italy. Why did Mussolini have to get involved with Hitler? Nunzio put his hands in his pocket, the car key clenched in his right hand. "Starting to feel real cold now," he said aloud as he walked faster to the car. Traffic was heavier than usual for a Thursday, he considered, as he sat in the car, holding his topcoat closed to keep warm.

The billboard ahead was plastered with a picture of a man sporting a funny beard and red and white striped hat, his finger pointing forward, with the caption, 'Uncle Sam Wants You'. Nunzio stared hypnotized. "Uncle Sam doesn't want me," he said out loud.

Rose and Alberto greeted Nunzio at the door. Jim Kelly, Jr. was standing behind Rose.

"I just got off the phone with Loretta, Nunzio," Rose said. "She's here in Boston at her father's house. Stanley stayed in California. She's wants to come over. Everybody on Hanover Street is upset with the war news."

"Everybody, everywhere, is upset," he replied turning toward his brother-in-law. "Haven't seen you for a while, Jim. Nice to see you."

"Likewise, Nunzio. I came to say goodbye. I joined the Marines today. I'm leaving for boot camp Monday morning."

"What about the police force? How could you give up a good job like that?" Nunzio asked.

"They still got my father, and the job will be there when the war is over. Got to do my duty."

"Are you going, too, daddy?" Alberto asked.

"Somebody has got to mind the store, son," Nunzio said, pulling his son close to him.

"Not everyone goes to fight the war, Alberto," Rose said. "Your father is needed here."

Nunzio walked into the parlor to pour himself a brandy. He stared at the painting of his brother Bruno on the wall over the fireplace. Life changes so fast, he thought. "Everyone is going to war, Bruno," he said to the picture. "For you the war is over. For me, well, who knows?"

Loretta arrived and quietly walked into the parlor. She watched Nunzio as he talked to his brother. She came behind him and put her hands on his shoulders, startling him.

"Loretta, I didn't hear you come in. I was going to pick you up a little later. How did you get here?"

"Took a taxi. I'm rich, too, in case you forgot," she laughed.

The New Patriots

"How come Stanley didn't come to Boston with you?"

"Stanley has a lot to do at the hospital. He's a doctor, remember? And, I wanted to see my father, and you and Rose."

"Aren't you doing any films?"

"Nope. I've been a good housewife, and I haven't had a drink in ages. I've been so happy with Stanley, Nunzio. He's such a wonderful man."

"I'm glad for you, Loretta. You deserve to be happy. Have you spoken to David?"

"I called him several times, but he was not available, and he doesn't return my calls. What about you?"

"It's been a while. Maybe tonight we will try to reach him. I'm sure the news of the war has him upset."

"Everyone's upset, Nunzio. And frightened. Do you see the newsreels? There's brutal fighting in Russia, and constant bombing in England. What if that happens here? It's awful."

"And what about Hawaii?" he asked. "Did you see the newsreels of the West Virginia and the Tennessee sinking? What about the Japanese? Isn't your housekeeper and his wife Japanese?"

"Yes, and we are Italian, so what?" she replied. "We have to stand united against the wrong. We are Americans now, aren't we?"

"I hope Americans will feel that way, Loretta. I hope they will look at us as Americans," Nunzio replied and poured another glass of brandy.

"This war is not our doing, Nunzio. People will realize that. We have been in this country for fourteen years."

"Yes, fourteen years is right Loretta, and its been a wonderful fourteen years. Anyway, you are six months pregnant, aren't you? How come you flew all the way from California?"

"The doctor said I could if I took it easy. I'm going home Saturday. The baby is due at the end of February."

"Pregnancy becomes you, Loretta. You look radiant."

"Thank you for saying that, Nunzio. I almost feel guilty about bringing another child into this world."

"This is a beautiful world, Loretta. There are problems, there always were and always will be. A lot of people are going to die before this war is over. A lot of people. And our children will replace some of them, and maybe things will get better. Let's go into the other room. Rose is probably wondering about us."

"Nunzio. You, me and David, we have a special relationship, a bond that will last until the end of time."

"That sounds like a song, Loretta. Maybe you could make a movie about us, call it 'Until the End of Time'. I do love you, Loretta. Sometimes, when I'm with Rose, you know, well... I fantasize it's you. Don't get me wrong, no matter what, Rose is my wife, I love her dearly, it's just that..."

"I understand, Nunzio. But to me you are like a brother. And I love you as I would a brother. If it were any other way, it wouldn't have lasted as long as fourteen years. You have seen how many lovers I've gone through since we met. I want this marriage to Stanley to work, but I am scared that something will happen."

"This time I think it will work. Stanley is a good man. Do you know what just came to my mind, Loretta?"

"What's that?" She asked.

"There are only fourteen more days until Christmas, and so many men are going to be leaving for the army. What kind of Christmas do you think its going to be for them?"

"I never thought of that, Nunzio. I'm going to spend Christmas praying. Stanley doesn't celebrate Christmas, he celebrates Channukah, the festival of lights, but he says his people are being slaughtered all over Europe, so there is no joy." She paused to reflect. "Let's drop this subject and join your family."

As they entered the main room where Rose was standing, they noticed the annoyed look on Rose's face.

"You two were in there quite a while, is something wrong?" Rose asked.

"No. We had some things to talk about," Nunzio answered. "Nothing important, just about what's going on with the war and such."

"I guess I'll be leaving now," Jim said.

"God go with you Jim," Nunzio replied. "That sounds corny, but I don't know what else to say. Be sure you write, and we will send you Italian salamis.

Jim laughed and hugged Nunzio. "Take care of my sister," he replied as he left the house.

"Kill one of those bad guys for me Uncle Jimmy," Alberto yelled to him.

Jim turned and smiled at the young boy in the doorway. Outside, he leaned on his car and stared at the mansion, broke a branch off the bush next to the tire, and drove away.

CHAPTER FORTY-THREE
Fort Benning, Georgia   February 8, 1942

Major Vito Natali stood at attention outside the Post Headquarters Building along with ten other officers who were to be commanders, the first of the Fifth Army under Lt. General Mark W. Clark to be shipped overseas. Vito was shivering. The icy cold air was going right through him. As he looked at the officer standing next to him, he got an eerie feeling. The man, a young Lieutenant by the name of Frank Dano, reminded him of Angelo Donatto. If these men knew they were standing next to Vito Natali, killer, bootlegger and mob boss turned bakery entrepreneur, what would they say? That's all bullshit anyway. We got a bunch of Germans to kill and a war to win, he thought to himself.

"At ease," the General commanded. Vito was relieved. "Dismissed," sounded even better. He put his hands in his pockets, and headed toward the Bachelors Officer's quarters.

Lt. Dano approached him before they reached the building. "Excuse me, Major," he said. "I noticed you kept staring at me before. Any reason?"

"You look like someone I used to know, Lieutenant. That's all. We ship out tomorrow. Going over there."

"I'm a little nervous, Major, but I am anxious at the same time," the lieutenant replied. "I'm glad to be serving under an Italian Major, sir."

"I'm an American Major, Lieutenant. It's important to remember that over there. Italy is the enemy in this war, same as the Germans and the Japs I fought in the last war. For me, this is just a reunion."

Vito went to his room and started packing his gear.

He was glad to be inside for a while, where it was nice and warm. Might as well get everything ready tonight, he figured. After he completed his packing, he decided to get some dinner and go into town for a little social drinking. After all, he thought. This is his last night in the States. Maybe I'll ask that Dano kid to go with me. Damn, it's haunting me how much he looks like Donato. He looked out his window and watched the buses being lined up for the trip to the ship. "Reality is upon us," he whispered. "Get ready you bastards. Natali is coming."

CHAPTER FORTY-FOUR
March 3, 1942   Los Angeles, California

Loretta and Stanley listened to the radio in disbelief. The news commentator was describing the plan in which all those of Japanese descent were to be evacuated. It made no difference whether they were American citizens or not.

Fuji was holding Judy on her lap while Tomo just stared at them.

"I feel the baby kicking," Loretta said, hoping to change the atmosphere in the room. "I think the baby wants to come out. Oh my God, look at the world it has to face," she started cry.

Stanley went over to comfort her.

"What this mean?" Tomo asked. "This General DeWitt, him say all Japanese to be put in camp until war is over. There is many of us here. What we do? I am American, good American. What they mean?"

Fuji just looked at her, fear in her face. She didn't say a word.

"Don't you worry, Tomo," Loretta said. "I'll never let them take you. You're part of this family. My God, Stanley. The pains are getting sharper. I think its time."

"One of the advantages of being a doctor, darling," he answered. "I can always deliver my own baby. Tomo, go call the hospital to let them know we are on the way and to get everything ready, the big moment is about here. And don't worry about the order. I have some friends. I'll work it out."

"Thank you, sir. Thank you very much," Tomo replied. "I go call now."

Loretta lay, forcing the child out of her body with the

help of her husband at her side. Several hours later, Stanley was slapping his seven pound baby boy on the rear. "Daniel Fryman, welcome to the world," he said as he sponged the crying baby. "I hope it will be a better one now that you are here."

CHAPTER FORTY-FIVE
MAY 8, 1942   The Coral Sea

None of the airplanes engaged in the fierce fighting would return to the sinking aircraft carrier Lexington. It was the first time in history that enemy naval ships were engaged in battle without seeing each other. The ships served only as launch pads for the fighter planes. It was the first major setback for the Japanese since they bombed Pearl Harbor.

Lt. Stefano Martinelli was treading water with the donut shaped life preserver around his chest. "Thank God the rescue ships have arrived," he said to himself. "Maria, I want so badly to return to your arms. What the hell am I doing here in the construction battalions, a fucking Marine?" he cried out in hysteria. "I didn't want to live in Lexington, and here I am watching the Lexington go down. Just a name, right, God? This water is so cold," he continued speaking out loud to himself trying to keep afloat. "The ropes. They're throwing me a rope." He tied the rope to his life preserver. He could feel himself being pulled out of the water.

"Are you all right, Lieutenant?" Chief Petty Officer Scott asked.

"So cold, so tired and so cold," he answered.

"Get him out of that wet uniform, and into the infirmary with the rest," the petty officer said to one of the crew members. "Most of your crew is alive," he added to Stefano. "Damned miracle."

After a full day's sleep, Stefano sat drinking hot soup in the infirmary, and tried to read the wet letter from Maria. It was the only thing he didn't leave in his quarters on the Lexington. The ink had run and he couldn't make out the words, but he had read it so many times he had it memorized. Her picture in his wallet was too soggy to make out, but he could see her in his mind, so beautiful, standing naked in front of him.

"All I want out of life is to love you, Maria. To have lots of healthy children, to give you a good life. What am I doing here wrapped in a blanket on some navy ship 10,000 miles from you, my Maria?" The tears were running down his face, and he was not ashamed. The medical officer offered him a cigarette. Stefano shook his head no.

"If you're all right, Lieutenant, we would appreciate you leaving the infirmary. There are so many others. Besides the Lexington, there are survivors from a destroyer and a tanker."

"Where do I go, sir?" Stefano asked.

"All those without need of medical attention are waiting on the deck to be transported to other ships. You will be issued an entire new set of supplies and will be reassigned to another construction battalion unit. When we take some of these islands from the Nips, we're going to need you guys."

Stefano wrapped the blanket around him and proceeded to the main deck to join the others. The only thing he wanted to think about was Maria. It was the only thing that kept him going. He fantasized of making love and recalled the times they had. He asked for a pen and paper and wrote a letter to Maria.

My Maria,

We are separated by distance, but my thoughts are always of you. My mind allows me to caress you in the night. I'm sure by now you have heard the news that my ship sank. But God has kept me alive so that I could return to you. I will love you forever.

Stefano.

CHAPTER FORTY-SIX
June 10, 1942 Warsaw, Poland

After ten months of running and hiding, Sally Fairchild was tired and worn out. Both her grandmother and grandfather were shot by the SS near the Russian Border. Sally was brought to the Warsaw Ghetto to await her destiny. The SS cared not that she was an American. To them she was only a Jewess. Besides, America was the enemy of the Third Reich.

"I will never see you again, my David, and my children. Oh God, what have I done?" She squeezed the piece of bread in her hands. The bugs crawling on it made her gag, but it was the only thing between life and death. She took a bite. Watching her was a girl about five years old, whose mother was stabbed to death by an SS that morning. She looked pathetically hungry. Sally handed her the bread. The child took it and ran into a hallway to hide.

Each day the trucks came, and the selections were made for those Jews to be deported to the camps.

"Resettlement," the Germans said. But everyone knew the truth. News of the death camps, of the starvation, the brutality, the horrors was all over Warsaw. Nobody escaped alive.

Sally walked to her quarters where six families shared the room she slept in. She carefully avoided passing the dresser with the broken mirror, so she wouldn't have to look at herself. The once radiant face and figure was skin and bones and wrinkles. The hair that was treated to a beauty salon visit once a week was dry and stringy. Her teeth hurt so much that she wished they would just fall out. She stepped over so many dead bodies the last few months that she didn't think twice about it any more. How could this be happening, she asked herself. How could anyone allow this to happen? Why? She was crying again.

Hershal Ginsberg noticed Sally crying and tried to comfort her.

"Did you eat anything today?" he asked.

"What difference does it make?" she replied. "We're all going to die."

"And who told you that lie?" he said. "You must not give up hope. We must do what we can to stay alive. Here, take this potato. It's fresh and it's good."

"I can't take your food. You're going to need it. What about your wife?"

"Take it. I have some connections to get food. Please, don't worry. Just don't give up."

"If only I could get word to my husband," Sally said.

"That, unfortunately, is impossible. And even if you could, what could he do? It's better your husband should think that there is a chance you are well and with your family, than to know you are here."

Sounds of gunfire came from the next room.

"Quick! Hide the potato," Hershal warned. "Maybe they won't come in here, but better to be careful."

They faked being asleep. The four SS officers looked in, yelled some profanities, and left.

"They were drunk," Sally whispered turning toward Hershal. He was weeping.

CHAPTER FORTY-SEVEN
November 18, 1942   Boston

Rose sat in the parlor of Dianne Peter's house while Alberto was finishing his piano lesson. She tried to read the newspaper while listening to the new piece Alberto was learning. She couldn't figure out what it was, but the tune sounded familiar. Where is Nunzio? she wondered. He said he would meet me here at three o'clock, and it's almost four.

"That was a good lesson," she heard Dianne saying, coming into the room. "Alby learns fast. He will be ready for a recital soon."

"That's good, Dianne. Thank you for being such a good teacher," Rose replied. "Come, Alby, let's wait for your father downstairs... and speaking of the devil," she added as Nunzio entered the parlor.

"Hello, Diane. Sorry I'm late. And, how was your lesson, Mr. Chopin?" he asked Alby.

"Fine, Papa. Can we go for some ice cream?"

"Sure."

"So what happened at the meeting?" Rose asked as they walked outside toward the car.

"Well, it's going to be tough for a while. Everything is going to be rationed, so besides being hard to get men to work, it's going to be hard to get supplies and fuel. Vito used to take care of problems like this. Of course, there is a war, but he would know what to do."

"Isn't Vito somewhere in North Africa? Why don't you just call General Eisenhower's office? The papers said he was in Morocco. Ask to speak to Vito and you can say 'Vito, I hate to interrupt your war, but I'm a little low on vanilla extract and shortening. What should I do?'"

"Very funny. You ever think about going on the radio? Maybe you can replace Jack Benny," he laughed.

"I got a letter from Stefano today," she said as they approached the ice cream parlor.

"Yeah, and Uncle Stefano said to say hello to me, all the way from... what's the name of that place, mommy?" Alberto asked.

"Guadalcanal. He's on an island called Guadalcanal," she answered.

"Where is that?" Nunzio asked.

"Where is that? Somewhere in the Pacific Ocean, that's all I know. He only wrote four lines."

"I called Maria. All she does is cry and tell me how worried she is. I told her she can move back to Lexington, but she says she likes New York. She's as stubborn as a mule."

"When is the war going to be over, Daddy?" Alberto asked.

" I wish I knew, son," Nunzio answered. "God only knows. By the way, I spoke to Loretta. She sounded really down. First off, Stanley is going into the army medical corps after the first of the year, and her Japanese maid and her husband have been interned in one of those camps. Loretta sounded a little wishy washy, like she was drinking again. She said she called David before she called me, and that David was busy with government contracts, and still no word on Sally."

"It's sad," said Rose. "Sometimes I can't believe the whole thing. You would think that life could be so beautiful, but if it isn't one thing its another. I'm scared, Nunzio, about this war, everything."

"I wish I could say there was nothing to be scared about Rose, but there is a lot to be scared about. I'm scared, too, believe me, but I still have a business to run. I'm going to drop you and Alby at the house and go back to the office."

"Can't you forget the office and stay home tonight?" she said taking his hand.

"It sounds tempting as hell, but I really have to get some papers signed and mailed. I won't be home until late."

"There was a time, Nunzio dear, that you would drop everything to please me. Remember those times?" she laughed putting her hand on his lap."

"Rose... Alby?" he whispered.

"Come on. You can go to the office early in the morning to sign your papers."

"You win," said Nunzio. He kissed her gently and the three of them went into the house.

CHAPTER FORTY-EIGHT
January 11, 1943

The bottle of Jack Daniels on David Fairchild's desk had become an old friend, a friend that David could not do without. "I am not an alcoholic," he would shout at anyone who would dare insinuate that he was.

"It... it just helps me relax," he would say and leave it at that. He had come to grips with the idea that Sally might not return, and he had an obligation to raise his sons. And now that he was Chairman of Continental Electric, he had an even greater responsibility to the stockholders.

Eric Hampton was the key lobbyist for Continental, and with FDR seeking a one-hundred billion dollar budget, David wanted to make damn sure Continental got its share.

With development of new communications equipment vital to the war effort, and the successful ability of Continental to mass produce television sets after the war, David envisioned Continental as one of the future giants of American industry. He was already experimenting with computers that could be programmed to do the work of a hundred men; machines that could store information that would fill up entire file rooms, and an operator who would push a button and all the information requested would be summoned in seconds.

Nothing is impossible in electronics. David took a swig of the Jack Daniels, and opened the door of his office to peek at his secretary, Dorothy Ann. He thought about last night, the wonderful dinner she had prepared and the passionate love making after dinner. He felt as if Sally was watching from wherever she was. It's been so long, he was lonely, and Dorothy Ann was here and willing.

She's crazy about me, and would do anything I asked, he thought. Besides, 'there's a war going on', was the popular phrase of the day, so you could rationalize anything; having an affair, drinking too much, whatever.

Those five words allowed you to be pardoned for the loss of values and principles. How many girls have lost their virginity because 'there's a war going on'? David wanted to smile at his thoughts, but felt guilty at the prospect of being cheerful. After all, a man whose wife is missing somewhere in the world should be sad.

But David had passed sad, and was into angry. Angry at Sally for having placed her grandparents above her husband and children. So David sought comfort from his friend Jack Daniels, and love from his secretary. He walked over to the window, and watched the snow beginning to stick to the ground of the parking lot.

Dorothy Ann walked into the office with a folder in her hand. "Are we going to acknowledge the Winthrop proposals, David?"

David stood there staring at her, "Dorothy," he replied, "when we are at work you will continue to call me Mr. Fairchild. You will also knock as you used to do before we were intimate. I hope that is clear. And, yes, we will acknowledge the Winthrop proposal."

Dorothy Ann froze. She put the folder on his desk and replied, "Whatever you say, sir," and left the office.

David wanted to slap himself for snapping at her. He called her back into the room. "I'm sorry for talking to you like that. I've got a lot on my mind and, well, there's a war going on, you know."

CHAPTER FORTY-NINE
March 7, 1943

The years were starting to show on Father Di Salvo's face. Gray hair and wrinkles, Nunzio thought to himself. He had not been to church for a long time and remembered the priest with his young appearance and jet-black hair. The Sunday morning's Mass was also a memorial service for Vito Natali, Lt. Col. U.S. Army, who on February 26, led his troops up the mountains of the Kasserine Pass in central Tunisia as Field Marshall Rommel's columns were retreating. The allies were victorious, but poor Vito bought the farm. "The North End of Boston will mourn the death of Vito Natali for a long time," Father Di Salvo declared.

"I wish I was the German that pulled the trigger," a voice from the middle of the church yelled.

"May God forgive you as he did Vito," Father Di Salvo said.

Nunzio thought about the partnership agreement that gave him full ownership of La Bella Rosa on the death of Vito. Vito had no heirs, nobody to contest. "A new ball game," Nunzio said to himself.

The allies were having some victories, turning the tide of the war both in the European theater and in the Pacific.

The smart money in the United States was preparing for peace, for the return of millions of men. Nunzio was buying options on land to be developed into new communities with low-cost housing. He opened fifteen more Ace Milk and Bread Stops, and formed two new corporations with Joe Allen. The war is making me richer than I could have ever imagined, he thought to himself, not paying attention to the sermon from the pulpit. Rose and the children, and his father and mother, chose to go to Mass at the new church in Lexington.

"I do not belong with the North End crowd," Rose had said. "And, frankly, I'm glad Vito is dead, and so are you, Nunzio," she told him that morning. "Vito was a gangster. He died for his country doing what he loved to do, kill. He will probably be awarded the Congressional Medal of Honor, and who would be chosen to receive it? He has no family that admits to being his family. You, Nunzio, his closest friend would have to receive Vito's Medal."

"Vito was a Lieutenant Colonial in the United States Army, and died in battle," he told her. "And that's how we will remember him. Also, without him I would never be where I am in business. He helped us get rich."

Nunzio left the church and walked along Hanover Street, past the old bakery. There was a familiar face. Loretta's father was standing on the corner under the lamp post. Nunzio took his hand in his and held it. "Mr. Camarco, how are you?" he asked.

"Old and tired," he answered. "My daughter is a cheesecake queen now, you know, Nunzio? A pin-up, they call her."

"Yes, I know," Nunzio answered. "The GI's have Loretta Bonet posters in their lockers. Betty Grable is also a pin-up. It's okay. Do you hear from her?"

"Very seldom, Nunzio. Her husband is in the Army Medical Corps, and she travels around visiting the troops. The movie star, and who knows who she leaves the children with. Strangers. And what's new with you, Nunzio? You went to the Mass for the gangster?"

"Yes, I went to Vito's memorial service," he said.

"You know who came to see me, Nunzio? Paul Bonet, the first Jew husband. He's making a killing with his factory. War contracts, making uniforms. He said he never stopped loving my Loretta, and just wanted to talk to me. I told him she couldn't forget him because she kept his name. I have no happiness from my daughter. Why couldn't she have fallen in love with you, Nunzio? I wish you were my son-in-law."

"It is nice to see you, Mr. Camarco," Nunzio stuttered, and walked away, his hands in his pockets, heading down Hanover Street. He stopped into Regina's for a plate of spaghetti and a glass of wine before returning to Lexington.

"Did you check the mail?" Rose asked.

"No mail on Sundays," he answered.

"Oh, yes. With both my brother and brother-in-law in the Solomon Islands, I'm just anxious. How was the memorial for Vito?"

"As expected. I ate lunch. I'm going to lie down for a while, then I have an important meeting with Joe and a few land developers. How do like the name Rose Gardens for a village of small homes?"

"Rose Gardens. It's got a nice ring to it. Are you naming it after me?"

"None other, dear," Nunzio smiled.

"How can you run the bakery and the stores and build houses? You're dancing at too many weddings."

"I have to, Rose. It's just the way things are developing. The little wop is going to be the biggest tycoon this country has seen. Ten years from today, Rose Gardens will be a city with it's own mayor and police department. Our city, Rose. An empire to pass to our children. A dynasty, I believe they call it."

"Nunzio, how much do we need? You are changing into someone I don't know, and I don't know how to deal with it. All you think about anymore is money. Why?"

"I don't know, Rose. It's just that once I started to make big money, I had to keep going. It's just the way it is. This country is going to be the major power after the war and we are going to be a major power in this country."

CHAPTER FIFTY
April 19, 1943 Warsaw, Poland

Under the command of SS General Jurgen Stroop, the SS attacked the ghetto with orders to seize the 60,000 Jews still living there. There were half a million Jews in the ghetto only a year before. Each of the 60,000, including Sally Fairchild, knew that if they did not die in their homes, they would die in a gas chamber in one of the concentration camps, so they had nothing to lose by fighting back.

The fighting was fierce. The Jews were throwing Molotov cocktails, and used what little weapons they were able to steal from the Nazi guards.

Hershal Ginsberg, Shlomo Abrams and Yossil Jacobs were going house to house to warn the people when the Nazis were approaching.

Sally was too weak to go on, and hid in the corner of the basement. She was tired and hungry. Her hands clung to the only possession she had left, a picture of David and her sons. She stared at the picture, knowing she would never see them again. The reality of what was going on around her was still uncomprehended by her. "All of us share this planet. Germany, New Hampshire, all humans, why is this happening? Why God, do you allow this to happen? What have I done?" she pleaded.

Sally was coughing from the dust that was coming from the ceilings. She could hear the shooting and the SS troops shouting. A rat was nibbling at her leg, but she didn't have the strength to move.

The basement door opened, and the soldier told her to get on her feet. She just stared at him. He aimed the rifle at her head.

She looked right into his eyes. "These are my children in America," she said to the soldier. "After you lose the war and have to answer to America for all this, maybe you could find my children and explain to them why you did this."

The soldier looked at her. Three of his comrades entered the room as he pulled the trigger.

CHAPTER FIFTY-ONE
April 20, 1943 Manchester, N.H.

David opened the door of his office and invited Dorothy Ann to see the first official program on a Continental Television. The little seven-inch, round screen sat on his desk. The black and white picture showed David and the Chief Engineer, explaining how television worked, was as clear as a movie, except for the little white dots that looked like snow.

"It's fabulous," said Dorothy Ann.

"After the war there will be one in every home in America," David said. He walked over to the door and locked it. Turning to Dorothy Ann, "I want to make love to you now. Get undressed."

"That's what I like most about you, David, you're so romantic." Mimicking him, "I want to make love to you now. Get undressed. Why don't you just say, 'hey, baby, let's fuck'? That would really turn me on."

David reached for the Jack Daniels, took a drink without offering Dorothy Ann any, and just looked at her. "You're very beautiful, Dorothy, and I believe I'm in love with you, but..."

"But you're married. Well, I don't care. I love you, too. What if your wife comes home? What then?"

"I guess we will have to worry about it then," he replied. "Please, go get undressed. I want to look at you naked. I enjoy looking at your beautiful body."

"Did you enjoy looking at Sally's body?" she asked.

"Sally is skinny and doesn't have much on top. I loved her, but when it came to sex, she didn't do the things you do."

Dorothy Ann smiled and got undressed. On her

knees, she opened the top button of David's pants and gently pulled them down. "Can we televise this encounter, lover boy?" she asked.

"I don't think so," he replied. "I feel so good, Dorothy Ann. You make me very happy."

"Well, I feel like I'm just a release. You look like your mind is somewhere else. Like you're doing a physical thing with me while you're thinking..."

"Maybe I just feel guilty," he interrupted.

"Sally left you. For whatever her reasons, she left her family to go where she shouldn't have gone, and it's been a long time. I didn't want to say this, but I think she's dead. If not, you would have heard something by now."

David didn't answer her, nor the telephone that was ringing.

"Let me answer it," Dorothy Ann said. "After all, I'm still your secretary." She lifted the receiver. "Mr. Fairchild's office. Yes, sir, one moment, please." She turned to David. "It's Mr. Cappolla in Boston."

He grabbed the phone while putting on his pants. "Nunzio, how are you?" he greeted his friend.

"I'm fine. We're all fine. How come I haven't heard from you for so long, David?"

"This place keeps me busy. I've just been watching a television program we made."

"Have you heard anything from Sally?"

"No, nothing, Nunzio. Nothing at all."

"Listen, I'm investing in a project. I bought some land and I'm building a village of homes. Calling it Rose Gardens. Would you come to the ground breaking ceremony on Saturday."

"Saturday? Saturday. That's the 24th. Let me see. Just a second." He held the phone away for a second and glanced at his secretary before returning to the conversation. "Sure, Nunzio, I'll be at your house Saturday morning. What time is the ceremony?"

"At noon. We'll be serving lunch. And, of course, we'll be featuring some of the new La Bella Rosa products."

"Of course. Rose Gardens. If you ever take over the world, we will be living on the planet 'Rose' instead of Earth, the way you name things after your wife."

"Rose is my life, David. What can I say? As long as I have her, there is nothing I can't do. I would name the universe after her if I could, and even heaven, if God let me."

"You're something else, Nunzio. I'll see you Saturday, paesano.

"Ciao, David".

"Ciao," David replied. He placed the receiver on the hook and once again embraced Dorothy Ann.

"Horny, aren't you," she laughed. "Haven't you had enough? It's time to get back to work."

"Who's the boss here?" he asked.

"You were the boss until you started dunking your donut in my coffee," she laughed. "Now, we're sort of, you know."

"I think I'm going to go over your application again. None of this shit is on there. I'm trying to figure out why I hired you. You can't type worth a damn and you're a smart ass. So, why did I hire you?"

"Big tits," she laughed again.

"That must be it. I knew there was a good reason," he said.

CHAPTER FIFTY-TWO
Christmas 1943   Pearl Harbor

Stefano Martinelli finished his drink and started to get dressed to go to the show at the outdoor theater. He glanced at the program for the USO Christmas show, 'Loretta Bonet - Cheesecake Queen'. Will the guys believe me when I tell them I know her?

He held the shirt in his hand and admired the emblem of his newly acquired rank of Major. The fighting Seebees. Only thirty days ago he left the Gilbert Islands. Twenty-seven hundred out of five thousand men died taking Tarawa. But here he was, alive and promoted, and three days of R and R to do whatever he pleased. He'd just finished reading the letter from Maria telling him all about Nunzio's new passion, Rose Gardens, and all of his plans for the future. "Please, God, let this fucking war end already. I want to go home. I'm so tired of destroying things. And, God, don't ever make me look at another island again unless it's Manhattan or Nantucket."

The outdoor theater was wall-to-wall uniforms. Army, Navy and Marines. Stefano, pushing his way backstage, gave the liaison officer a message to deliver to Loretta.

"She told me to send you right in, Major," the officer told Stafano when he returned.

Loretta's dressing room was very small, with just a table, an army cot and one chair.

"Thank you for the roses, Stefano," Loretta said throwing her arms around him in a big hug. It's good to see someone I know out here."

"It's nice to see you too, Miss Bonet. It's a far cry from Boston and Nunzio's house. And how is your husband, Colonial Fryman? I met him at the Officer's Club before I left the States."

"Oh, my husband is well, thank you. He was supposed to be here for Christmas, the poor thing, but with all the casualties on those islands, they needed him. They're working him to death. Why the hell don't those damn Japs give up already?"

"Miss Bonet, do you think after the show we could have a drink at the Officer's Club?"

"Well, Stefano, the band is having a Christmas party with all the top brass. You can be my guest. And please, call me Loretta. By the way, how's that sweet little wife of yours, Maria?"

"She's fine. I just got a letter from her. She moved back to Lexington with her parents and Nunzio."

"Yes," Loretta answered. "Nunzio does have a rather large family, but then he has a rather large estate."

"I'm going to write to Maria and tell her I saw you. Nunzio will be surprised."

"Give him my love when you write. It's time for me to go on. I'll see you after the show, Stefano."

"Okay, Loretta, but please, call me Steve. The guys all know me as Steve. I don't use the name Stefano, too much."

"Okay, Steve," she smiled.

Stefano sat in his seat in the fourth row daydreaming while Lenny Barton was breaking up the audience with his one-liners. Finally, he announced, "And here's the moment you've been waiting for. The gorgeous, talented, the one and only, Loretta Bonet."

The guys were on their feet, whistling and applauding. A chill went up Stefano's spine. He felt very proud, just the thought that she was his friend. He knew her from Boston. And he would be with her tonight as her guest at the party. He wanted all the guys to know it. Then, feeling a little guilty, wondered why he was so excited. After all, she was a married lady and I'm married too, he thought. So what? This is here and now. There's a war on and there may not be any tomorrow. Why am I thinking like this? All we are going to do is talk, have some drinks and mingle with the brass. Here I am having a fantasy about Loretta Bonet. What the hell, so are all the other guys, he was thinking, noticing her tight, very low-cut gown. Teasing all these men who haven't been with a woman in years, except maybe the prostitutes here in Honolulu. And how many of those whores will be playing the part of Loretta Bonet tonight, he wondered.

After the show, Stefano waited by the stage entrance for Loretta.

"Oh, there you are Steve. You can ride with me in the staff car, if you like."

Stefano smiled and climbed into the khaki army car with Loretta and a colonel he did not know. The party was at the home of Admiral Walling.

At the party, Stefano sat on the sofa, nursing a gin and tonic, waiting for Loretta to spend some time with him. She was busy making conversation with all the officers who caught her attention. Finally, he went up to her and interrupted her conversation with a Navy Captain. "I wonder if I can have a minute of your time?" he asked.

"I'm sorry if I seem to be ignoring you Steve, but I am the wife of a Colonel and I must mingle with these people."

"Well, Loretta, can we at least have a dance?"

"They're playing a waltz. I don't waltz."

"Then can we go for a walk?" Stefano persisted.

"Major, if you are trying to put the make on me, I'm flattered, but it won't work," she said, somewhat abruptly. "Somewhere in time it will come back to haunt you. Enjoy the party and enjoy the notoriety you will receive from your fellow Seebees when they find out you escorted Loretta Bonet to a Christmas Party. And do have a very

Merry Christmas, Major Martinelli."

Stefano smiled, backing into reality, "And, Merry Christmas to you, Mrs. Fryman."

CHAPTER FIFTY-THREE
February 18, 1944   Boston

The members of the board were seated at the table, Nunzio, Joe Allen, Earl Tannenbaum, the lawyer, Donald Wolff, Bryan Wiseman and Peter Jascowitz. La Bella Rosa was a private corporation, solely owned by Nunzio. Only he could vote, and his decision was final, but he respected the advice and input of the board members, and all areas were represented; the Union, the market places, the bank and the legal profession.

"Gentlemen," Nunzio began. "The war will be over soon, and there is no doubt we are going to be the winner. There is going to be a new America, a prosperous America. This company is going to be a major part of that America. We will be expanding with new products and we will be building bakeries across the country. This will take enormous amounts of money, and there is only one way of raising that kind of money. We must go public. Mr. Jascowitz will fill you in on the details. By this time next year, La Bella Rosa will be a public corporation, and all of you on the board will be stockholders with voting power. I will be the majority stockholder and I will remain Chairman of the Board, however, I am sure we will continue working well together. I now turn the floor over to Mr. Peter Jasowitz."

"Thank you, Mr. Cappolla. Gentlemen, if you read the report in front of you, you will notice that we are running at about a 35% profit margin, and our annual sales have doubled in the last two years in spite of the rationing and the war. By going public with our stock, or rather Mr. Cappolla's stock, the corporation can raise five million dollars to be used for expansion, and Mr. Cappolla would be able to pay back the loans that he used to build the Rose Gardens complex. We are also negotiating to buy Penn Brothers Bakeries, which would give us coverage on the entire eastern seaboard. We are looking forward to opening twelve more convenience stores. This company is on the move. Arrowton and Emerson will handle the stock deal. Employees and customers will be able to buy the new issues without paying a commission. All questions on that will be answered by Mr. Emerson. Thank you."

Nunzio shook Jascowitz's hand, and turned back to the members. "As far as Rose Gardens is concerned, I own that outright and I will pay the interest on the loans until the war is over and the units are sold. And they will sell. Seventeen years ago, when I first arrived in Boston, I couldn't speak two words of English..."

"Nunzio," Earl Tannenbaum interrupted. "I would like to make a suggestion. La Bella Rosa is a beautiful name and for our Italian products it's fine. But I think the corporation would have more clout and attract more investors with a, well, Americanized name."

"I won't hear of it. I named the company La Bella Rosa, The Beautiful Rose, and I came this far with that name, thanks to your help, of course, and Vito, may he rest in peace. But, the name stays."

"How about just calling the company The Rose Corporation. Roseco for short," Tannenbaum added.

"Rose Corporation, Roseco. Yes, yes, I like it. Roseco. That might work."

"Gentlemen," Tannenbaum shouted. "I raise my cup in a toast to The Rose Corporation."

"To The Rose Corporation," the rest of the men chanted.

Nunzio picked up the phone and asked the receptionist to get his wife on the line.

Alberto answered.

"I have your son on the line, Mr. Cappolla. Would you like to speak with him?"

"Yes, that's fine, thank you," he answered. "Alberto, where's mother?"

"She went with Grandpa Kelly into town, Daddy. Uncle Jimmy sent a package from England, and they have to pick it up at the post office."

"I see," Nunzio said. "Why aren't you in school today?"

"Tuesday is George Washington's birthday, Daddy, and the school is closed so the teachers can get their paperwork done. Who's Wendle Wilkie, Daddy? He wants to be President and take Mr. Roosevelt's job."

"I doubt very seriously that it will happen, son," Nunzio replied. "Have Mother call me when she gets home."

"Okay, and Father DiSalvi wants to see you Sunday. Remember, I'm going to be twelve next month. My confirmation? I told him the whole family would be in church Sunday. Is that okay, Daddy?"

"Yes, of course," Nunzio whispered into the phone. "I'll see you tonight, son." He put the receiver down. Twelve years old, he thought to himself. It won't be long before the children come into the business. They will never feel what it is to give birth to something like this and watch it grow. Nunzio looked at the five men still seated at the table discussing plans for the Rose Corporation. My Rose Corporation, he said to himself. "Gentlemen," he interrupted, "if you need to see me, I'll be in my office. I still have to run La Bella Rosa Bakery today so there will be bread on the tables of America tomorrow." Nunzio smiled as he walked toward his office.

CHAPTER FIFTY-FOUR
MAY 7, 1945   Boston

News of Germany's unconditional surrender had the population of Boston dancing and cheering in the streets. There was still Japan left to defeat, but for the most part the war was over. With FDR's death in April, and the revelation of the horrors of the Nazi regime's crimes against humanity, there was as much mourning as there was celebrating.

But the end of the war in Europe had come after five years, eight months and six days. Hitler was dead. But for Nunzio, it was just another Monday morning.

Rose Corporation's CEO was at the office discarding the war news and checking on the opening figures on Roseco stock. Eight and a half, up one quarter. That's good, he thought to himself. He glanced over the rest of the newspaper. There was a spread in the real estate section on Rose Gardens. Twenty percent of the homes were already sold. "Wait until the boys come home," he said to himself. "With the GI loans, I'll have every unit sold within a week. He noticed a picture of his brother-in-law, Jim Kelly, at the bottom of the front page. *'Local Hero - Medal of Honor, Captain James L. Kelly, Jr., a Boston police officer before the war, was awarded the Congressional Medal of Honor for bravery above and beyond the call of duty in the invasion of Normandy. On June 6, 1944, in the town of Caen, Captain Kelly, without any regard for his own safety, single handedly knocked out a Nazi stronghold and carried two of his own men to safety while under enemy fire. Miraculously, he was not wounded and is now part of the Allied Forces that will be occupying what is left of Germany.'*

Wow, Nunzio said to himself. He grabbed the phone and called home. "Rose, did you see the article on your brother in today's newspaper?" he asked.

"Yes, my father is here right now," she answered. "Imagine, the Medal of Honor, my brother. Nunzio, I'm so proud. We're all so proud. This is the greatest thing to ever happen in our family. I'm sending him a telegram right now. We're having a dinner party tonight, darling. Loretta is in town with her children and she is going to join us. Maria and your parents will be here too. By the way, we just heard from Stephano in the Philippines. There really is so much to celebrate. Please come home early."

"I'll try, Rose."

Nunzio put the phone down and stared at the newspaper. 'Local Hero'. The greatest thing to ever happen to our family, she said. Why do I feel so envious? After all, look what I did with the bakery. I've built an empire. This is the greatest thing that ever happened.

Nunzio began to fantasize that he could have been a great general and single-handedly won the war. He thought about Il Duce, and their hanging the bastard by his feet. He envisioned a framed picture hanging in his office next to a picture of Bruno.

Then snapping back to reality, he found himself talking to the newspaper. "War. Grown men acting like animals. Fools become heroes. A policeman, whose main job was to collect the bribes from the local peddlers and bring the money to the station to be divided up, gets the highest award this country can give. And a man who builds a giant public corporation, providing security for thousands of people, gets investigated by the Internal Revenue Service once a year."

Nunzio thought about calling David. Perhaps he'd heard something about Sally, now that Germany surrendered, but he figured that David would call him if he had heard anything. "Not in the mood to talk to him, anyway," he said to himself. "So much work to do, and yet I don't feel like doing anything," he heard himself say aloud.

He walked around the plant and watched the men packing the breads and pastries. He picked up a package of bread sticks with sesame seeds and tore it open. He took out a bread stick and put it between his teeth like a cigar, and offered one to the lady packing the carton.

"Thank you, Mr. Cappolla," the lady said taking one of the sticks.

"They are delicious, if I have to say so myself," he smiled at her.

"Isn't it great that Germany has surrendered, Mr. Cappolla? I hope my husband comes home soon."

"Your husband is in the Army, Mrs.... Geez, I'm sorry, I don't remember your name."

"Santoro, Elena Santoro. My husband is in the Marine Corps. He is in the Pacific."

"My brother-in-law, Stefano, is in the Marine Corps, the Seebees. My other brother-in-law, my wife's brother, is in the Army. He won the Congressional Medal of Honor."

"Yes, I know Mr. Cappolla. Captain Kelly. I saw today's paper."

"And you knew that Captain Kelly is my brother-in-law?"

"Yes, sir. I know a lot about you. I've been working here since the war started and, well you know, people talk and I just heard a lot about you."

"Do you have any children, Elena? You don't mind me calling you Elena, do you?"

"Not at all Mr. Cappolla. I have two girls, nine and ten. My mother watches them after school. She works part-time in a defense plant downtown. It's rough making ends meet, even with this job and the allotment I get from my husband."

"Do you speak Italian Elena?"

"I was born in Naples, Mr. Cappolla. I speak fluently, even though I was three years old when we came to Boston."

"Elena, you know how the Generals give soldiers promotions on the spot because they like them? Well, I like you, and I'm going to make you the head of a department and double your salary. What do you say to that?"

"I say you're kidding, of course. Why would you do that?"

"Because, my dear, I am the General of this army and you are one of my soldiers, and I want to do it."

"I don't know what to say. Thank you, Mr. Cappolla. I'll probably wake up soon to find this is just a dream. Right?"

"No, Elena, this is not a dream. Listen, we're having a dinner party at my house tonight. I'll send my chauffeur to pick you up at seven o'clock. You can have the rest of the day off. I'll get someone else to finish packing those bread sticks."

"Mr. Cappolla...."

"Call me Nunzio. Write down your home address, your dress size and your shoe size. Give it to my secretary. My chauffeur will be at your house early enough with your new clothes so that you will have time to change."

"Oh, my. Thank you, but..."

"What is it now?"

"My place is a dump. It's all I could afford. I have never invited anyone. Your chauffeur? Well..."

"Don't worry about it. You're moving tomorrow. You will be living in Rose Gardens, in your own home. Your husband will really be surprised. I'll see to it you get a mortgage, and with your new job, you should be able to handle it."

"Why are you doing this Mr. Capp... I mean Nunzio? What do you want in return? Surely you wouldn't do all this just to seduce me? You could have any girl you wanted for a lot less, and to be honest, after over five years of being without my husband, I would attack you in a heartbeat."

Nunzio stared at her and laughed. "You are very pretty Elena, and I am flattered, but I don't know why I am doing this. It makes me feel good, that's all. Perhaps it's for me as well as for you. Don't look a gift horse in the mouth. Enjoy it. Do a good job as a manager."

"You know, my husband is not going to believe this. He's going to think... you know what."

"That's something you'll have to work out with him."

"Nunzio, this is the best thing that has ever happened to me in my life."

"Honestly?" he shot back. "The very best thing? You don't by any chance have any relatives who won the Congressional Medal of Honor, do you?"

"No, but why do you ask? I don't get it."

Nunzio just smiled. "Don't worry about it. I'll see you tonight."

He called out to the receptionist as he walked out of the building, "Have my car brought around front, please."

CHAPTER FIFTY-FIVE
September 3, 1945   Los Angeles

Loretta waited anxiously at the train station for the 3:06 from Phoenix. It had been four hard years of the most horrible war ever. The dropping of two atomic bombs on the Japanese cities of Hiroshima and Nagasaki forced Japan to unconditionally surrender, and finally, the war had ended.

Nagasaki was Fuji's hometown in Japan. Four years she and Tomo spent in the God-awful interment camp. Her family in Japan was possibly dead or mutilated. Millions on both sides were murdered for no reason, and now it's over. Fuji and Tomo would be on that train.

It will never be over, Loretta thought. Not in the minds of those who have lost their loved ones. On Friday, Stanley will be coming home. No more movies. From now on I am going to be Mrs. Stanley Fryman, housewife, mother, and perhaps, even a civic leader. Why not?

She continued to nervously pace the depot. It's after three o'clock. The train will be here in just minutes. So many people here. There must be a lot of soldiers on that train. The ones who aren't part of the occupation forces.

So far, thank goodness, nobody recognizes me with this wig and dark glasses. Here comes the train now. Right on time.

The crowd went wild with a thousand reunions.

Loretta spotted Tomo among the hundreds of Japanese Americans getting off the train. The crowd was yelling insults at them. "Go back to Japan. We don't need you here. We showed you a thing or two."

Finally, fighting her way through the crowd, she wrapped her arms around Fugi. Tomo was standing behind her with their one suitcase. He was leaning on a crutch.

"What happened to your leg?" Loretta asked.

"I cut pretty bad. At camp. Lucky I not lose it. But it not heal right. I will be walking with this crutch always."

"I'm sorry. It must have been awful for the two of you, and I missed you so," Loretta said. "Come on, let's go home."

"Home. Home," Fuji cried. "This not home for me. I used to love this country. I would have died for America. You see what America do for Fuji? We are leaving, Miss Bonet. We just want to see beautiful daughter Judy, and stay with you short while, and then we go."

"Please, Fuji, I know you've been through hell," Loretta replied. "But the war is over, and time will heal all wounds. I will take care of you and Tomo for the rest of your lives. I need you."

"Yes, dear missy," Tomo answered, "you take care of us. We clean your house, make dinner for guests, clean toilets. Fuji and Tomo want different life. Chance to build. I study hard in camp. I learn new trade, making brooms and brushes. I start my own business, but not in this country."

"Where will you go? Japan?" Loretta asked.

"No Japan. I find place somewhere. We see," answered Tomo.

"Please, the war is over. Fuji, you and Tomo always have a home with me. You want to start a business? Okay, do it in Los Angeles. I'll lend you whatever you need. This country did you a terrible disservice, but look at all the people who were done a much more terrible disservice than you. Things too horrible to mention. We have to get on with our lives. Let's go home now, okay?"

"We are grateful to you, Missy. It will be good to sleep in nice house tonight," Tomo smiled. "And Fuji will cook nice shrimp tempura, just like you like Missy. You still big movie star, right?"

"Well, no one's throwing any big parts at me lately, but I suppose I'm still a star. Really, I just want to be a mother and wife."

Loretta helped Fuji put her suitcase in the car and the three of them headed home. They tried to pretend they did not hear the obscene remarks being hurled at them from passing motorists who noticed a Japanese couple sitting in the back of a Rolls Royce.

Nobody recognized Loretta Bonet as the driver. Her sunglasses and her wig with the wide-brimmed hat were an excellent disguise.

"I think I will call Nunzio tonight. Maybe, when Stanley comes home, we could plan on a white Christmas in Boston. Listen to me. It's only September, and I'm planning Christmas. Fuji, this is the first time I ever drove this car, I don't think I'll need a chauffeur any more. I want a family car and I want to do the shopping and cook and all those wonderful things. Things I did when I was poor."

"We see how long that last, Missy," Tomo laughed. He stopped and realized what he was doing. "That is the first time I laugh in years," he added.

CHAPTER FIFTY-SIX
Lexington February 11, 1946

Nunzio looked out of the window at the endless hills of white snow and wondered how he was going to drive to work. He poured himself another cup of coffee and looked through the financial section of the evening paper he had brought home last night. The Rose Corporation stock was up two points. He tried to figure in his head what that meant in terms of his personal wealth but could not calculate it.

Rose Gardens was one-hundred percent sold, and plans were being made for a second Rose Gardens in Worcester, with Stephano handling construction.

Nunzio thought about Jim Kelly, Jr., the hero, now head of security at Rose Corporation. "No more Boston cop. No more war hero captain. He works for me, under me, like everyone else at the Rose Corporation," Nunzio smiled, the newspaper in his hand.

"Are you going to the office?" Rose asked, as she walked into the dining room with a cup of coffee in her hand.

"I'll serve ma'am," the maid pleaded, standing behind her, trying to relieve her of the cup.

"That's quite all right, Ethel. You have other things to do. Anyway, Nunzio, are you going to the office?" She asked again.

"If I can get out of here, and the roads are clear, I will," Nunzio answered.

"Daddy," Alberto screamed from the family room, "Mr. Allen is on the phone for you."

"Thank you, Alby. I'll get it in the study," Nunzio answered.

"Joe, what is it?" Nunzio asked.

"I don't mean to bother you at home Nunzio, but I called your office and they said you hadn't arrived, so I figured you might be snowed in there in Lexington. I guess I was right."

"Yeah, looks like ten inches at least. I kept the kids home from school today. But, I'm going to try to get to the office. Anyway, what's up?"

"Strike talk, Nunzio," Joe Allen replied. "The Union refused your offer. Times are changing, and now that the war is over, everyone wants to be your partner. You know the steel workers are on strike, and they're striking at General Motors and General Electric; even your buddy up there in New Hampshire at Continental Electric is on strike. Everyone's getting into the act. We need to have a meeting, snow or no snow."

"I'll get there sometime today. Schedule the meeting for three o'clock. All the shop stewards, make sure they're there."

"Okay. You know that girl you promoted, that Elena? She's in charge of packaging, and she's a shop steward, Local 42. She could be of some help."

"How can she be of help?" Nunzio asked.

"She's loyal and you gave her husband, Frank, a job as a driver. She can talk to the membership and convince them to accept a contract."

"That's true. Frank is a teamster, and we have a new contract with the teamsters. It's your union we don't have a new contract with. That's your responsibility, Joe. That's what I've been buying you fucking Cadillacs for."

"Times are changing, Nunzio. I'll see you at three o'clock. Try to have a snowmobile sent over. Arriva..., whatever you Italian guys say. ...derrci. That's it. Arrivederci."

Nunzio put down the phone and walked back to the window. "I might as well chance it and get down to the plant," he said to himself. He put on his heavy coat and boots. It was a task just driving onto the main road. There's a certain thrill in maneuvering a car in deep snow, a challenge, he thought. It took him two hours, but he made it to the plant.

Joe Allen greeted Nunzio at the entrance to the conference room. "Glad you were able to get here. I gotta talk to you before we go in. You know, as a public corporation, there are obligations to stockholders, and you have to think like a Chief Executive Officer. You can't just make decisions that are good for Nunzio Cappolla. We have to go in there and make certain concessions to the union, so that we can get a contract and keep the ship sailing. Capisce?"

"At the rate things are going, Joe, we're going to have to charge twenty cents for a loaf of bread," Nunzio replied. "It's dubots. Crazy. You mark my word, prices will be going up and up on everything in this country. They keep holding us up, and we keep giving in. So they hold us up again and again and again. Before long, a peanut butter and jelly sandwich is two dollars. Me and you, we could pay five dollars, we're big shots, right? But the little people, they're gonna eat dogshit. We have to make a stand. Show the unions they can't hold us up."

"Then they will strike, and we won't be able to deliver."

"Fuck them, Joe," Nunzio shouted. "Let them strike. I used to deliver the bread by myself. No union. I worked eighteen hours a day, seven days a week. I built a business, now everyone wants to tell me how to run the fucking business. This envelope I hold here has the proposals for what I am willing to concede to the union. Hours, pay scale and benefits. This will enable us to increase our prices a small percentage and keep the profit structure in line. If they reject it, let them freeze their fucking asses off walking the streets with 'Rose Corporation Unfair to Labor' signs until their little toes and fingers freeze up and drop off. I'll be in my office. Capisce?" Nunzio walked away, happy with himself. Not my day for eating shit, he thought to himself.

CHAPTER FIFTY-SEVEN
February 15, 1946

There it was on the front page of the Boston Newspapers, *ROSE CORPORATION ON STRIKE. Workers at the Boston-based bakery walked out yesterday after the CEO, Nunzio Cappolla, refused to listen to their demands. The only comment Mr. Cappolla would make was that he offered them a fair package and they refused. U.S. steel settled their strike with a record across-the-board 18.5% raise.*

Rose was getting Alby ready for a school when Nunzio charged into the room. "If the damned press calls, I'm out of town, Rose," he shouted.

"Why don't you just go down to your office and deal with the strike, darling?" she replied.

"Because I've been thinking. With all the GIs coming home from the occupation both in Europe and Japan, there will be plenty of labor available. It don't take much brains to drive a truck or work the ovens. I'm going to break the goddamn union."

"But you have a contract with the Teamsters. Why can't Joe Allen get you a contract with the bakers?"

"Because Joe Allen is full of shit. Sure, he can make deals to line his pockets, and he can bullshit the politicians, but when it comes time to deliver, it's only what suits Joe Allen. His intentions were always to take over this company from the start. Jascowitz, Tannenbaum and Allen are in this together, board of directors, public corporation stockholders. What happened to La Bella Rosa, the Rose Corporation? I'm losing control."

"But Nunzio, we're rich. We don't need anything, and you're still the chairman."

"We're rich, yes. But not as rich as we could be and

should be. Suddenly I'm not the major stockholder. Those boys played a scam on me with the stock issues and all that other bullshit. I just wasn't knowledgeable enough on that stuff and they knew it. Goddamn, did they know it! They knew I wouldn't give in to those ridiculous demands of the paper union that the bastard, Joe Allen, runs. I'm going to fight the whole bunch of them."

"Nunzio, be careful, please. Rose Gardens is doing well. You don't need to worry. Alby, you go to school now."

"Are you going to be all right, Daddy?" Alby asked.

Nunzio stared into the fourteen year old's eyes. He grabbed him into his arms. "We're going to be fine, son. Make sure you keep your gloves and scarf on. It's bitter cold outside."

Nunzio picked up the phone and called Elena. "I'm glad you're at home. I need to have a meeting with you."

"Well, where else would I be? I would never walk a picket line against you, Mr. Cappolla. Would you like me to meet you at your office?"

"No, that wouldn't be good. Meet me at the Lobster Shack, at noon, for lunch. There's a booth in the back on the far right. You make the reservations. Use Kelly as the name."

"Kelly. Yes, Mr. Cappolla. I'll see you there."

Elena was already at the table when Nunzio arrived. It was the first time he had seen her away from the plant. She looked much more attractive then usual. "You look real nice, Elena," Nunzio remarked, biting his tongue for having said it.

"Thank you, Mr. Cappolla. It was nice of you to say that. What is it I can do for you?" she asked.

"Let's order some lunch first. Would you care for a drink?" he asked.

"Just a coca-cola for me," she answered.

"One coca-cola and a Pabst Blue Ribbon for me," he

said to the waitress. "And bring a platter of shrimp and oysters. That okay?" he asked Elena.

"Wonderful, I love shrimp. Oysters I can live without," she laughed.

"The reason I needed to see you today is that I need your help. I want you to call every one of the strikers and tell them I will offer them a deal if they are willing to defy the union and cross the picket line. Whoever refuses will be replaced by a non-union worker. Violence will be met with violence. They will come out ahead in the long run, assure them that. I will rent a banquet room at the Regency for this Sunday. There will be sandwiches and beer. Let those who want to work for the Rose Corporation be there. Can you do that Elena?"

"That's pretty strong, Mr. Cappolla. Strikebreaking. But yes, I will do it, because you asked me. I would do anything you ask me to, Mr. Cappolla, anything at all. She looked into his eyes when she said that, and pouted just enough, so there was no mistaking her meaning.

"Thank you, Elena. I will keep that in mind. If you handle it right for me and we get the plant opened next week, you will be rewarded handsomely. Here comes the food, let's eat."

"Thank you Mr. Cappolla. Thank you," she smiled.

"I've told you before to call me Nunzio."

CHAPTER FIFTY- EIGHT
February 18, 1946. Manchester, NH

Shlomo Abrams sat in the reception area outside David Fairchild's office holding the picture of Sally's children. The dried blood she left on it made it almost impossible to recognize them. But what did it matter, he thought.

"Mr. Fairchild just called," the secretary told him. "He will be here in about fifteen minutes. Would you care for a cup of coffee?" she asked very slowly, as he had mentioned that his English was poor.

"A glass of tea perhaps," he replied, trying to force a smile.

"Tea, of course. I'll have it in a moment."

"Thank you," again trying to smile. He recalled how easy it was to smile before the war. Hannah and Chaim were alive, and he and Esther would play in the meadow, running and laughing. And now, like Sally, they were just memories.

Reaching into his shirt pocket, he took out the medal the Russians had given him. He clenched it in his palm, as he did several times each day. The medal represented the revenge, the small amount of revenge he had when he escaped the ghetto and joined the partisans, and finally the Red Army. He marched into Poland killing Germans. He marched into Germany and right into Berlin, killing as many Germans as he could.

The hate was in his eyes, and in his soul and heart. He lived for revenge, but it did not bring back Esther or Chaim or beautiful little Hannah or the rest of his relatives or the six million others. They were gone. They know nothing of his heroics, of his revenge. "Six months in America, and finally I have reached Manchester, New

Hampshire, for you, Sally," he whispered.

"Did you say something?" the receptionist asked.

"Just thinking out loud," he said as David walked into the reception area.

Reaching out his hand, David said, "Mr. Abrams, I'm so happy to meet you. Please come into my office."

"Thank you, Mr. Fairchild," he replied.

"Mr. Abrams, you have been through so much and you have survived. You mentioned on the telephone that you were with my wife when she..."

"Your wife was a very brave women," Mr. Abrams said. "Everyone loved her. The SS officer that shot her, Lt. Fritz Holtzner, committed suicide after we captured him. I was there. He was a coward. For him it was easy to kill women and children, and defenseless Jews. So many of them were cowards. This picture of your children was all that Sally had in her possession when I found her, before I escaped. I wanted you to have it."

"God bless you, Mr. Abrams. Thank you. Is there anything I can do for you? Anything?" David offered.

"I would love to meet your children. Perhaps a meal at your house. My children and my wife are gone. I live in a small rooming house in New York City. It would be nice to..."

"We would be honored to have you, Mr. Abrams. I am remarried now. My new wife, Dorothy Ann, is not Jewish, but she is wonderful, and the children love her. I know you are probably saying to yourself, 'how could he have forgotten Sally and married someone else so soon', but things happen, Mr. Abrams."

"I did not come here to judge. I am anxious to meet the children."

"Give me about an hour to get my work in order and we will leave. I'll call my wife and tell her you are coming home with me. We are not kosher, do you have requirements?"

"Listen, I served in the Russian Army and ate rat droppings. Don't worry about my requirements," he smiled. This time it was genuine.

Shlomo sat on the couch in the reception room drinking his tea while waiting for David. "A toast to you, Sally," he said lifting his cup.

CHAPTER FIFTY-NINE
The next day. Lexington

Nunzio lay in bed looking over at Rose, his eyes half opened. She was so beautiful in the morning. I'm glad I didn't take Elena up on her obvious offer, he thought to himself. I could never live with the guilt. People think Italians all have mistresses. Well, not Nunzio Cappolla. The bakery, that's my mistress. Only it looks like I'm the one getting fucked now. I could lie here in bed all day. Then I wouldn't have to face anyone. Let them strike. I have enough money to last for years without worrying. Fuck you, Joe Allen. Ahhhh. A couple more minutes of shut-eye, and then I'll get up.

Two minutes later the phone startled him awake.

"Want me to get it?" Rose asked.

"That's all right, Rose. Go back to sleep, I'll get it." He picked up the phone. "Hello? David? Good morning. Good to hear your voice. What's new?"

"I don't know where to begin, Nunzio," David whispered into the phone. "I know what happened to Sally, how she died, everything. I have a houseguest. His name is Shlomo Abrams. He was there, but he escaped. It's a long story. I need someone to talk to, Nunzio. I haven't told the children the whole story. They're not too happy with having Shlomo at the house. He's different. I can't explain it. And Dorothy Ann keeps giving me looks. I'm coming to Boston for a meeting in the morning. Can we have breakfast?"

"Yes, of course, David. I'm in the middle of a strike, you know."

"Yes, Nunzio. I read about it in the paper. And they're making you look like the new Hitler. How come?"

"How come? Because some mother-you-know-what,

by the name of Joe Allen, is putting all the shit on yours truly."

"Well, you know Nunzio, I've been thinking. Why don't you settle the strike. Look like a hero, and then sell your interest in the Rose Corporation."

"What? Sell my Rose Corporation? La Bella Rose? I built that company. You know that. It's my life. What would I do? David, you're crazy."

"Think about it, Nunzio. You have the Rose Gardens project. Stefano is back, right? You can concentrate on building housing developments all over the country. Get investors. I'll invest. Loretta would invest, she has all kinds of money and contacts. You can become one of the richest men in the world. To hell with the bakery. Let some asshole union boss run it. Anyway, I'll discuss it with you tomorrow. Today, you think about it. You'll see I'm right."

"Okay, David. I'll think. Nunzio Cappolla, the richest man in the world. Rose, you awake? How would you like to be married to the richest man in the world?" Nunzio put down the phone, and leaned over to kiss her on the forehead. "Got to get up. Things to do today," he said.

"What I would like is just to have my husband to stay in bed with me a little longer."

How much is enough? Nunzio was thinking as he got dressed. In the old country a fraction of what he had would be a fortune. Why this obsession with wealth? It's becoming a disease. Uncontrollable. Yes, David, perhaps you are right.

With that, Nunzio felt the weight of the world lift from his shoulders. I wish Bruno were here. And Uncle Alberto. I would love to share this feeling with them. Yes, God, I have Rose and the children. I have my sister, I have... I have the world. Me, Nunzio Cappolla, and no unions, no Joe Allens are going to take this from me.

He walked out into the street, took a deep breath of

fresh air and stared at the acres that were his.

"I have it all, thanks to you God. I have it all."